Classics *for*
Christmastime

*Five Novels*
*About the Spirit*
*of the Holiday*

*Including*

The Story of the
Other Wise Man
*by Henry van Dyke*

The Birds'
Christmas Carol
*by Kate Douglas Wiggin*

Brotherly House
*by Grace S. Richmond*

The Romance of
a Christmas Card
*by Kate Douglas Wiggin*

A Christmas Carol
*by Charles Dickens*

# Classics *for*

# Christmastime

*Five Novels*
*About the Spirit*
*of the Holiday*

A Ballantine/Epiphany Book

Ballantine Books • New York

A Ballantine/Epiphany Book
Published by Ballantine Books

Preface copyright © 1989 by Random House, Inc.
Illustrations copyright © 1989 by Lawrence Schwinger
Publishing Company. Copyright 1916 by Kate Douglas Wiggin.

Library of Congress Cataloging-in-Publication Data
Classics for Christmastime: five novels about the spirit of
the holiday. — 1st Ballantine Books/Epiphany Omnibus Ed.
      p.    cm.
   "A Ballantine/Epiphany book."
   ISBN: 0-345-36343-4
   1. Christmas stories, American.  2. Christmas stories, English.
PS648.C45C5   1989
813.008′033–dc20                                    89-90637
                                                         CIP

Manufactured in the United States of America
Design by Holly Johnson
Borders and ornaments © 1989 by Holly Johnson

THE STORY OF THE OTHER WISE MAN: First Ballantine/Epiphany Books
Edition: December 1984

THE BIRDS' CHRISTMAS CAROL: First Ballantine/Epiphany Books Edition: December 1987

BROTHERLY HOUSE: First Ballantine/Epiphany Books Edition: December 1988

THE ROMANCE OF A CHRISTMAS CARD: First Ballantine/Epiphany Books Edition: December 1989

First Ballantine/Epiphany Books Omnibus Edition: November 1989

10 9 8 7 6 5 4 3 2

"I will honor Christmas in my heart and try to keep it all the year."
—Ebeneezer Scrooge
*A Christmas Carol,* 1843

# Contents

The Story of the Other Wise Man      1
*by Henry van Dyke*

The Birds' Christmas Carol      49
*by Kate Douglas Wiggin*

Brotherly House      109
*by Grace S. Richmond*

The Romance of a Christmas Card      155
*by Kate Douglas Wiggin*

A Christmas Carol      231
*by Charles Dickens*

# Preface

Does your heart soften at memories of Christmas long ago? Are you partial to Currier & Ives scenes of horse-drawn sleighs in the snow and quiet evening streets bathed in the warm glow of oil lamps?

Styles and methods of celebrating may change, but the spirit of Christmas does not. It beckons us to remember the forgotten, to love the unloved, to spread joy even among strangers. Here we have gathered five favorite Christmas classics that capture the essence of the season. The first four stories were originally published at the turn of the century, while the first edition of *A Christmas Carol* gladdened readers in 1843.

Although holly-crested figgy puddings and yule logs may be scarce nowadays, *Classics for Christmastime* will infuse you with nostalgia and a renewed gratitude for the miracle of Christmas. May these five stories work magic in *your* soul.

# The Story
## *of the*

# Other Wise Man

*by*
# Henry
# van Dyke

I t is now some years since this little story was set afloat on the sea of books. It is not a man-of-war, nor even a high-sided merchantman; only a small, peaceful sailing-vessel. Yet it has had rather an adventurous voyage. Twice it has fallen into the hands of pirates. The tides have carried it to far countries. It has been passed through the translator's port of entry into German, French, Armenian, Turkish, and perhaps some other foreign regions. Once I caught sight of it flying the outlandish flag of a brand-new phonetic language along the coasts of France; and once it was claimed by a dealer in antiquities as a long-lost legend of the Orient. Best of all, it has slipped quietly into many a far-away harbor that I have never seen, and found a kindly welcome, and brought back messages of good cheer from unknown friends.

Now it has turned home to be new-rigged and fitted for further voyaging. Before it is sent out again I have been asked to tell where the story came from and what it means.

I do not know where it came from—out of the air, perhaps. One thing is certain, it is not written in any other book, nor is it to be found among the ancient lore of the East. And yet I have never felt as if it were my own. It was a gift. It was sent to me; and it seemed as if I knew the Giver, though His name was not spoken.

The year had been full of sickness and sorrow. Every day brought trouble. Every night was tormented with pain. They are very long—those nights when one lies awake, and hears the laboring heart pumping wearily at its task, and watches for the morning, not knowing whether it will ever dawn. They are not nights of fear; for the thought of death grows strangely familiar when you have lived with it for a year. Besides, after a time you come to feel like a soldier who has been long standing still under fire; any change would be a relief. But they are lonely nights; they are very heavy nights. And their heaviest burden is this:

You must face the thought that your work in the world may be almost ended, but you know that it is not nearly finished.

You have not solved the problems that perplexed you. You have not reached the goal that you aimed at.

You have not accomplished the great task that you set for yourself. You are still on the way; and perhaps your journey must end now—nowhere—in the dark.

Well, it was in one of these long lonely nights that this story came to me. I had studied and loved the curious tales of the Three Wise Men of the East as they are told in the "Golden Legend" of Jacobus de Voragine and other medieval books. But of the Fourth Wise Man I had never heard until that night. Then I saw him distinctly, moving through the shadows in a little circle of light. His countenance was as clear as the memory of my father's face as I saw it for the last time a few months before. The narrative of his journeyings and trials and disappointments ran without a break. Even certain sentences came to me complete and unforgettable, clear-cut like a cameo. All that I had to do was to follow Artaban, step by step, as the tale went on, from the beginning to the end of his pilgrimage.

Perhaps this may explain some things in the story. I have been asked many times why I made the Fourth Wise Man tell a lie, in the cottage at Bethlehem, to save the little child's life.

I did not make him tell a lie.

What Artaban said to the soldiers he said for himself, because he could not help it.

Is a lie ever justifiable? Perhaps not. But may it not sometimes seem inevitable?

And if it were a sin, might not a man confess it,

and be pardoned for it more easily than for the greater sin of spiritual selfishness, or indifference, or the betrayal of innocent blood? That is what I saw Artaban do. That is what I heard him say. All through his life he was trying to do the best that he could. It was not perfect. But there are some kinds of failure that are better than success.

Though the story of the Fourth Wise Man came to me suddenly and without labor, there was a great deal of study and toil to be done before it could be written down. An idea arrives without effort; a form can only be wrought out by patient labor. If your story is worth telling, you ought to love it enough to be willing to work over it until it is true—true not only to the ideal, but true also to the real. The light is a gift; but the local color can only be seen by one who looks for it long and steadily. Artaban went with me while I toiled through a score of volumes of ancient history and travel. I saw his figure while I journeyed on the motionless sea of the desert and in the strange cities of the East.

And now that his story is told, what does it mean?

How can I tell? What does life mean? If the meaning could be put into a sentence there would be no need of telling the story.

Henry van Dyke

*Who seeks for heaven alone to save his soul,*
*May keep the path, but will not reach the goal;*
*While he who walks in love may wander far,*
*Yet God will bring him where the blessed are.*

 **Y**ou know the story of the Three Wise Men of the East, and how they traveled from far away to offer their gifts at the manger-cradle in Bethlehem. But have you ever heard the story of the Other Wise Man, who also saw the star in its rising, and set out to follow it, yet did not arrive with his brethren in the presence of the young child Jesus? Of the great desire of this fourth pilgrim, and how it was denied, yet accomplished in the denial; of his many wanderings and the probations of his soul; of the long way of his seeking, and the strange way of his finding, the One whom he sought— I would tell the tale as I have heard fragments of it in the Hall of Dreams, in the palace of the Heart of Man.

# The Sign in the Sky

**I** n the days when Augustus Caesar was master of many kings and Herod reigned in Jerusalem, there lived in the city of Ecbatana, among the mountains of Persia, a certain man named Artaban, the Median. His house stood close to the outermost of the seven walls which encircled the royal treasury. From his roof he could look over the rising battlements of black and white and crimson and blue and red and silver and gold, to the hill where the summer palace of the Parthian emperors glittered like a jewel in a sevenfold crown.

Around the dwelling of Artaban spread a fair garden, a tangle of flowers and fruit trees, watered by a score of streams descending from the slopes of Mount Orontes, and made musical by innumerable birds. But all color was lost in the soft and odorous darkness of the late September night, and all sounds were hushed in the deep charm of its silence, save the plashing of the water, like a voice half sobbing and half laughing under the shadows. High above the trees a dim glow of light shone through the curtained arches of the upper chamber, where the master of the house was holding council with his friends.

He stood by the doorway to greet his guests—a tall, dark man of about forty years, with brilliant eyes set near together under his broad brow, and firm lines graven around his fine, thin lips; the brow of a dreamer and the mouth of a soldier, a man of sensitive feeling but inflexible will—one of those who, in whatever age they may live, are born for inward conflict and life of quest.

His robe was of pure white wool, thrown over a tunic of silk; and a white pointed cap, with long lapels at the sides, rested on his flowing black hair. It was the dress of the ancient priesthood of the Magi, called the fire-worshipers.

"Welcome!" he said, in his low, pleasant voice, as one after another entered the room—"welcome, Abdus; peace be with you, Rhodaspes and Tigranes, and with you my father, Abgarus. You are all welcome, and this house grows bright with the joy of your presence."

There were nine of the men, differing widely in age, but alike in the richness of their dress of many-colored silks, and in the massive golden collars around their necks, marking them as Parthian nobles, and the winged circles of gold resting upon their breasts, the sign of the followers of Zoroaster.

They took their places around a small black altar at the end of the room, where a tiny flame was burning. Artaban, standing beside it, and waving a barsom of thin tamarisk branches above the fire, fed it with dry sticks of pine and fragrant oils. Then he began the ancient chant of the Yasna, and the voices of his companions joined in the beautiful hymn to Ahura-Mazda:

We worship the Spirit Divine,
all wisdom and goodness possessing,
Surrounded by Holy Immortals,
the givers of bounty and blessing,
We joy in the works of His hands,
His truth and His power confessing.

We praise all the things that are pure,
for these are His only Creation;
The thoughts that are true,
and the words and deeds that have won
    approbation;
These are supported by Him and
for these we make adoration.

Hear us, O Mazda!
Thou livest in truth and in heavenly
    gladness;

Cleanse us from falsehood,
and keep us from evil and bondage to
  badness;
Pour out the light and the joy of
Thy life on our darkness and sadness.

Shine on our gardens and fields,
Shine on our working and weaving;
Shine on the whole race of man,
Believing and unbelieving;
Shine on us now through the night,
Shine on us now in Thy might,
The flame of our holy love and
the song of our worship receiving.

The fire rose with the chant, throbbing as if it were made of musical flame, until it cast a bright illumination through the whole apartment, revealing its simplicity and splendor.

The floor was laid with tiles of dark blue veined with white; pilasters of twisted silver stood out against the blue walls; the clear-story of round-arched windows above them was hung with azure silk; the vaulted ceiling was a pavement of sapphires, like the body of heaven in its clearness, sown with silver stars. From the four corners of the roof hung four golden magic-wheels, called the tongues of the gods. At the eastern end, behind the altar, there were two dark-red pillars of porphyry; above them a lintel of the same stone, on which was carved the figure of a winged archer, with his arrow set to the string and his bow drawn.

The doorway between the pillars, which opened upon the terrace of the roof, was covered with a heavy curtain of the color of a ripe pomegranate, embroidered with innumerable golden rays shooting upward from the floor. In effect the room was like a quiet, starry night, all azure and silver, flushed in the east with rosy promise of the dawn. It was, as the house of a man should be, an expression of the character and spirit of the master.

He turned to his friends when the song was ended, and invited them to be seated on the divan at the western end of the room.

"You have come to-night," said he, looking around the circle, "at my call, as the faithful scholars of Zoroaster, to renew your worship and rekindle your faith in the God of Purity, even as this fire has been rekindled on the altar. We worship not the fire, but Him of whom it is the chosen symbol, because it is the purest of all created things. It speaks to us of one who is Light and Truth. Is it not so, my father?"

"It is well said, my son," answered the venerable Abgarus. "The enlightened are never idolaters. They lift the veil of the form and go into the shrine of the reality, and new light and truth are coming to them continually through the old symbols."

"Hear me, then, my father and my friends," said Artaban, very quietly, "while I tell you of the new light and truth that have come to me through the most ancient of all signs. We have searched the secrets of nature together, and studied the healing virtues of water and fire and the plants. We have read also the books of prophecy in which the future is dimly foretold in words that are hard to understand. But the highest of all learning is the knowledge of the stars. To trace their courses is to untangle the threads of the mystery of life from the beginning to the end. If we could follow them perfectly, nothing would be hidden from us. But is not our knowledge of them still incomplete? Are there not many stars still beyond our horizon—lights that are known only to the dwellers in the far southland, among the spice-trees of Punt and the gold-mines of Ophir?"

There was a murmur of assent among the listeners.

"The stars," said Tigranes, "are the thoughts of the Eternal. They are numberless. But the thoughts of man can be counted, like the years of his life. The wisdom of the Magi is the greatest of all wisdoms on earth, because it knows its own ignorance. And that is the secret of power. We keep men always looking and waiting for a new sunrise. But we ourselves know that the darkness is equal to the light, and that the conflict between them will never be ended."

"That does not satisfy me," answered Artaban, "for, if the waiting must be endless, if there could be no fulfilment of it, then it would not be wisdom to look and wait. We should become like those new teachers of the Greeks, who say that there is no truth, and that the only wise men are those who spend their lives in discovering and exposing the lies that have been believed in the world. But the new sunrise will certainly dawn in the appointed time. Do not our own books tell us that this will come to pass, and that men will see the brightness of a great light?"

"That is true," said the voice of Abgarus; "every faithful disciple of Zoroaster knows the prophecy of the Avesta and carries the word in his heart. 'In that day Sosiosh the Victorious shall arise out of the number of the prophets in the east country. Around him shall shine a mighty brightness, and he shall make life everlasting, incorruptible, and immortal, and the dead shall rise again.' "

"This is a dark saying," said Tigranes, "and it may be that we shall never understand it. It is better to consider the things that are near at hand, and to increase the influence of the Magi in their own country, rather than to look for one who may be a stranger, and to whom we must resign our power."

The others seemed to approve these words. There

was a silent feeling of agreement manifest among them; their looks responded with that indefinable expression which always follows when a speaker has uttered the thought that has been slumbering in the hearts of his listeners. But Artaban turned to Abgarus with a glow on his face, and said:

"My father, I have kept this prophecy in the secret place of my soul. Religion without a great hope would be like an altar without a living fire. And now the flame has burned more brightly, and by the light of it I have read other words which also have come from the fountain of Truth, and speak yet more clearly of the rising of the Victorious One in his brightness."

He drew from the breast of his tunic two small rolls of fine linen, with writing upon them, and unfolded them carefully upon his knee.

"In the years that are lost in the past, long before our fathers came into the land of Babylon, there were wise men in Chaldea, from whom the first of the Magi learned the secret of the heavens. And of these Balaam the son of Beor was one of the mightiest. Hear the words of his prophecy: 'There shall come a star out of Jacob, and a scepter shall arise out of Israel.' "

The lips of Tigranes drew downward with contempt, as he said:

"Judah was a captive by the waters of Babylon, and the sons of Jacob were in bondage to our kings. The tribes of Israel are scattered through the mountains like lost sheep, and from the remnant that dwells in Judea under the yoke of Rome neither star nor scepter shall arise."

"And yet," answered Artaban, "it was the Hebrew Daniel, the mighty searcher of dreams, the counselor of kings, the wise Belteshazzar, who was most honored and beloved of our great King Cyrus. A prophet of sure things and a reader of the thoughts of God, Daniel proved himself to our people. And these are the words that he wrote." (Artaban read from the second roll:) " 'Know, therefore, and understand that from the going forth of the commandment to restore Jerusalem, unto the Anointed One, the Prince, the time shall be seven and threescore and two weeks.' "

"But, my son," said Abgarus, doubtfully, "these are mystical numbers. Who can interpret them, or who can find the key that shall unlock their meaning?"

Artaban answered: "It has been shown to me and to my three companions among the Magi—Caspar, Melchior, and Balthazar. We have searched the ancient tablets of Chaldea and computed the time. It falls in this year. We have studied the sky, and in the spring of the year we saw two of the greatest stars draw near together in the sign of the Fish, which is the house of the Hebrews. We also saw a new star there, which shone for one night and then vanished. Now again the two great planets are meeting. This night is their conjunction. My three brothers are watching at the ancient

Temple of the Seven Spheres, at Borsippa, in Babylonia, and I am watching here. If the star shines again, they will wait ten days for me at the temple, and then we will set out together for Jerusalem, to see and worship the promised one who shall be born King of Israel. I believe the sign will come. I have made ready for the journey. I have sold my house and my possessions, and bought these three jewels—a sapphire, a ruby, and a pearl—to carry them as tribute to the King. And I ask you to go with me on the pilgrimage, that we may have joy together in finding the Prince who is worthy to be served."

While he was speaking he thrust his hand into the inmost fold of his girdle and drew out three great gems—one blue as a fragment of the night sky, one redder than a ray of sunrise, and one as pure as the peak of a snow mountain at twilight—and laid them on the outspread linen scrolls before him.

But his friends looked on with strange and alien eyes. A veil of doubt and mistrust came over their faces, like a fog creeping up from the marshes to hide the hills. They glanced at each other with looks of wonder and pity, as those who have listened to incredible sayings, the story of a wild vision, or the proposal of an impossible enterprise.

At last Tigranes said: "Artaban, this is a vain dream. It comes from too much looking upon the stars and the cherishing of lofty thoughts. It would be wiser to spend the time in gathering money for the new fire-temple at Chala. No king will ever rise from the broken race of Israel, and no end will ever come to the eternal strife of light and darkness. He who looks for it is a chaser of shadows. Farewell."

And another said: "Artaban, I have no knowledge of these things, and my office as guardian of the royal treasure binds me here. The quest is not for me. But if thou must follow it, fare thee well."

And another said: "In my house there sleeps a new bride, and I cannot leave her nor take her with me on this strange journey. This quest is not for me. But may thy steps be prospered wherever thou goest. So farewell."

And another said: "I am ill and unfit for hardship, but there is a man among my servants whom I will send with thee when thou goest, to bring me word how thou farest."

But Abgarus, the oldest and the one who loved Artaban the best, lingered after the others had gone, and said, gravely: "My son, it may be that the light of truth is in this sign that has appeared in the skies, and then it will surely lead to the Prince and the mighty brightness. Or it may be that it is only a shadow of the light, as Tigranes has said, and then he who follows it will have only a long pilgrimage and an empty search. But it is better to follow even the shadow of the best than to remain content with the worst. And those who would see wonderful things must often be ready to travel alone. I am too old for this journey, but my heart shall be a companion of the pilgrimage day and night, and I shall know the end of my quest. Go in peace."

So one by one they went out of the azure chamber with its silver stars, and Artaban was left in solitude.

He gathered up the jewels and replaced them in his girdle. For a long time he stood and watched the flame that flickered and sank upon the altar. Then he crossed the hall, lifted the heavy curtain, and passed out between the dull red pillars of porphyry to the terrace on the roof.

The shiver that thrills through the earth ere she rouses from her night sleep had already begun, and the cool wind that heralds the daybreak was drawing downward from the lofty snow-traced ravines of Mount Orontes. Birds, half awakened, crept and chirped among the rustling leaves and the smell of ripened grapes came in brief wafts from the arbors.

Far over the eastern plain a white mist stretched like a lake. But where the distant peak of Zagros serrated the western horizon the sky was clear. Jupiter and Saturn rolled together like drops of lambent flame about to blend in one.

As Artaban watched them, behold! an azure spark was born out of the darkness beneath, rounding itself with purple splendors to a crimson sphere, and spiring upward through rays of saffron and orange into a point of white radiance. Tiny and infinitely remote, yet perfect in every part, it pulsated in the enormous vault as if the three jewels in the Magian's breast had mingled and been transformed into a living heart of light.

He bowed his head. He covered his brow with his hands.

"It is the sign," he said. "The King is coming, and I will go to meet him."

# By the Waters of Babylon

**A**ll night long Vasda, the swiftest of Artaban's horses, had been waiting, saddled and bridled, in her stall, pawing the ground impatiently and shaking her bit as if she shared the eagerness of her master's purpose, though she knew not its meaning.

Before the birds had fully roused to their strong, high, joyful chant of morning song, before the white mist had begun to lift lazily from the plain, the Other Wise Man was in the saddle, riding swiftly along the highroad, which skirted the base of Mount Orontes, westward.

How close, how intimate is the comradeship between a man and his favorite horse on a long journey. It is a silent, comprehensive friendship, an intercourse beyond the need of words.

They drink at the same wayside spring, and sleep

under the same guardian stars. They are conscious together of the subduing spell of nightfall and the quickening joy of daybreak. The master shares his evening meal with his hungry companion, and feels the soft, moist lips caressing the palm of his hand as they close over the morsel of bread. In the gray dawn he is roused from his bivouac by the gentle stir of a warm, sweet breath over his sleeping face, and looks up into the eyes of his faithful fellow-traveler, ready and waiting for the toil of the day. Surely, unless he is a pagan and an unbeliever, by whatever name he calls upon his God, he will thank Him for this voiceless sympathy, this dumb affection, and his morning prayer will embrace a double blessing—God bless us both, and keep our feet from falling and our souls from death!

And then, through the keen morning air, the swift hoofs beat their spirited music along the road, keeping time to the pulsing of two hearts that are moved with the same eager desire—to conquer space, to devour the distance, to attain the goal of the journey.

Artaban must, indeed, ride wisely and well if he would keep the appointed hour with the other Magi; for the route was a hundred and fifty parasangs, and fifteen was the utmost that he could travel in a day. But he knew Vasda's strength, and pushed forward without anxiety, making the fixed distance every day, though he must travel late into the night, and in the morning long before sunrise.

He passed along the brown slopes of Mount Orontes, furrowed by the rocky courses of a hundred torrents.

He crossed the level plains of the Nisaeans, where the famous herds of horses, feeding in the wide pastures, tossed their heads at Vasda's approach and galloped away with a thunder of many hoofs, and flocks of wild birds rose suddenly from the swampy meadows, wheeling in great circles with a shining flutter of innumerable wings and shrill cries of surprise.

He traversed the fertile fields of Concabar, where the dust from the threshing-floors filled the air with a golden mist, half hiding the huge Temple of Astarte with its four hundred pillars.

At Baghistan, among the rich gardens watered by fountains from the rock, he looked up at the mountain thrusting its immense rugged brow out over the road, and saw the figure of King Darius trampling upon his fallen foes, and the proud list of his wars and conquests graven high upon the face of the eternal cliff.

Over many a cold and desolate pass, crawling painfully across the windswept shoulders of the hills; down many a black mountain gorge, where the river roared and raced before him like a savage guide; across many a smiling vale, with terraces of yellow limestone full of vines and fruit trees; through the oak groves of Carine and the dark Gates of Zagros, walled in by precipices; into the ancient city of Chala, where the peo-

25

ple of Samaria had been kept in captivity long ago; and out again by the mighty portal, riven through the encircling hills, where he saw the image of the High Priest of the Magi sculptured on the wall of rock, with hand uplifted as if to bless the centuries of pilgrims; past the entrance of the narrow defile, filled from end to end with orchards of peaches and figs, through which the river Gyndes foamed down to meet him; over the broad rice-fields, where the autumnal vapors spread their deathly mists; following along the course of the river, under tremulous shadows of poplar and tamarind, among the lower hills; and out upon the flat plain, where the road ran straight as an arrow through the stubble-fields and parched meadows; past the city of Ctesiphon, where the Parthian emperors reigned, and the vast metropolis of Seleucia which Alexander built; across the swirling floods of Tigris and the many channels of Euphrates, flowing yellow through the corn-lands—Artaban pressed onward until he arrived, at nightfall of the tenth day, beneath the shattered walls of populous Babylon.

Vasda was almost spent, and he would gladly have turned into the city to find rest and refreshment for himself and for her. But he knew that it was three hours' journey yet to the Temple of the Seven Spheres, and he must reach the place by midnight if he would find his comrades waiting. So he did not halt, but rode steadily across the stubble-fields.

A grove of date-palms made an island of glooms in the pale yellow sea. As she passed into the shadow Vasda slackened her pace, and began to pick her way more carefully.

Near the farther end of the darkness an access of caution seemed to fall upon her. She scented some danger or difficulty; it was not in her heart to fly from it—only to be prepared for it, and to meet it wisely as a good horse should do. The grove was close and silent as the tomb; not a leaf rustled, not a bird sang.

She felt her steps before her delicately, carrying her head low, and sighing now and then with apprehension. At last she gave a quick breath of anxiety and dismay, and stood stock-still, quivering in every muscle, before a dark object in the shadow of the last palm-tree.

Artaban dismounted. The dim starlight revealed the form of a man lying across the road. His humble dress and the outline of his haggard face showed that he was probably one of the poor Hebrew exiles who still dwelt in great numbers in the vicinity. His pallid skin, dry and yellow as parchment, bore the mark of the deadly fever which ravaged the marshlands in autumn. The chill of death was in his lean hand, and, as Artaban released it, the arm fell back inertly upon the motionless breast.

He turned away with a thought of pity, consigning the body to that strange burial which the Magians deemed most fitting—the funeral of the desert, from which the kites and vultures rise on dark wings, and the beasts of prey slink furtively away, leaving only a heap of white bones in the sand.

But, as he turned, a long, faint, ghostly sigh came from the man's lips. The brown, bony fingers closed convulsively on the hem of the Magian's robe and held him fast.

Artaban's heart leaped to his throat, not with fear, but with a dumb resentment at the importunity of this blind delay.

How could he stay here in the darkness to minister to a dying stranger? What claim had this unknown fragment of human life upon his compassion or his service? If he lingered but for an hour he could hardly reach Borsippa at the appointed time. His companions would think he had given up the journey. They would go without him. He would lose his quest.

But if he went on now, the man would surely die. If he stayed, life might be restored. His spirit throbbed and fluttered with the urgency of the crisis. Should he risk the great reward of his divine faith for the sake of a single deed of human love? Should he turn aside, if only for a moment, from the following of the star, to give a cup of cold water to a poor, perishing Hebrew?

"God of truth and purity," he prayed, "direct me in the holy path, the way of wisdom which only Thou knowest."

Then he turned back to the sick man. Loosening the grasp of his hand, he carried him to a little mound at the foot of the palm-tree.

He unbound the thick folds of the turban and opened the garment above the sunken breast. He brought water from one of the small canals near by, and moistened the sufferer's brow and mouth. He mingled a draught of one of those simple but potent remedies which he carried always in his girdle—for the Magians were physicians as well as astrologers—and poured it slowly between the colorless lips. Hour after hour he labored as only a skilful healer of disease can do; and, at last, the man's strength returned; he sat up and looked about him.

"Who art thou?" he said, in the rude dialect of the country, "and why hast thou sought me here to bring back my life?"

"I am Artaban the Magian, of the city of Ecbatana, and I am going to Jerusalem in search of one who is to be born King of the Jews, a great Prince and Deliverer of all men. I dare not delay any longer upon my journey, for the caravan that has waited for me may depart without me. But see, here is all that I have left of bread and wine, and here is a potion of healing herbs. When thy strength is restored thou canst find the dwellings of the Hebrews among the houses of Babylon."

The Jew raised his trembling hand solemnly to heaven.

"Now may the God of Abraham and Isaac and Jacob bless and prosper the journey of the merciful, and bring him in peace to his desired haven. But stay; I have nothing to give thee in return—only this: that I can tell thee where the Messiah must be sought. For our prophets have said that he should be born not in Jerusalem, but in Bethlehem of Judah. May the Lord bring thee in safety to that place, because thou hast had pity upon the sick."

It was already long past midnight. Artaban rode in haste, and Vasda, restored by the brief rest, ran eagerly through the silent plain and swam the channels of the river. She put forth the remnant of her strength, and fled over the ground like a gazelle.

But the first beam of the sun sent her shadow before her as she entered upon the final stadium of the journey, and the eyes of Artaban, anxiously scanning the great mound of Nimrod and the Temple of the Seven Spheres, could discern no trace of his friends.

The many-colored terraces of black and orange and red and yellow and green and blue and white, shattered by the convulsions of nature, and crumbling under the repeated blows of human violence, still glittered like a ruined rainbow in the morning light.

Artaban rode swiftly around the hill. He dismounted and climbed to the highest terrace, looking out toward the west.

The huge desolation of the marshes stretched away to the horizon and the border of the desert. Bitterns stood by the stagnant pools and jackals skulked through the low bushes; but there was no sign of the caravan of the wise men, far or near.

At the edge of the terrace he saw a little cairn of broken bricks, and under them a piece of parchment. He caught it up and read: "We have waited past the midnight and can delay no longer. We go to find the King. Follow us across the desert."

Artaban sat down upon the ground and covered his head in despair.

"How can I cross the desert," said he, "with no food and with a spent horse? I must return to Babylon, sell my sapphire, and buy a train of camels, and provision for the journey. I may never overtake my friends. Only God the merciful knows whether I shall not lose the sight of the King because I tarried to show mercy."

## For the Sake of a Little Child

T here was a silence in the Hall of Dreams, where I was listening to the story of the Other Wise Man. And through this silence I saw, but very dimly, his figure passing over the dreary undulations of the desert, high upon the back of his camel, rocking steadily onward like a ship over the waves.

The land of death spread its cruel net around him. The stony wastes bore no fruit but briers and thorns. The dark ledges of rock thrust themselves above the surface here and there, like the bones of perished monsters. Arid and inhospitable mountain ranges rose before him, furrowed with dry channels of ancient torrents, white and ghastly as scars on the face of nature. Shifting hills of treacherous sand were heaped like tombs along the horizon. By day, the fierce heat pressed its intolerable burden on the quivering air; and no living creature moved on the dumb, swooning earth but tiny jerboas scuttling through the parched bushes, or lizards vanishing in the clefts of the rock. By night the jackals prowled and barked in the distance, and the lion made the black ravines echo with his hollow roaring, while a bitter, blighting chill followed the fever of the day. Through heat and cold, the Magian moved steadily onward.

Then I saw the gardens and orchards of Damascus, watered by the streams of Aldana and Pharpar, with their sloping swards inlaid with bloom, and their thickets of myrrh and roses. I saw also the long, snowy ridge of Hermon, and the dark groves of cedars, and the valley of the Jordan, and the blue waters of the Lake of Galilee, and the fertile plain of Esdraelon and the hills of Ephraim, and the highlands of Judah. Through all these I followed the figure of Artaban moving steadily onward, until he arrived at Bethlehem. And it was the third day after the three wise men had come to that place and had found Mary and Joseph, with the young child, Jesus, and had lain their gifts of gold and frankincense and myrrh at his feet.

Then the Other Wise Man drew near, weary, but full of hope, bearing his ruby and his pearl to offer to the King. "For now at last," he said, "I shall surely find him, though it be alone, and later than my brethren. This is the place of which the Hebrew exile told me that the prophets had spoken, and here I shall behold the rising of the great light. But I must inquire about the visit of my brethren, and to what house the star directed them, and to whom they presented their tribute."

The streets of the village seemed to be deserted, and Artaban wondered whether the men had all gone up to the hill-pastures to bring down their sheep. From the open door of a low stone cottage he heard the sound of a woman's voice singing softly. He entered and found a young mother hushing her baby to rest. She told him of the strangers from the Far East who had appeared in the village three days ago, and how they said that a star had guided them to the place where Joseph of Nazareth was lodging with his wife and her new-born child, and how they had paid reverence to the child and given him many rich gifts.

"But the travelers disappeared again," she continued, "as suddenly as they had come. We were afraid at the strangeness of their visit. We could not understand it. The man of Nazareth took the babe and his mother and fled away that same night secretly, and it was whispered that they were going far away to Egypt. Ever since there has been a spell upon the village; something evil hangs over it. They say that the Roman soldiers are coming from Jerusalem to force a new tax from us, and the men have driven the flocks and herds far back among the hills, and hidden themselves to escape it."

Artaban listened to her gentle, timid speech and the child in her arms looked up in his face and smiled, stretching out its rosy hands to grasp at the winged circle of gold on his breast. His heart warmed to the touch. It seemed like a greeting of love and trust to one who had journeyed long in loneliness and perplexity, fighting with his own doubts and fears, and following a light that was veiled in clouds.

"Might not this child have been the promised Prince?" he asked within himself, as he touched its soft cheek. "Kings have been born ere now in lowlier houses than this, and the favorite of the stars may rise even from a cottage. But it has not seemed good to the God of wisdom to reward my search so soon and so easily. The one whom I seek has gone before me; and now I must follow the King to Egypt."

The young mother laid the babe in its cradle, and rose to minister to the wants of the strange guest that fate had brought into her house. She set food before him, the plain fare of peasants, but willingly offered, and therefore full of refreshment for the soul as well as for the body. Artaban accepted it gratefully; and, as he ate, the child fell into a happy slumber, and murmured sweetly in its dreams, and a great peace filled the quiet room.

But suddenly there came the noise of a wild confusion and uproar in the streets of the village, a shrieking and wailing of women's voices, a clangor of swords, and a desperate cry: "The soldiers! The soldiers of Herod! They are killing our children."

The young mother's face grew white with terror. She clasped her child to her bosom, and crouched motionless in the darkest corner of the room, covering him with the folds of her robe, lest he should wake and cry.

But Artaban went quickly and stood in the doorway of the house. His broad shoulders filled the portal from side to side, and the peak of his white cap all but touched the lintel.

The soldiers came hurrying down the street with bloody hands and dripping swords. At the sight of the stranger in his imposing dress they hesitated with surprise. The captain of the band approached the threshold to thrust him aside. But Artaban did not stir. His face was as calm as though he were watching the stars, and in his eyes there burned that steady radiance before which even the half-tamed hunting-leopard shrinks and the fierce bloodhound pauses in his leap. He held the soldier silently for an instant, and then said, in a low voice:

"I am all alone in this place, and I am waiting to give this jewel to the prudent captain who will leave me in peace."

He showed the ruby, glistening in the hollow of his hand like a great drop of blood.

36

The captain was amazed at the splendor of the gem. The pupils of his eyes expanded with desire, and the hard lines of greed wrinkled around his lips. He stretched out his hand and took the ruby.

"March on!" he cried to his men. "There is no child here. The house is still."

The clamor and the clang of arms passed down the street as the headlong fury of the chase sweeps by the secret covert where the trembling deer is hidden. Artaban re-entered the cottage. He turned his face to the east and prayed:

"God of truth, forgive my sin! I have said the thing that is not, to save the life of a child. And two of my gifts are gone. I have spent for man that which was meant for God. Shall I ever be worthy to see the face of the King?"

But the voice of the woman, weeping for joy in the shadow behind him, said, very gently:

"Because thou hast saved the life of my little one, may the Lord bless thee and keep thee; the Lord make His face to shine upon thee and be gracious unto thee; the Lord lift up His countenance upon thee and give thee peace."

# In the Hidden Way of Sorrow

T hen again there was a silence in the Hall of Dreams, deeper and more mysterious than the first interval, and I understood that the years of Artaban were flowing very swiftly under the stillness of that clinging fog, and I caught only a glimpse, here and there, of the river of his life shining through the shadows that concealed its course.

I saw him moving among the throngs of men in populous Egypt, seeking everywhere for traces of the household that had come down from Bethlehem, and finding them under the spreading sycamore-trees of Heliopolis, and beneath the walls of the Roman fortress of New Babylon beside the Nile—traces so faint and dim that they vanished before him continually, as footprints on the hard river-sand glisten for a moment with moisture and then disappear.

I saw him again at the foot of the pyramids, which lifted their sharp points into the intense saffron glow of the sunset sky, changeless monuments of the perishable glory and the imperishable hope of man. He looked up into the vast countenance of the crouching Sphinx and vainly tried to read the meaning of the calm eyes and smiling mouth. Was it, indeed, the mockery of all effort and all aspiration, as Tigranes had said—the cruel jest of a riddle that has no answer, a search that never can succeed? Or was there a touch of pity and encouragement in that inscrutable smile—a promise that even the defeated should attain a victory, and the disappointed should discover a prize, and the ignorant should be made wise, and the blind should see, and the wandering should come into the haven at last?

I saw him again in an obscure house of Alexandria, taking counsel with a Hebrew rabbi. The venerable man, bending over the rolls of parchment on which the prophecies of Israel were written, read aloud the pathetic words which foretold the sufferings of the promised Messiah—the despised and rejected of men, the man of sorrows and the acquaintance of grief.

"And remember, my son," said he, fixing his deep-set eyes upon the face of Artaban, "the King whom you are seeking is not to be found in a palace, nor among the rich and powerful. If the light of the world and the glory of Israel had been appointed to come with the greatness of earthly splendor, it must have appeared long ago. For no son of Abraham will ever again rival the power which Joseph had in the palaces of Egypt, or the magnificence of Solomon throned between the lions in Jerusalem. But the light for which the world is waiting is a new light, the glory that shall rise out of patient and triumphant suffering. And the kingdom which is to be established forever is a new kingdom, the royalty of perfect and unconquerable love.

"I do not know how this shall come to pass, nor how the turbulent kings and peoples of earth shall be brought to acknowledge the Messiah and pay homage to him. But this I know. Those who seek Him will do well to look among the poor and the lowly, the sorrowful and the oppressed."

So I saw the Other Wise Man again and again, traveling from place to place, and searching among the people of the dispersion, with whom the little family from Bethlehem might, perhaps, have found a refuge. He passed through countries where famine lay heavy upon the land, and the poor were crying for bread. He made his dwelling in plague-stricken cities where the sick were languishing in the bitter companionship of helpless misery. He visited the oppressed and the afflicted in the gloom of subterranean prisons, and the crowded wretchedness of slave-markets, and the weary toil of galley-ships. In all this populous and intricate world of anguish, though he found none to worship, he found many to help. He fed the hungry, and clothed the naked, and healed the sick, and comforted the captive; and his years went by more swiftly than the weaver's shuttle that flashes back and forth through the loom while the web grows and the invisible pattern is completed.

It seemed almost as if he had forgotten his quest. But once I saw him for a moment as he stood alone at sunrise, waiting at the gate of a Roman prison. He had taken from a secret resting-place in his bosom the pearl, the last of his jewels. As he looked at it, a mellower luster, a soft and iridescent light, full of shifting gleams of azure and rose, trembled upon its surface. It seemed to have absorbed some reflection of the colors of the lost sapphire and ruby. So the profound, secret purpose of a noble life draws into itself the memories of past joy and past sorrow. All that has helped it, all that has hindered it, is transfused by a subtle magic into its very essence. It becomes more luminous and precious the longer it is carried close to the warmth of the beating heart.

Then, at last, while I was thinking of this pearl, and of its meaning, I heard the end of the story of the Other Wise Man.

# A Pearl of Great Price

Three-and-thirty years of the life of Artaban had passed away, and he was still a pilgrim, and a seeker after light. His hair, once darker than the cliffs of Zagros, was now white as the wintry snow that covered them. His eyes, that once flashed like flames of fire, were dull as embers smoldering among the ashes.

Worn and weary and ready to die, but still looking for the King, he had come for the last time to Jerusalem. He had often visited the holy city before, and had searched through all its lanes and crowded hovels and black prisons without finding any trace of the family of Nazarenes who had fled from Bethlehem long ago. But now it seemed as if he must make one more effort, and something whispered in his heart that, at last, he might succeed.

It was the season of the Passover. The city was thronged with strangers. The children of Israel, scattered in far lands all over the world, had returned to the Temple for the great feast, and there had been a confusion of tongues in the narrow streets for many days.

But on this day there was a singular agitation visible in the multitude. The sky was veiled with a portentous gloom, and currents of excitement seemed to flash through the crowd like the thrill which shakes the forest on the eve of a storm. A secret tide was sweeping them all one way. The clatter of sandals, and the soft, thick sound of thousands of bare feet shuffling over the stones, flowed unceasingly along the street that leads to the Damascus gate.

Artaban joined company with a group of people from his own country, Parthian Jews who had come up to keep the Passover, and inquired of them the cause of the tumult, and where they were going.

"We are going," they answered, "to the place called Golgotha, outside the city walls, where there is to be an execution. Have you not heard what has happened? Two famous robbers are to be crucified, and with them another, called Jesus of Nazareth, a man who has done many wonderful works among the people, so that they love him greatly. But the priests and elders have said that he must die, because he gave himself out to be the Son of God. And Pilate has sent him to the cross because he said that he was the 'King of the Jews.' "

How strangely these familiar words fell upon the tired heart of Artaban! They had led him for a lifetime over land and sea. And now they came to him darkly and mysteriously like a message of despair. The King had arisen, but He had been denied and cast out. He was about to perish. Perhaps He was already dying. Could it be the same who had been born in Bethlehem thirty-three years ago, at whose birth the star had appeared in heaven, and of whose coming the prophets had spoken?

Artaban's heart beat unsteadily with that troubled, doubtful apprehension which is the excitement of old age. But he said within himself: "The ways of God are stranger than the thoughts of men, and it may be that I shall find the King, at last, in the hands of His enemies, and shall come in time to offer my pearl for His ransom before He dies."

So the old man followed the multitude with slow and painful steps toward the Damascus gate of the city. Just beyond the entrance of the guardhouse a troop of Macedonian soldiers came down the street, dragging a young girl with torn dress and disheveled hair. As the Magian paused to look at her with compassion she broke suddenly from the hands of her tormentors and threw herself at his feet, clasping him around the knees. She had seen his white cap and the winged circle on his breast.

"Have pity on me," she cried, "and save me, for the sake of the God of Purity! I also am a daughter of the true religion which is taught by the Magi. My father was a merchant of Parthia, but he is dead, and I am seized for his debts to be sold as a slave. Save me from worse than death."

Artaban trembled.

It was the old conflict in his soul, which had come to him in the palm grove of Babylon and in the cottage at Bethlehem—the conflict between the expectation of faith and the impulse of love. Twice the gift which he had consecrated to the worship of religion had been drawn from his hand to the service of humanity. This was the third trial, the ultimate probation, the final and irrevocable choice.

Was it his great opportunity, or his last temptation? He could not tell. One thing only was clear in the darkness of his mind—it was inevitable. And does not the inevitable come from God?

One thing only was sure to his divided heart—to rescue this helpless girl would be a true deed of love. And is not love the light of the soul?

He took the pearl from his bosom. Never had it seemed so luminous, so radiant, so full of tender, living luster. He laid it in the hand of the slave.

"This is thy ransom, daughter! It is the last of my treasures which I kept for the King."

While he spoke, the darkness of the sky thickened, and shuddering tremors ran through the earth, heaving convulsively like the breast of one who struggles with mighty grief.

The walls of the houses rocked to and fro. Stones were loosened and crashed into the street. Dust-clouds filled the air. The soldiers fled in terror, reeling like drunken men. But Artaban and the girl whom he had ransomed crouched helpless beneath the wall of the Praetorium.

What had he to fear? What had he to live for? He had given away the last remnant of his tribute for the King. He had parted with the last hope of finding Him. The quest was over, and it had failed. But, even in that thought, accepted and embraced, there was peace. It was not resignation. It was not submission. It was something more profound and searching. He knew that all was well, because he had done the best that he could, from day to day. He had been true to the light that had been given to him. He had looked for more. And if he had not found it, if a failure was all that came out of his life, doubtless that was the best that was possible. He had not seen the revelation of "life everlasting, incorruptible, and immortal." But he knew that even if he could live his earthly life over again, it could not be otherwise than it had been.

One more lingering pulsation of the earthquake quivered through the ground. A heavy tile, shaken from the roof, fell and struck the old man on the temple. He lay breathless and pale, with his gray head resting on the young girl's shoulder, and the blood trickling from the wound. As she bent over him, fearing that he was dead, there came a voice through the twilight, very small and still, like music sounding from a distance, in which the notes are clear but the words are lost. The girl turned to see if someone had spoken from the window above them, but she saw no one.

Then the old man's lips began to move, as if in answer, and she heard him say in the Parthian tongue:

"Not so, my Lord: For when saw I thee anhungered and fed thee? Or thirsty, and gave thee drink? When saw I thee a stranger, and took thee in? Or naked, and clothed thee? When saw I thee sick or in prison, and came unto thee? Three-and-thirty years have I looked for thee; but I have never seen thy face, nor ministered to thee, my King."

He ceased, and the sweet voice came again. And again the maid heard it, very faintly and far away. But now it seemed as though she understood the words:

*"Verily I say unto thee, Inasmuch as thou hast done it unto one of the least of these my brethren, thou hast done it unto me."*

A calm radiance of wonder and joy lighted the pale face of Artaban like the first ray of dawn on a snowy mountainpeak. One long, last breath of relief exhaled gently from his lips.

His journey was ended. His treasures were accepted. The Other Wise Man had found the King.

# The *Birds'*

# Christmas Carol

## by
## Kate
## Douglas
## Wiggin

## 1

# A Little Snow Bird

I t was very early Christmas morning, and in the stillness of the dawn, with the soft snow falling on the house-tops, a little child was born in the Bird household.

They had intended to name the baby Lucy, if it were a girl; but they had not expected her on Christmas morning, and a real Christmas baby was not to be lightly named—the whole family agreed in that.

They were consulting about it in the nursery. Mr. Bird said that he had assisted in naming the three boys, and that he should leave this matter entirely to Mrs. Bird; Donald wanted the child called "Dorothy," after a pretty, curly-haired girl who sat next him in school; Paul chose "Luella," for Luella was the nurse who had been with him during his whole babyhood, up to the time of his first trousers, and the name suggested all sorts of comfortable things. Uncle Jack said that the first girl should always be named for her mother, no matter how hideous the name happened to be.

Grandma said that she would prefer not to take any part in the discussion, and everybody suddenly remembered that Mrs. Bird had thought of naming the baby Lucy, for Grandma herself; and, while it would be indelicate for her to favor that name, it would be against human nature for her to suggest any other, under the circumstances.

Hugh, the "hitherto baby," if that is a possible term, sat in one corner and said nothing, but felt, in some mysterious way, that his nose was out of joint; for there was a newer baby now, a possibility he had never taken into consideration; and the "first girl," too,—a still higher development of treason, which made him actually green with jealousy.

But it was too profound a subject to be settled then and there, on the spot; besides, Mamma had not been asked, and everybody felt it rather absurd, after all, to forestall a decree that was certain to be absolutely wise, just, and perfect.

The reason that the subject had been brought up at all so early in the day lay in the fact that Mrs. Bird never allowed her babies to go overnight unnamed. She was a person of so great decision of character that she would have blushed at such a thing; she said that to let blessed babies go dangling and dawdling about without names, for months and months, was enough to ruin them for life. She also said that if one could not make up one's mind in twenty-four hours it was a sign that— But I will not repeat the rest, as it might prejudice you against the most charming woman in the world.

So Donald took his new velocipede and went out to ride up and down the stone pavement and notch the shins of innocent people as they passed by, while Paul spun his musical top on the front steps.

But Hugh refused to leave the scene of action. He seated himself on the top stair in the hall, banged his head against the railing a few times, just by way of uncorking the vials of his wrath, and then subsided into gloomy silence, waiting to declare war if more "first girl babies" were thrust upon a family already surfeited with that unnecessary article.

Meanwhile dear Mrs. Bird lay in her room, weak, but safe and happy, with her sweet girl baby by her side and the heaven of motherhood opening again before her. Nurse was making gruel in the kitchen, and the room was dim and quiet. There was a cheerful open fire in the grate, but though the shutters were closed, the side windows that looked out on the Church of Our Saviour, next door, were a little open.

Suddenly a sound of music poured out into the bright air and drifted into the chamber. It was the boy choir singing Christmas anthems. Higher and higher rose the clear, fresh voices, full of hope and cheer, as children's voices always are. Fuller and fuller grew the burst of melody as one glad strain fell upon another in joyful harmony:—

> "Carol, brothers, carol,
>     Carol joyfully,
> Carol the good tidings,
>     Carol merrily!
> And pray a gladsome Christmas
>     For all your fellow-men:
> Carol, brothers, carol,
>     Christmas Day again."

One verse followed another, always with the same sweet refrain:—

> "And pray a gladsome Christmas
>     For all your fellow-men:
> Carol, brothers, carol,
>     Christmas Day again."

Mrs. Bird thought, as the music floated in upon her gentle sleep, that she had slipped into heaven with her new baby, and that the angels were bidding them welcome. But the tiny bundle by her side stirred a little, and though it was scarcely more than the ruffling of a feather, she awoke; for the mother-ear is so close to the heart that it can hear the faintest whisper of a child.

She opened her eyes and drew the baby closer. It looked like a rose dipped in milk, she thought, this pink and white blossom of girlhood, or like a pink cherub, with its halo of pale yellow hair, finer than floss silk.

"Carol, brothers, carol,
　　Carol joyfully,
Carol the good tidings,
　　Carol merrily!"

The voices were brimming over with joy.

"Why, my baby," whispered Mrs. Bird in soft surprise, "I had forgotten what day it was. You are a little Christmas child, and we will name you 'Carol'—mother's Christmas Carol!"

"What!" said Mr. Bird, coming in softly and closing the door behind him.

"Why, Donald, don't you think 'Carol' is a sweet name for a Christmas baby? It came to me just a moment ago in the singing, as I was lying here half asleep and half awake."

"I think it is a charming name, dear heart, and sounds just like you, and I hope that, being a girl, this baby has some chance of being as lovely as her mother;"—at which speech from the baby's papa, Mrs.

Bird, though she was as weak and tired as she could be, blushed with happiness.

And so Carol came by her name.

Of course, it was thought foolish by many people, though Uncle Jack declared laughingly that it was very strange if a whole family of Birds could not be indulged in a single Carol; and Grandma, who adored the child, thought the name much more appropriate than Lucy, but was glad that people would probably think it short for Caroline.

Perhaps because she was born in holiday time, Carol was a very happy baby. Of course, she was too tiny to understand the joy of Christmas-tide, but people say there is everything in a good beginning, and she may have breathed in unconsciously the fragrance of evergreens and holiday dinners; while the peals of sleigh-bells and the laughter of happy children may have fallen upon her baby ears and wakened in them a glad surprise at the merry world she had come to live in.

Her cheeks and lips were as red as hollyberries; her hair was for all the world the color of a Christmas candle-flame; her eyes were bright as stars; her laugh like a chime of Christmas-bells, and her tiny hands forever outstretched in giving.

Such a generous little creature you never saw! A spoonful of bread and milk had always to be taken by Mama or nurse before Carol could enjoy her supper;

whatever bit of cake or sweetmeat found its way into her pretty fingers was straightway broken in half to be shared with Donald, Paul, or Hugh; and when they made believe nibble the morsel with affected enjoyment, she would clap her hands and crow with delight.

"Why does she do it?" asked Donald thoughtfully. "None of us boys ever did."

"I hardly know," said Mamma, catching her darling to her heart, "except that she is a little Christmas child, and so she has a tiny share of the blessedest birthday the world ever knew!"

*2*

# Drooping Wings

**I**t was December, ten years later.

Carol had seen nine Christmas trees lighted on her birthdays, one after another; nine times she had assisted in the holiday festivities of the household, though in her babyhood her share of the gayeties was somewhat limited.

For five years, certainly, she had hidden presents for Mamma and Papa in their own bureau drawers, and harbored a number of secrets sufficiently large to burst a baby brain, had it not been for the relief gained by whispering them all to Mamma, at night, when she was in her crib, a proceeding which did not in the least lessen the value of a secret in her innocent mind.

For five years she had heard " 'Twas the night before Christmas," and hung up a scarlet stocking many sizes too large for her, and pinned a sprig of holly on her little white nightgown, to show Santa Claus that she was a "truly" Christmas child, and dreamed of fur-coated saints and toy-packs and reindeer, and wished everybody a "Merry Christmas" before it was light in the morning, and lent every one of her new toys to the neighbors' children before noon, and eaten turkey and plum-pudding, and gone to bed at night in a trance of happiness at the day's pleasures.

Donald was away at college now. Paul and Hugh were great manly fellows, taller than their mother. Papa Bird had gray hairs in his whiskers; and Grandma, God bless her, had been four Christmases in heaven.

But Christmas in the Birds' Nest was scarcely as merry now as it used to be in the bygone years, for the little child, that once brought such an added blessing to the day, lay month after month a patient, helpless invalid, in the room where she was born. She had never been very strong in body, and it was with a pang of terror her mother and father noticed, soon after she was five years old, that she began to limp, ever so slightly; to complain too often of weariness, and to nestle close to her mother, saying she "would rather not go out to play, please." The illness was slight at first, and hope was always stirring in Mrs. Bird's heart. "Carol would feel stronger in the summer-time;" or, "She would be better when she had spent a year in the country;" or, "She would outgrow it;" or, "They would try a new physician;" but by and by it came to be all too sure that no physician save One could make Carol strong again, and that no "summer-time" nor "country air," unless it were the everlasting summer-time in a heavenly country, could bring back the little girl to health.

The cheeks and lips that were once as red as holly-berries faded to faint pink; the star-like eyes grew softer, for they often gleamed through tears; and the gay child-laugh, that had been like a chime of Christmas bells, gave place to a smile so lovely, so touching, so tender and patient, that it filled every corner of the house with a gentle radiance that might have come from the face of the Christ-child himself.

Love could do nothing; and when we have said that we have said all, for it is stronger than anything else in the whole wide world. Mr. and Mrs. Bird were talking it over one evening, when all the children were asleep. A famous physician had visited them that day, and told them that some time, it might be in one year, it might be in more, Carol would slip quietly off into heaven, whence she came.

"It is no use to close our eyes to it any longer," said Mr. Bird, as he paced up and down the library floor; "Carol will never be well again. It almost seems as if I could not bear it when I think of that loveliest child doomed to lie there day after day, and, what is still more, to suffer pain that we are helpless to keep away from her. Merry Christmas, indeed; it gets to be the saddest day in the year to me!" and poor Mr. Bird sank into a chair by the table, and buried his face in his hands to keep his wife from seeing the tears that would come in spite of all his efforts.

"But, Donald, dear," said sweet Mrs. Bird, with trembling voice, "Christmas Day may not be so merry with us as it used, but it is very happy, and that is better, and very blessed, and that is better yet. I suffer chiefly for Carol's sake, but I have almost given up being sorrowful for my own. I am too happy in the child, and I see too clearly what she has done for us and the other children. Donald and Paul and Hugh were three strong, willful, boisterous boys, but now you seldom see such tenderness, devotion, thought for others, and self-denial in lads of their years. A quarrel or a hot word is almost unknown in this house, and why? Carol would hear it, and it would distress her, she is so full of love and goodness. The boys study with all their might and main. Why? Partly, at least, because they like to teach Carol, and amuse her by telling her what they read. When the seamstress comes, she likes to sew in Miss Carol's room, because there she forgets her own troubles, which, Heaven knows, are sore enough! And as for me, Donald, I am a better woman every day for Carol's sake; I have to be her eyes, ears, feet, hands—her strength, her hope; and she, my own little child, is my example!"

"I was wrong, dear heart," said Mr. Bird more

cheerfully; "we will try not to repine, but to rejoice instead, that we have an 'angel of the house.' "

"And as for her future," Mrs. Bird went on, "I think we need not be over-anxious. I feel as if she did not belong altogether to us, but that when she has done what God sent her for, He will take her back to Himself—and it may not be very long!" Here it was poor Mrs. Bird's turn to break down, and Mr. Bird's turn to comfort her.

## 3

## The Birds' Nest

C arol herself knew nothing of motherly tears and fatherly anxieties; she lived on peacefully in the room where she was born.

But you never would have known that room; for Mr. Bird had a great deal of money, and though he felt sometimes as if he wanted to throw it all in the sea, since it could not buy a strong body for his little girl, yet he was glad to make the place she lived in just as beautiful as it could be.

The room had been extended by the building of a large addition that hung out over the garden below, and was so filled with windows that it might have been a conservatory. The ones on the side were thus still nearer the Church of Our Saviour than they used to be; those in front looked out on the beautiful harbor, and those in the back commanded a view of nothing in particular but a narrow alley; nevertheless, they were pleasantest of all to Carol, for the Ruggles family lived in the alley, and the nine little, middle-sized, and big Ruggles children were a source of inexhaustible interest.

The shutters could all be opened and Carol could take a real sun-bath in this lovely glass house, or they could all be closed when the dear head ached or the dear eyes were tired. The carpet was of soft gray, with clusters of green bay and holly leaves. The furniture was of white wood, on which an artist had painted snow scenes and Christmas trees and groups of merry children ringing bells and singing carols.

Donald had made a pretty, polished shelf, and screwed it on the outside of the foot-board, and the boys always kept this full of blooming plants, which they changed from time to time; the head-board, too, had a bracket on either side, where there were pots of maiden-hair ferns.

Love-birds and canaries hung in their golden houses in the windows, and they, poor caged things, could hop as far from their wooden perches as Carol could venture from her little white bed.

On one side of the room was a bookcase filled with hundreds—yes, I mean it—with hundreds and hundreds of books; books with gay-colored pictures, books without; books with black and white outline sketches, books with none at all; books with verses, books with stories; books that made children laugh, and some, only a few, that made them cry; books with words of one syllable for tiny boys and girls, and books with words of fearful length to puzzle wise ones.

This was Carol's "Circulating Library." Every Saturday she chose ten books, jotting their names down in a diary; into these she slipped cards that said:—

"Please keep this book two weeks and read it.

With love, CAROL BIRD."

Then Mrs. Bird stepped into her carriage and took the ten books to the Children's Hospital, and brought home ten others that she had left there the fortnight before.

This was a source of great happiness; for some of the Hospital children that were old enough to print or write, and were strong enough to do it, wrote Carol sweet little letters about the books, and she answered them, and they grew to be friends. (It is very funny, but you do not always have to see people to love them. Just think about it, and tell me if it isn't so.)

There was a high wainscoting of wood about the room, and on top of this, in a narrow gilt framework, ran a row of illuminated pictures, illustrating fairy tales, all in dull blue and gold and scarlet and silver. From the door to the closet there was the story of "The

Fair One with Golden Locks;" from closet to book-case, ran "Puss in Boots;" from bookcase to fireplace, was "Jack the Giant-Killer;" and on the other side of the room were "Hop o' my Thumb," "The Sleeping Beauty," and "Cinderella."

Then there was a great closet full of beautiful things to wear, but they were all dressing-gowns and slippers and shawls; and there were drawers full of toys and games, but they were such as you could play with on your lap. There were no ninepins, nor balls, nor bows and arrows, nor bean bags, nor tennis rackets; but, after all, other children needed these more than Carol Bird, for she was always happy and contented, whatever she had or whatever she lacked; and after the room had been made so lovely for her, on her eighth Christmas, she always called herself, in fun, a "Bird of Paradise."

On these particular December days she was happier than usual, for Uncle Jack was coming from England to spend the holidays. Dear, funny, jolly, loving, wise Uncle Jack, who came every two or three years, and brought so much joy with him that the world looked as black as a thunder-cloud for a week after he went away again.

The mail had brought this letter:—

LONDON, November 28, 188—.
Wish you merry Christmas, you dearest

birdlings in America! Preen your feathers, and stretch the Birds' nest a trifle, if you please, and let Uncle Jack in for the holidays. I am coming with such a trunk full of treasures that you'll have to borrow the stockings of Barnum's Giant and Giantess; I am coming to squeeze a certain little ladybird until she cries for mercy; I am coming to see if I can find a boy to take care of a black pony that I bought lately. It's the strangest thing I ever knew; I've hunted all over Europe, and can't find a boy to suit me! I'll tell you why. I've set my heart on finding one with a dimple in his chin, because this pony particularly likes dimples! ["Hurrah!" cried Hugh; "bless my dear dimple; I'll never be ashamed of it again."]

Please drop a note to the clerk of the weather, and have a good, rousing snowstorm—say on the twenty-second. None of your meek, gentle, nonsensical, shilly-shallying snow-storms; not the sort where the flakes float lazily down from the sky as if they didn't care whether they ever got here or not and then melt away as soon as they touch the earth, but a regular businesslike whizzing, whirring, blurring, cutting snowstorm, warranted to freeze and stay on!

I should like rather a LARGE Christmas tree, if it's convenient: not one of those "sprigs," five or six feet high, that you used to have three or four years ago, when the birdlings were not fairly feathered out; but a tree of some size. Set it up in the garret, if necessary, and then we can cut a hole in the roof if the tree chances to be too high for the room.

Tell Bridget to begin to fatten a turkey. Tell her that by the twentieth of December that turkey must not be able to stand on its legs for fat, and then on the next three days she must allow it to recline easily on its side, and stuff it to bursting. (One ounce of stuffing beforehand is worth a pound afterwards.)

The pudding must be unusually huge, and darkly, deeply, lugubriously blue in color. It must be stuck so full of plums that the pudding itself will ooze out into the pan and not be brought on to the table at all. I expect to be there by the twentieth, to manage these little things myself,—remembering it is the early Bird that catches the worm,— but give you the instructions in case I should be delayed.

And Carol must decide on the size of

the tree—she knows best, she was a Christmas child; and she must plead for the snowstorm—the "clerk of the weather" may pay some attention to her; and she must look up the boy with the dimple for me—she's likelier to find him than I am, this minute. She must advise about the turkey, and Bridget must bring the pudding to her bedside and let her drop every separate plum into it and stir it once for luck, or I'll not eat a single slice—for Carol is the dearest part of Christmas to Uncle Jack, and he'll have none of it without her. She is better than all the turkeys and puddings and apples and spare-ribs and wreaths and garlands and mistletoe and stockings and chimneys and sleighbells in Christendom! She is the very sweetest Christmas Carol that was ever written, said, sung, or chanted, and I am coming as fast as ships and railway trains can carry me, to tell her so.

Carol's joy knew no bounds. Mr. and Mrs. Bird laughed like children and kissed each other for sheer delight, and when the boys heard it they simply whooped like wild Indians; until the Ruggles family, whose back yard joined their garden, gathered at the door and wondered what was "up" in the big house.

## "Birds of a Feather Flock Together"

ncle Jack did really come on the twentieth. He was not detained by business, nor did he get left behind nor snowed up, as frequently happens in stories, and in real life too, I am afraid. The snow-storm came also; and the turkey nearly died a natural and premature death from overeating. Donald came, too; Donald, with a line of down upon his upper lip, and Greek and Latin on his tongue, and stores of knowledge in his handsome head, and stories—bless me, you couldn't turn over a chip without reminding Donald of something that happened "at College." One or the other was always at Carol's bedside, for they fancied her paler than she used to be, and they could not bear her out of sight. It was Uncle Jack, though, who sat beside her in the winter twilights. The room was quiet, and almost dark, save for the snow-light outside, and the flickering flame of the fire, that danced over the "Sleeping Beauty's" face and touched the Fair One's golden locks with ruddier glory. Carol's hand (all too thin and white these latter days) lay close clasped in Uncle Jack's, and they talked together quietly of many, many things.

"I want to tell you all about my plans for Christmas this year, Uncle Jack," said Carol, on the first evening of his visit, "because it will be the loveliest one I ever had. The boys laugh at me for caring so much about it; but it isn't altogether because it is Christmas, nor because it is my birthday; but long, long ago, when I first began to be ill, I used to think, the first thing when I waked on Christmas morning, "To-day is Christ's birthday—*and mine!*' I did not put the words close together, you know, because that made it seem too bold; but I first said, 'Christ's birthday,' out loud, and then, in a minute, softly to myself—'*and mine!*' 'Christ's birthday—*and mine!*' And so I do not quite feel about Christmas as other girls do. Mamma says she supposes that ever so many other children have been born on that day. I often wonder where they are, Uncle Jack, and whether it is a dear thought to them, too, or whether I am so much in bed, and so often alone, that it means more to me. Oh, I do hope that none of them are poor, or cold, or hungry; and I wish— I wish they were all as happy as I, because they are really my little brothers and sisters. Now, Uncle Jack dear, I am going to try and make somebody happy every single Christmas that I live, and this year it is to be the 'Ruggleses in the rear.' "

"That large and interesting brood of children in the little house at the end of the back garden?"

"Yes; isn't it nice to see so many together?—and, Uncle Jack, why do the big families always live in the small houses, and the small families in the big houses? We ought to call them the Ruggles children, of course; but Donald began talking of them as the 'Ruggleses in the rear,' and Papa and Mamma took it up, and now we cannot seem to help it. The house was built for Mr. Carter's coachman, but Mr. Carter lives in Europe, and the gentleman who rents his place for him doesn't care what happens to it, and so this poor family came to live there. When they first moved in, I used to sit in my window and watch them play in their back yard; they are so strong, and jolly, and good-natured;—and then, one day, I had a terrible headache, and Donald asked them if they would please not scream quite so loud, and they explained that they were having a game of circus, but that they would change and play 'Deaf and Dumb Asylum' all the afternoon."

"Ha, ha, ha!" laughed Uncle Jack, "what an obliging family, to be sure!"

"Yes, we all thought it very funny, and I smiled at them from the window when I was well enough to be up again. Now, Sarah Maud comes to her door when the children come home from school, and if Mamma nods her head, 'Yes,' that means 'Carol is very well,' and then you ought to hear the little Ruggleses yell,— I believe they try to see how much noise they can make; but if Mamma shakes her head, 'No,' they always play at quiet games. Then, one day, 'Cary,' my pet canary, flew out of her cage, and Peter Ruggles caught her and brought her back, and I had him up here in my room to thank him."

"Is Peter the oldest?"

"No; Sarah Maud is the oldest—she helps do the washing, and Peter is the next. He is a dressmaker's boy."

"And which is the pretty little red-haired girl?"

"That's Kitty."

"And the fat youngster?"

"Baby Larry."

"And that—most freckled one?"

"Now, don't laugh—that's Peoria."

"Carol, you are joking."

"No, really, Uncle dear. She was born in Peoria; that's all."

"And is the next boy Oshkosh?"

"No," laughed Carol, "the others are Susan, and Clement, and Eily, and Cornelius; they all look exactly alike, except that some of them have more freckles than the others."

"How did you ever learn all their names?"

"Why, I have what I call a 'window-school.' It is

too cold now; but in warm weather I am wheeled out
on my balcony, and the Ruggleses climb up and walk
along our garden fence, and sit down on the roof of
our carriage-house. That brings them quite near, and I
tell them stories. On Thanksgiving Day they came up
for a few minutes,—it was quite warm at eleven
o'clock,—and we told each other what we had to be
thankful for; but they gave such queer answers that
Papa had to run away for fear of laughing; and I
couldn't understand them very well. Susan was thankful for *'trunks,'* of all things in the world; Cornelius,
for 'horse-cars;' Kitty, for 'pork steak;' while Clem,
who is very quiet, brightened up when I came to
him, and said he was thankful for *'his lame puppy.'*
Wasn't that pretty?"

"It might teach some of us a lesson, mightn't it,
little girl?"

"That's what Mamma said. Now I'm going to
give this whole Christmas to the Ruggleses; and, Uncle
Jack, I earned part of the money myself."

"You, my bird; how?"

"Well, you see, it could not be my own, own
Christmas if Papa gave me all the money, and I thought
to really keep Christ's birthday I ought to do something of my very own; and so I talked with Mamma.
Of course she thought of something lovely; she always
does: Mamma's head is just brimming over with lovely

thoughts,—all I have to do is ask, and out pops the very one I want. This thought was to let her write down, just as I told her, a description of how a child lived in her room for three years, and what she did to amuse herself; and we sent it to a magazine and got twenty-five dollars for it. Just think!"

'Well, well," cried Uncle Jack, "my little girl a real author! And what are you going to do with this wonderful 'own' money of yours?"

"I shall give the nine Ruggleses a grand Christmas dinner here in this very room—that will be Papa's contribution,—and afterwards a beautiful Christmas tree, fairly blooming with presents—that will be my part; for I have another way of adding to my twenty-five dollars, so that I can buy nearly anything I choose. I should like it very much if you would sit at the head of the table, Uncle Jack, for nobody could ever be frightened of you, you dearest, dearest, dearest thing that ever was! Mamma is going to help us, but Papa and the boys are going to eat together downstairs for fear of making the little Ruggleses shy; and after we've had a merry time with the tree we can open my window and all listen together to the music at the evening church-service, if it comes before the children go. I have written a letter to the organist, and asked him if I might have the two songs I like best. Will you see if it is all right?"

BIRDS' NEST, December 21, 188—.

DEAR MR. WILKIE,—I am the little girl who lives next door to the church, and, as I seldom go out, the music on practice days and Sundays is one of my greatest pleasures.

I want to know if you can have "Carol, brothers, carol," on Christmas night, and if the boy who sings "My ain countree" so beautifully may please sing that too. I think it is the loveliest thing in the world, but it always makes me cry; doesn't it you?

If it isn't too much trouble, I hope they can sing them both quite early, as after ten o'clock I may be asleep.

Yours respectfully, CAROL BIRD

P.S.—The reason I like "Carol, brothers, carol," is because the choir-boys sang it eleven years ago, the morning I was born, and put it into Mamma's head to call me Carol. She didn't remember then that my other name would be Bird, because she was half asleep, and could only think of one thing at a time. Donald says if I had been born on the Fourth of July they would have named me "Independence," or if on the twenty-second of February, "Georgina," or even "Cherry," like Cherry in "Martin

Chuzzlewit;" but I like my own name and birthday best.

Yours truly, CAROL BIRD

Uncle Jack thought the letter quite right, and did not even smile at her telling the organist so many family items.

The days flew by as they always fly in holiday time, and it was Christmas Eve before anybody knew it. The family festival was quiet and very pleasant, but almost overshadowed by the grander preparations for the next day. Carol and Elfrida, her pretty German nurse, had ransacked books, and introduced so many plans, and plays, and customs, and merrymakings from Germany, and Holland, and England, and a dozen other countries, that you would scarcely have known how or where you were keeping Christmas. Even the dog and the cat had enjoyed their celebration under Carol's direction. Each had a tiny table with a lighted candle in the centre, and a bit of Bologna sausage placed very near it; and everybody laughed till the tears stood in their eyes to see Villikins and Dinah struggle to nibble the sausages, and at the same time to evade the candle flame. Villikins barked, and sniffed, and howled in impatience, and after many vain attempts succeeded in dragging off the prize, though he singed his nose in doing it. Dinah, meanwhile, watched him placidly, her delicate nostrils quivering with expectation, and, after all excitement had subsided, walked with dignity to the table, her beautiful gray satin trail sweeping behind her, and, calmly putting up one velvet paw, drew the sausage gently down, and walked out of the room without turning a hair, so to speak. Elfrida had scattered handfuls of seed over the snow in the garden, that the wild birds might have a comfortable breakfast next morning, and had stuffed bundles of dry grasses in the fireplaces, so that the reindeer of Santa Claus could refresh themselves after their long gallops across country. This was really only done for fun, but it pleased Carol.

And when, after dinner, the whole family had gone to the church to see the Christmas decorations, Carol limped out on her slender crutches, and with Elfrida's help, placed all the family boots in a row in the upper hall. That was to keep the dear ones from quarreling all through the year. There were Papa's stout top boots; Mamma's pretty buttoned shoes next; then Uncle Jack's, Donald's, Paul's, and Hugh's; and at the end of the line her own little white worsted slippers. Last, and sweetest of all, like the children in Austria, she put a lighted candle in her window to guide the dear Christ-child, lest he should stumble in the dark night as he passed up the deserted street. This done, she dropped into bed, a rather tired, but very happy Christmas fairy.

*5*

## Some Other Birds are Taught to Fly

**B**efore the earliest Ruggles could wake and toot his five-cent tin horn, Mrs. Ruggles was up and stirring about the house, for it was a gala day in the family. Gala day! I should think so! Were not her nine "children" invited to a dinner-party at the great house, and weren't they going to sit down free and equal with the mightiest in the land? She had been preparing for this grand occasion ever since the receipt of Carol Bird's invitation, which, by the way, had been speedily enshrined in an old photograph frame and hung under the looking-glass in the most prominent place in the kitchen, where it stared the occasional visitor directly in the eye, and made him livid with envy:—

BIRDS' NEST, December 17, 188—.

DEAR MRS. RUGGLES,—I am going to have a

dinner-party on Christmas Day, and would like to have all your children come. I want them every one, please, from Sarah Maud to Baby Larry. Mamma says dinner will be at half past five, and the Christmas tree at seven; so you may expect them home at nine o'clock. Wishing you a Merry Christmas and a Happy New Year, I am

Yours truly, CAROL BIRD

Breakfast was on the table promptly at seven o'clock, and there was very little of it, too; for it was an excellent day for short rations, though Mrs. Ruggles heaved a sigh as she reflected that the boys, with their India-rubber stomachs, would be just as hungry the day after the dinner-party as if they had never had any at all.

As soon as the scanty meal was over, she announced the plan of the campaign: "Now, Susan, you an' Kitty wash up the dishes; an' Peter, can't yer spread up the beds, so't I can git ter cuttin' out Larry's new suit? I ain't satisfied with his clo'es, an' I thought in the night of a way to make him a dress out o' my old red plaid shawl—kind o' Scotch style, yer know, with the fringe 't the bottom.—Eily, you go find the comb and take the snarls out the fringe, that's a lady! You little young ones clear out from under foot! Clem, you and Con hop into bed with Larry while I wash yer

underflannins; t'won't take long to dry 'em.—Yes, I
know it's bothersome, but yer can't go int' s'ciety
'thout takin' some trouble, 'n' anyhow I couldn't git
round to 'em last night.—Sarah Maud, I think 'twould
be perfeckly han'som' if you ripped them brass buttons
off yer uncle's *policeman's* coat 'n' sewed 'em in a row
up the front o' yer green skirt. Susan, you must iron
out yours 'n' Kitty's apurns; 'n' there, I come mighty
near forgettin' Peory's stockin's! I counted the whole
lot last night when I was washin' of 'em, 'n' there ain't
but nineteen anyhow yer fix 'em, 'n' no nine pairs
mates nohow; 'n' I ain't goin' ter have my children
wear odd stockin's to a dinner-comp'ny, fetched up as
I was! —Eily, can't you run out and ask Mis' Cullen
ter lend me a pair o' stockin's for Peory, 'n' tell her if
she will, Peory'll give Jim half her candy when she gets
home. Won't yer, Peory?''

Peoria was young and greedy, and thought the
remedy so out of all proportion to the disease, that she
set up a deafening howl at the projected bargain—a
howl so rebellious and so entirely out of season that
her mother started in her direction with flashing eye
and uplifted hand; but she let it fall suddenly, saying,
"No, I vow I won't lick ye Christmas Day, if yer drive
me crazy; but speak up smart, now, 'n' say whether
yer'd ruther give Jim Cullen half yer candy or go bare-
legged ter the party?'' The matter being put so plainly,
Peoria collected her faculties, dried her tears, and chose

the lesser evil, Clem having hastened the decision by an affectionate wink, that meant he'd go halves with her on his candy.

"That's a lady!" cried her mother. "Now, you young ones that ain't doin' nothin', play all yer want ter before noontime, for after ye git through eatin' at twelve o'clock me 'n' Sarah Maud's goin' ter give yer sech a washin' 'n' combin' 'n' dressin' as yer never had before 'n' never will agin likely, 'n' then I'm goin' to set yer down 'n' give yer two solid hours trainin' in manners; 'n' 'twon't be no foolin' neither."

"All we've got ter do's go eat!" grumbled Peter.

"Well, that's enough," responded his mother; "there's more'n one way of eatin', let me tell yer, 'n' you've got a heap ter learn about it, Peter Ruggles. Land sakes, I wish you children could see the way I was fetched up to eat. I never took a meal o' vittles in the kitchen before I married Ruggles; but yer can't keep up that style with nine young ones 'n' yer Pa always off ter sea."

The big Ruggleses worked so well, and the little Ruggleses kept from "under foot" so successfully, that by one o'clock nine complete toilets were laid out in solemn grandeur on the beds. I say, "complete;" but I do not know whether they would be called so in the best society. The law of compensation had been well applied: he that had necktie had no cuffs; she that had sash had no handkerchief, and *vice versa*; but they all had shoes and a certain amount of clothing, such as it was, the outside layer being in every case quite above criticism.

"Now, Sarah Maud," said Mrs. Ruggles, her face shining with excitement, "everything's red up an' we can begin. I've got a boiler 'n' a kettle 'n' a pot o' hot water. Peter, you go into the back bedroom, 'n' I'll take Susan, Kitty, Peory, 'n' Cornelius; 'n' Sarah Maud, you take Clem, 'n' Eily, 'n' Larry, one to a time. Scrub 'em 'n' rinse 'em, or, 't any rate, git's fur's yer can with 'em, and then I'll finish 'em off while you do yerself."

Sarah Maud couldn't have scrubbed with any more decision and force if she had been doing floors, and the little Ruggleses bore it bravely, not from natural heroism, but for the joy that was set before them. Not being satisfied, however, with the "tone" of their complexions, and feeling that the number of freckles to the square inch was too many to be tolerated in the highest social circles, she wound up operations by applying a little Bristol brick from the knife-board, which served as the proverbial "last straw," from under which the little Ruggleses issued rather red and raw and out of temper. When the clock struck four they were all clothed, and most of them in their right minds, ready for those last touches that always take the most time.

Kitty's red hair was curled in thirty-four ringlets, Sarah Maud's was braided in one pig-tail, and Susan's and Eily's in two braids apiece, while Peoria's resisted all advances in the shape of hair oils and stuck out straight on all sides, like that of the Circassian girl of the circus—so Clem said; and he was sent into the bedroom for it, too, from whence he was dragged out forgivingly, by Peoria herself, five minutes later. Then, exciting moment, came linen collars for some and neckties and bows for others,—a magnificent green glass breastpin was sewed into Peter's purple necktie,—and Eureka! the Ruggleses were dressed, and Solomon in all his glory was not arrayed like one of these!

A row of seats was then formed directly through the middle of the kitchen. Of course, there were not quite chairs enough for ten, since the family had rarely wanted to sit down all at once, somebody always being out or in bed, or otherwise engaged, but the wood-box and the coal-hod finished out the line nicely, and nobody thought of grumbling. The children took their places according to age, Sarah Maud at the head and Larry on the coal-hod, and Mrs. Ruggles seated herself in front, surveying them proudly as she wiped the sweat of honest toil from her brow.

"Well," she exclaimed, "if I do say so as shouldn't, I never see a cleaner, more stylish mess o' children in my life! I do wish Ruggles could look at ye for a minute!—Larry Ruggles, how many times have I got ter tell yer not ter keep pullin' at yer sash? Haven't I told yer if it comes ontied, yer waist 'n' skirt'll part

comp'ny in the middle, 'n' then where'll yer be?
—Now look me in the eye, all of yer! I've of'en told
yer what kind of a family the McGrills was. I've got
reason to be proud, goodness knows! Your uncle is on
the *po*lice force o' New York city; you can take up the
paper most any day an' see his name printed right out—
James McGrill—'n' I can't have my children fetched
up common, like some folks'; when they go out
they've got to have clo'es, and learn to act decent! Now
I want ter see how yer goin' to behave when yer git
there to-night. 'Tain't so awful easy as you think 'tis.
Let's start in at the beginnin' 'n' act out the whole
business. Pile into the bedroom, there, every last one
o' ye, 'n' show me how yer goin' to go int' the parlor.
This'll be the parlor, 'n' I'll be Mis' Bird.''

The youngsters hustled into the next room in
high glee, and Mrs. Ruggles drew herself up in the chair
with an infinitely haughty and purse-proud expression
that much better suited a descendant of the McGrills
than modest Mrs. Bird.

The bedroom was small, and there presently ensued such a clatter that you would have thought a
herd of wild cattle had broken loose. The door opened,
and they straggled in, all the younger ones giggling,
with Sarah Maud at the head, looking as if she had
been caught in the act of stealing sheep; while Larry,
being last in line, seemed to think the door a sort of
gate of heaven which would be shut in his face if he

didn't get there in time; accordingly he struggled ahead of his elders and disgraced himself by tumbling in head foremost.

Mrs. Ruggles looked severe. "There, I knew yer'd do it in some sech fool way! Now go in there and try it over again, every last one o' ye, 'n' if Larry can't come in on two legs he can stay ter home,—d'yer hear?"

The matter began to assume a graver aspect; the little Ruggleses stopped giggling and backed into the bedroom, issuing presently with lock step, Indian file, a scared and hunted expression on every countenance.

"No, no, no!" cried Mrs. Ruggles, in despair. "That's worse yet; yer look for all the world like a gang o' pris'ners! There ain't no style ter that: spread out more, can't yer, 'n' act kind o' carelesslike—nobody's goin' ter kill ye! That ain't what a dinner-party is!"

The third time brought deserved success, and the pupils took their seats in the row. "Now, yer know," said Mrs. Ruggles impressively, "there ain't enough decent hats to go round, 'n' if there was I don' know's I'd let yer wear 'em, for the boys would never think to take 'em off when they got inside, for they never do—but anyhow, there ain't enough good ones. Now, look me in the eye. You're only goin' jest round the corner; you needn't wear no hats, none of yer, 'n' when yer get int' the parlor, 'n' they ask yer ter lay off yer hats, Sarah Maud must speak up 'n' say it was sech a pleasant evenin' 'n' sech a short walk that yer left yer hats to home. Now, can yer remember?"

All the little Ruggleses shouted, "Yes, marm!" in chorus.

"What have *you* got ter do with it?" demanded their mother; "did I tell *you* to say it? Warn't I talkin' ter Sarah Maud?"

The little Ruggleses hung their diminished heads. "Yes, marm," they piped, more discreetly.

"Now we won't leave nothin' to chance; git up, all of ye, an' try it.—Speak up, Sarah Maud."

Sarah Maud's tongue clove to the roof of her mouth.

"Quick!"

"Ma thought—it was—sech a pleasant hat that we'd—we'd better leave our short walk to home," recited Sarah Maud, in an agony of mental effort.

This was too much for the boys. An earthquake of suppressed giggles swept all along the line.

"Oh, whatever shall I do with yer?" moaned the unhappy mother; "I s'pose I've got to learn it to yer!"— which she did, word for word, until Sarah Maud thought she could stand on her head and say it backwards.

"Now, Cornelius, what are *you* goin' ter say ter make yerself good comp'ny?"

"Do? Me? Dunno!" said Cornelius, turning pale, with unexpected responsibility.

"Well, ye ain't goin' to set there like a bump on a log 'thout sayin' a word ter pay for yer vittles, air ye? Ask Mis' Bird how she's feelin' this evenin', or if Mr. Bird's hevin' a busy season, or how this kind o' weather agrees with him, or somethin' like that. —Now we'll make b'lieve we've got ter the dinner— that won't be so hard, 'cause yer'll have somethin' to do—it's awful bothersome to stan' round an' act stylish.—If they have napkins, Sarah Maud down to Peory may put em in their laps, 'n' the rest of ye can tuck 'em in yer necks. Don't eat with yer fingers— don't grab no vittles off one 'nother's plates; don't reach out for nothin', but wait till yer asked, 'n' if you never *git* asked don't git up and grab it.—Don't spill nothin' on the tablecloth, or like's not Mis' Bird'll send yer away from the table—'n' I hope she will if yer do! (Susan! keep your handkerchief in your lap where Peory can borry it if she needs it, 'n' I hope she'll know when she does need it, though I don't expect it.) Now we'll try a few things ter see how they'll go! Mr. Clement, do you eat cramb'ry sarse?"

"Bet yer life!" cried Clem, who in the excitement of the moment had not taken in the idea exactly and had mistaken this for an ordinary bosom-of-the-family question.

"Clement McGrill Ruggles, do you mean to tell

me that you'd say that to a dinner-party? I'll give ye one more chance. Mr. Clement, will you take some of the cramb'ry?"

"Yes, marm, thank ye kindly, if you happen ter have any handy."

"Very good, indeed! But they won't give yer two tries to-night,—yer just remember that!—Miss Peory, do you speak for white or dark meat?"

"I ain't perticler as ter color,—anything that no-body else wants will suit me," answered Peory with her best air.

"First-rate! Nobody could speak more genteel than that. Miss Kitty, will you have hard or soft sarse with your pudden?"

"Hard or soft? Oh! A little of both, if you please, an' I'm much obliged," said Kitty, bowing with de-cided ease and grace; at which all the other Ruggleses pointed the finger of shame at her, and Peter *grunted* expressively, that their meaning might not be mis-taken.

"You just stop your gruntin', Peter Ruggles; that weren't greedy, that was all right. I wish I could git it inter your heads that it ain't so much what yer say, as the way you say it. And don't keep starin' cross-eyed at your necktie pin, or I'll take it out 'n' sew it on to Clem or Cornelius: Sarah Maud'll keep her eye on it, 'n' if it turns broken side out she'll tell yer. Gracious! I shouldn't think you'd ever seen nor worn no jool'ry in your life.—Eily, you an' Larry's too little to train, so you just look at the rest an' do's they do, 'n' the Lord have mercy on ye 'n' help ye to act decent! Now, is there anything more ye'd like to practice?"

"If yer tell me one more thing, I can't set up an' eat," said Peter gloomily; "I'm so cram full o' manners now, I'm ready ter bust, 'thout no dinner at all."

"Me, too," chimed in Cornelius.

"Well, I'm sorry for yer both," rejoined Mrs. Ruggles sarcastically; "if the 'mount o' manners yer've got on hand now troubles ye, you're dreadful easy hurt! Now, Sarah Maud, after dinner, about once in so often, you must git up 'n' say, 'I guess we'd better be goin',' 'n' if they say, 'Oh, no, set a while longer,' yer can set; but if they don't say nothin' you've got ter get up 'n' go.—Now hev yer got that int' yer head?"

*About once in so often!* Could any words in the language be fraught with more terrible and wearing uncertainty?

"Well," answered Sarah Maud mournfully, "seems as if this whole dinner-party set right square on top o' me! Mebbe I could manage my own manners, but to manage nine mannerses is worse'n staying to home!"

"Oh, don't fret," said her mother, good-naturedly, now that the lesson was over; "I guess you'll git along. I wouldn't mind if folks would only say, 'Oh, childern will be childern;' but they won't. They'll say, 'Land o' Goodness, who fetched them childern up?'—It's quarter past five, 'n' yer can go now: —remember 'bout the hats,—don't all talk ter once, —Susan, lend yer han'k'chief ter Peory,—Peter, don't keep screwin' yer scarf-pin,—Cornelius, hold yer head up straight,—Sarah Maud, don't take yer eyes off o' Larry, 'n' Larry you keep holt o' Sarah Maud 'n' do jest as she says,—'n' whatever you do, all of yer, never forgit for one second that yer mother was a McGrill."

# 6

## "When The Pie Was Opened, The Birds Began To Sing!"

T he children went out of the back door quietly, and were presently lost to sight, Sarah Maud slipping and stumbling along absent-mindedly, as she recited rapidly under her breath, "Itwassuchapleasantevenin'n'suchashortwalk, thatwethoughtwe'dleaveourhatstohome. — Itwassuchapleasantevenin'n'suchashortwalk, thatwethoughtwe'dleaveourhatstohome."

Peter rang the door-bell, and presently a servant admitted them, and, whispering something in Sarah's ear, drew her downstairs into the kitchen. The other Ruggleses stood in horror-stricken groups as the door closed behind their commanding officer; but there was no time for reflection, for a voice from above was heard, saying, "Come right upstairs, please!"

"Theirs not to make reply,
Theirs not to reason why,
Theirs but to do or die."

Accordingly they walked upstairs, and Elfrida, the nurse, ushered them into a room more splendid than anything they had ever seen. But, oh woe! where was Sarah Maud! and was it Fate that Mrs. Bird should say, at once, "Did you lay your hats in the hall?" Peter felt himself elected by circumstance the head of the family, and, casting one imploring look at tongue-tied Susan, standing next him, said huskily, "It was so very pleasant—that—that—" "That we hadn't good hats enough to go 'round," put in little Susan, bravely, to help him out, and then froze with horror that the ill-fated words had slipped off her tongue.

However, Mrs. Bird said, pleasantly, "Of course you wouldn't wear hats such a short distance—I forgot when I asked. Now will you come right in to Miss Carol's room? She is so anxious to see you."

Just then Sarah Maud came up the back stairs, so radiant with joy from her secret interview with the cook that Peter could have pinched her with a clear conscience; and Carol gave them a joyful welcome. "But where is Baby Larry?" she cried, looking over the group with searching eye. "Didn't he come?"

"Larry! Larry!" Good gracious, where was Larry?

They were all sure that he had come in with them, for Susan remembered scolding him for tripping over the door-mat. Uncle Jack went into convulsions of laughter. "Are you sure there were nine of you?" he asked, merrily.

"I think so, sir," said Peoria, timidly; "but anyhow, there was Larry;" and she showed signs of weeping.

"Oh, well, cheer up!" cried Uncle Jack. "Probably he's not lost—only mislaid. I'll go and find him before you can say Jack Robinson!"

"I'll go, too, if you please, sir," said Sarah Maud, "for it was my place to mind him, an' if he's lost I can't relish my vittles!"

The other Ruggleses stood rooted to the floor. Was this a dinner-party, forsooth; and if so, why were such things ever spoken of as festive occasions?

Sarah Maud went out through the hall, calling, "Larry! Larry!" and without any interval of suspense a thin voice piped up from below, "Here I be!"

The truth was that Larry, being deserted by his natural guardian, dropped behind the rest, and wriggled into the hat-tree to wait for her, having no notion of walking unprotected into the jaws of a fashionable entertainment. Finding that she did not come, he tried to crawl from his refuge and call somebody, when— dark and dreadful ending to a tragic day—he found that he was too much intertwined with umbrellas and canes to move a single step. He was afraid to yell (when I have said this of Larry Ruggles I have pictured a state of helpless terror that ought to wring tears from every eye); and the sound of Sarah Maud's beloved voice, some seconds later, was like a strain of angel music in his ears. Uncle Jack dried his tears, carried him upstairs, and soon had him in breathless fits of laughter, while Carol so made the other Ruggleses forget themselves that they were presently talking like accomplished diners-out.

Carol's bed had been moved into the farthest corner of the room, and she was lying on the outside, dressed in a wonderful dressing-gown that looked like a fleecy cloud. Her golden hair fell in fluffy curls over her white forehead and neck, her cheeks flushed delicately, her eyes beamed with joy, and the children told their mother, afterwards, that she looked as beautiful as the angels in the picture books.

There was a great bustle behind a huge screen in another part of the room, and at half past five this was taken away, and the Christmas dinnertable stood revealed. What a wonderful sight it was to the poor little Ruggles children, who ate their sometimes scanty meals on the kitchen table! It blazed with tall colored candles, it gleamed with glass and silver, it blushed with flowers, it groaned with good things to eat; so it was not strange that the Ruggleses, forgetting altogether that their mother was a McGrill, shrieked in admira-

tion of the fairy spectacle. But Larry's behavior was
the most disgraceful, for he stood not upon the order
of his going, but went at once for a high chair that
pointed unmistakably to him, climbed up like a squir-
rel, gave a comprehensive look at the turkey, clapped
his hands in ecstasy, rested his fat arms on the table,
and cried with joy, "I beat the hull lot o' yer!" Carol
laughed until she cried, giving orders, meanwhile,—
"Uncle Jack, please sit at the head, Sarah Maud at
the foot, and that will leave four on each side;
Mamma is going to help Elfrida, so that the children
need not look after each other, but just have a good
time."

A sprig of holly lay by each plate, and nothing
would do but each little Ruggles must leave his seat
and have it pinned on by Carol, and as each course was
served, one of them pleaded to take something to her.
There was hurrying to and fro, I can assure you, for it
is quite a difficult matter to serve a Christmas dinner
on the third floor of a great city house; but if it had
been necessary to carry every dish up a rope ladder the
servants would gladly have done so. There were turkey
and chicken, with delicious gravy and stuffing, and
there were half a dozen vegetables, with cranberry jelly,
and celery, and pickles; and as for the way these deli-
cacies were served, the Ruggleses never forgot it as long
as they lived.

Peter nudged Kitty, who sat next him, and said, "Look, will yer, ev'ry feller's got his own partic'lar butter; I s'pose that's to show you can eat that 'n' no more. No, it ain't either, for that pig of a Peory's just gettin' another helpin'!"

"Yes," whispered Kitty, "an' the napkins is marked with big red letters! I wonder if that's so nobody'll nip 'em; an' oh, Peter, look at the pictures stickin' right on ter the dishes! Did yer ever?"

"The plums is all took out o' my cramb'ry sarse an' it's friz to a stiff jell'!" whispered Peoria, in wild excitement.

"Hi—yah! I got a wish-bone!" sang Larry, regardless of Sarah Maud's frown; after which she asked to have his seat changed, giving as excuse that he "gen'ally set beside her, an' would feel strange;" the true reason being that she desired to kick him gently, under the table, whenever he passed what might be termed "the McGrill line."

"I declare to goodness," murmured Susan, on the other side, "there's so much to look at I can't scarcely eat nothin'!"

"Bet yer life I can!" said Peter, who had kept one servant busily employed ever since he sat down; for, luckily, no one was asked by Uncle Jack whether he would have a second helping, but the dishes were quietly passed under their noses, and not a single Ruggles refused anything that was offered him, even unto the seventh time.

Then, when Carol and Uncle Jack perceived that more turkey was a physical impossibility, the meats were taken off and the dessert was brought in—a dessert that would have frightened a strong man after such a dinner as had preceded it. Not so the Ruggleses—for a strong man is nothing to a small boy—and they kindled to the dessert as if the turkey had been a dream and the six vegetables an optical delusion. There were plum-pudding, mince-pie, and ice-cream; and there were nuts, and raisins, and oranges. Kitty chose ice-cream, explaining that she knew it "by sight, though she hadn't never tasted none;" but all the rest took the entire variety, without any regard to consequences.

"My dear child," whispered Uncle Jack, as he took Carol an orange, "there is no doubt about the necessity of this feast, but I do advise you after this to have them twice a year, or quarterly perhaps, for the way these children eat is positively dangerous; I assure you I tremble for that terrible Peoria. I'm going to run races with her after dinner."

"Never mind," laughed Carol; "let them have enough for once; it does my heart good to see them, and they shall come oftener next year."

The feast being over, the Ruggleses lay back in their chairs languidly, like little gorged boa-constrictors, and the table was cleared in a trice. Then a door was opened into the next room, and there, in a corner facing Carol's bed, which had been wheeled as close as possible, stood the brilliantly lighted Christmas tree, glittering with gilded walnuts and tiny silver balloons, and wreathed with snowy chains of pop-corn. The presents had been bought mostly with Carol's story-money, and were selected after long consultations with Mrs. Bird. Each girl had a blue knitted hood, and each boy a red crocheted comforter, all made by Mamma, Carol, and Elfrida. ("Because if you buy everything, it doesn't show so much love," said Carol.) Then every girl had a pretty plaid dress of a different color, and every boy a warm coat of the right size. Here the useful presents stopped and they were quite enough; but Carol had pleaded to give them something "for fun." "I know they need the clothes," she had said, when they were talking over the matter just after Thanksgiving, "but they don't care much for them, after all. Now, Papa, won't you *please* let me go without part of my presents this year, and give me the money they would cost, to buy something to amuse the Ruggleses?"

"You can have both," said Mr. Bird, promptly; "is there any need of my little girl's going without her own Christmas, I should like to know? Spend all the money you like."

"But that isn't the thing," objected Carol, nestling close to her father; "it wouldn't be mine. What is the use? Haven't I almost everything already, and am I not the happiest girl in the world this year, with Uncle Jack and Donald at home? You know very well it is more blessed to give than to receive; so why won't you let me do it? You never look half as happy when you are getting your presents as when you are giving us ours. Now, Papa, submit, or I shall have to be very firm and disagreeable with you!"

"Very well, your Highness, I surrender."

"That's a dear Papa! Now what were you going to give me? Confess!"

"A bronze figure of Santa Claus; and in the 'little round belly that shakes when he laughs like a bowlful of jelly,' is a wonderful clock—oh, you would never give it up if you could see it!"

"Nonsense," laughed Carol; "as I never have to get up to breakfast, nor go to bed, nor catch trains, I think my old clock will do very well! Now, Mamma, what were you going to give me?"

"Oh, I hadn't decided. A few more books, and a gold thimble, and a smelling-bottle, and a music-box, perhaps."

"Poor Carol," laughed the child, merrily, "she can afford to give up these lovely things, for there will still be left Uncle Jack, and Donald, and Paul, and

Hugh, and Uncle Rob, and Aunt Elsie, and a dozen other people to fill her Christmas stocking!"

So Carol had her way, as she generally did; but it was usually a good way, which was fortunate, under the circumstances; and Sarah Maud had a set of Miss Alcott's books, and Peter a modest silver watch, Cornelius a tool-chest, Clement a dog-house for his lame puppy, Larry a magnificent Noah's ark, and each of the younger girls a beautiful doll.

You can well believe that everybody was very merry and very thankful. All the family, from Mr. Bird down to the cook, said that they had never seen so much happiness in the space of three hours; but it had to end, as all things do. The candles flickered and went out, the tree was left alone with its gilded ornaments, and Mrs. Bird sent the children downstairs at half past eight, thinking that Carol looked tired.

"Now, my darling, you have done quite enough for one day," said Mrs. Bird, getting Carol into her little nightgown. "I'm afraid you will feel worse to-morrow, and that would be a sad ending to such a charming evening."

"Oh, wasn't it a lovely, lovely time," sighed Carol. "From first to last, everything was just right. I shall never forget Larry's face when he looked at the turkey; nor Peter's when he saw his watch; nor that sweet, sweet Kitty's smile when she kissed her dolly;

nor the tears in poor, dull Sarah Maud's eyes when she thanked me for her books; nor"—

"But we mustn't talk any longer about it to-night," said Mrs. Bird, anxiously; "you are too tired, dear."

"I am not so very tired, Mamma. I have felt well all day; not a bit of pain anywhere. Perhaps this has done me good."

"Perhaps; I hope so. There was no noise or confusion; it was just a merry time. Now, may I close the door and leave you alone, dear? Papa and I will steal in softly by and by to see if you are all right; but I think you need to be very quiet."

"Oh, I'm willing to stay by myself; but I am not sleepy yet, and I am going to hear the music, you know."

"Yes, I have opened the window a little, and put the screen in front of it, so that you won't feel the air."

"Can I have the shutters open? and won't you turn my bed, please? This morning I woke ever so early, and one bright, beautiful star shone in that eastern window. I never noticed it before, and I thought of the Star in the East, that guided the wise men to the place where the baby Jesus was. Good-night, Mamma. Such a happy, happy day!"

"Good-night, my precious Christmas Carol— mother's blessed Christmas child."

"Bend your head a minute, mother dear," whispered Carol, calling her mother back. "Mamma, dear, I do think that we have kept Christ's birthday this time just as He would like it. Don't you?"

"I am sure of it," said Mrs. Bird, softly.

*7*

## The Birdling Flies Away

T he Ruggleses had finished a last romp in the library with Paul and Hugh, and Uncle Jack had taken them home and stayed a while to chat with Mrs. Ruggles, who opened the door for them, her face all aglow with excitement and delight. When Kitty and Clem showed her the oranges and nuts that they had kept for her, she astonished them by saying that at six o'clock Mrs. Bird had sent her in the finest dinner she had ever seen in her life; and not only that, but a piece of dress-goods that must have cost a dollar a yard if it cost a cent.

As Uncle Jack went down the rickety steps he looked back into the window for a last glimpse of the family, as the children gathered about their mother, showing their beautiful presents again and again,—and then upward to a window in the great house yonder.

"A little child shall lead them," he thought. "Well, if— if anything ever happens to Carol, I will take the Ruggleses under my wing."

"Softly, Uncle Jack," whispered the boys, as he walked into the library a while later. "We are listening to the music in the church. The choir has sung 'Carol, brothers, carol,' and now we think the organist is beginning to play 'My ain countree' for Carol."

"I hope she hears it," said Mrs. Bird; "but they are very late to-night, and I dare not speak to her lest she should be asleep. It is almost ten o'clock."

The boy soprano, clad in white surplice, stood in the organ loft. The light shone full upon his crown of fair hair, and his pale face, with its serious blue eyes, looked paler than usual. Perhaps it was something in the tender thrill of the voice, or in the sweet words, but there were tears in many eyes, both in the church and in the great house next door.

"I am far frae my hame,
    I am weary aften whiles
  For the langed-for hame-bringin',
    An' my Faether's welcome smiles;
  An' I'll ne'er be fu' content,
    until my e'en do see

The gowden gates o'heaven
　　In my ain countree.

"The earth is decked wi' flow'rs,
　　Mony tinted, fresh an' gay,
An' the birdies warble blythely,
　　For my Faether made them sae;
But these sights an' these soun's
　　Will as naething be to me,
When I hear the angels singin'
　　In my ain countree.

"Like a bairn to its mither,
　　A wee birdie to its nest,
I fain would be gangin' noo
　　Unto my Faether's breast;
For He gathers in His arms
　　Helpless, worthless lambs like me,
An' carries them to Himsel'
　　To his ain countree."

There were tears in many eyes, but not in Carol's. The loving heart had quietly ceased to beat, and the "wee birdie" in the great house had flown to its "home nest." Carol had fallen asleep! But as to the song, I think perhaps, I cannot say, she heard it after all!

———

So sad an ending to a happy day! Perhaps—to those who were left; and yet Carol's mother, even in the freshness of her grief, was glad that her darling had slipped away on the loveliest day of her life, out of its glad content, into everlasting peace.

She was glad that she had gone as she had come, on the wings of song, when all the world was brimming over with joy; glad of every grateful smile, of every joyous burst of laughter, of every loving thought and word and deed the dear last day had brought.

Sadness reigned, it is true, in the little house behind the garden; and one day poor Sarah Maud, with a courage born of despair, threw on her hood and shawl, walked straight to a certain house a mile away, up the marble steps into good Dr. Bartol's office, falling at his feet as she cried, "Oh, sir, it was me an' our children that went to Miss Carol's last dinner-party, an' if we made her worse we can't never be happy again!" Then the kind old gentleman took her rough hand in his and told her to dry her tears, for neither she nor any of her flock had hastened Carol's flight; indeed, he said that had it not been for the strong hopes and wishes that filled her tired heart, she could not have stayed long enough to keep that last merry Christmas with her dear ones.

And so the old years, fraught with memories, die, one after another, and the new years, bright with hopes, are born to take their places; but Carol lives again in every chime of Christmas bells that peal glad tidings, and in every Christmas anthem sung by childish voices.

# Brotherly House

*A Christmas
Story by*
Grace S.
Richmond

t seems to me," said Mr. Stephen Kingsley thoughtfully to himself, as he laid down his younger brother Samuel's letter, "that it would be a very good thing to get Sam and Sylvester together. Judging by this letter—and one I had not long ago from Syl— it must be some three or four years since they've met—voluntarily. And that is too long—altogether too long—for brothers to remain in relations—er—lacking harmony."

He perused the letter again. As he had observed, its general tenor certainly did suggest that the relations between Samuel and Sylvester lacked harmony, and that that was a very mild putting of the case. Samuel's terse phrases left the situation in no doubt whatever.

"I don't like to say it to you, Stephen,"
the letter ran in one portion, "but Sylvester
has acted not only unfairly, but contemptibly.
I could have forgiven him the act itself, but
the manner of the act—never. It was done too
deliberately, too designedly, to be overlooked.
I shall not overlook it. I shall—" etc.

In short, the letter had not been pleasant reading.
The white-haired brother who read it, lying back
among his invalid's pillows, with a wry little twist of
pain about his gentle lips as his eyes laboriously followed Samuel's vigorous scrawls and equally vigorous
language, felt it to be a matter in which it was time to
interfere. Men and brothers of the age of Samuel and
Sylvester—neither would see forty-five years again—
should not be allowed to feel in this way toward each
other if their elder brother could help it.

"He 'doesn't like to say it,' " commented Stephen
Kingsley with mild irony, "yet he seems to say it with
considerable relish, nevertheless. The question is—what
can I do?"

He closed his eyes and lay thinking. After a little
he put out his hand and touched an electric bell. Its
distant summons presently brought into the room the
tall and commanding figure of a woman with iron-gray
hair and a capable face. Mrs. Griggs had been Mr. Stephen Kingsley's housekeeper for thirty years; there

could be no person more fitting for an elderly bachelor to consult.

Mr. Kingsley opened his eyes and regarded Mrs. Griggs with an air of deliberation. His plans were made. He announced them. As one looked at Mrs. Griggs one would hardly have expected an employer so helpless as he to issue orders to a subject so powerful as she, in so firm a manner. Yet he gave the impression of consulting her, after all.

"Mrs. Griggs," said he, "I am thinking of having a Christmas house-party. Merely the family, you know. Yet that means a considerable number, including—er—er—all the babies. Should you think we could accommodate them?"

Mrs. Griggs's somewhat stern expression of face grew incredulous. Having served Mr. Kingsley so long, under conditions so peculiar, she was accustomed to take—and was allowed—liberties of speech which would have been sternly forbidden any other person outside the circle of kinship.

"The family!" said she. "You—they—why, there won't more'n half of them come. Your brother Sylvester and your brother Samuel—"

"I understand about Sylvester and Samuel. That is why I want a Christmas house-party."

"Your sister Clara and your sister Isabel—"

"That was not serious. They must be quite over it by now."

"Not over it at all. It's worse. I happen to know what they said to each other the last time they were here. Your sister Clara said—"

"Never mind, Mrs. Griggs. We must surely get them here. The others are certainly on the best of terms."

Mrs. Griggs pursed her lips. "I guess you've forgotten, Mr. Stephen, about that old fuss between George's family and William's. They've never been the same since. There's a coolness—"

"We will warm it up. Coolness can't exist in the Christmas warmth. If you feel that you can tuck everybody away somewhere—"

"Mr. Stephen"—Mrs. Griggs's tone was a trifle indignant—"there's eleven sleeping-rooms in this house."

"Are there? I had forgotten. I haven't been upstairs in—twenty years. I can't quite remember whether there are fireplaces in them all."

"All but two—and they have Franklin stoves."

"Have Israel fill all the woodboxes, Mrs. Griggs. Send him to the woods for ground-pine. I will order holly from the city. Tell Mary and Hannah to begin cooking and baking. But I must write my invitations. It's three weeks yet to Christmas. Plenty of time to plan. Please hand me my writing materials, Mrs. Griggs."

"Mr. Stephen"—the housekeeper's hand lingered on the leather tablet without taking it from the desk across the room—"do you think you'd better try to write all those letters to-day? There's considerable many of the family and—you didn't sleep much last night."

"Didn't I? I shall sleep better to-night, Mrs. Griggs, if the letters are posted. Let me get them off my mind."

Reluctantly she gave him the tablet and his fountain-pen. Then she propped him up among his pillows and lighted a reading-lamp at his elbow; the day was dull and his eyesight not of the keenest—his physical eyesight. The spiritual vision reached far and away, quite out of the world altogether.

The letters went out. With five of them went five others, appendices in the hand of Mrs. Griggs.

At Samuel Kingsley's breakfast-table, twenty-four hours later, letter and appendix produced their effect. But due credit must certainly be given to the appendix. Mr. Stephen Kingsley's letter read thus:

"*Dear Samuel*:

"I am thinking of having a Christmas house-party. It seems a long time since I have seen the family all together. There are at least three new babies among the children. I am asking everybody to come on the day before

**115**

Christmas—Wednesday—and remain over at least until Friday. Don't refuse me. I should write much more, but must send word to all the others, and you know my eyes.

"Believe me always
"Your loving brother,
Stephen."

"Sylvester will be there," was Samuel's comment. He closed his lips tight as he said it. They were firm-set lips beneath a close-trimmed gray moustache. He squared his broad shoulders. "Sylvester will be there"— *and I won't!* his keen brown eyes added.

Then he opened the appendix.

"*Respected Sir and Friend*," began Mrs. Griggs with dignity, "I take my pen in hand to send you a line in regard to Mr. Stephen's letter, hoping this finds you well and will reach you by the same mail. I hope you and Mrs. Samuel and the family will come as Mr. Stephen wishes, as he has set his mind on having this party, which I think is too much for him, but he will do it. Mr. Stephen is not as strong as he was. Hoping you will come.

"Respectfully yours,
"Sarah A. Griggs."

**116**

It could hardly be said that Mrs. Griggs's language possessed to a greater degree than Mr. Kingsley's the quality of persuasion. But one sentence in her letter, together with the fact that she had considered it a matter which called upon her to take her unaccustomed pen in hand at all, gave weight to the invitation. Mr. Samuel Kingsley handed both letters across the table to his wife, with the curt comment that it was a confounded nuisance, and he didn't see what had got into Stephen's head, but he supposed they'd have to consider it.

The other letters met with varied receptions. To all they were a surprise, for Stephen lived well out of town and had been a recluse for so long that nobody was in the habit of taking him much into consideration when it came to affairs social. There could be no question that he was well beloved by every member of his family, and sincerely pitied—when they took time to think about it, which was not often. But, except for brief, infrequent visits at his quiet home, inspired by a sense of duty, few of them felt him in their lives at all.

It interfered decidedly with previous plans, but nobody was quite willing to refuse the invitation—certainly not those to whom Mrs. Griggs, with shrewd grasp of various situations, had ventured to indite her supplementary lines. To each of these her appeal on the score of Mr. Stephen's failing health came as a sting to action and turned the scale. More or less grudgingly,

**117**

they all wrote that they would come. But not without mental reservations as to courses of procedure when on the spot. George's family need not be familiar with William's. Clara and Isabel would avoid each other all that it was possible to do without attracting the notice of a certain pair of mild blue eyes beneath a crown of thick white hair. And Samuel and Sylvester—would Samuel and Sylvester even so much as shake hands? Those who knew them best doubted it.

But the children were all glad to go. Family quarrels mattered nothing to them. And in the children lay Stephen's hope.


The house was ready. Dignified, even stately, with its tall pillars and lines of fine proportion, representing the best of the architecture of New England's early days, Stephen Kingsley's country home stood awaiting its guests. Far back from the road, its wide front entrance was festooned with hemlock and pine, a stout young tree fastened upon either side. The long-closed blinds of the upper story were all thrown wide; from each square chimney floated a welcoming banner of smoke. Passersby upon the road that morning, on their way to family reunions of their own, gazed and wondered. It was many a long day since "the old Kingsley place" had worn that hospitable air of habitation.

Inside, activity reigned from cellar to roof-tree—

the activity which is the fine flower of many previous days of preparation. Speaking of flowers, they were everywhere. It would seem as if Mr. Kingsley's orders must have stripped the nearest city of scarlet carnations, so lavishly were they combined with the holly and ground-pine of the decorations. Every guest-room smiled with a big bunch of them, reflected cheerily from quaint old mirrors above low dressing-tables. Downstairs they glowed even from obscure corners, lighting up the severely decorous order of the rooms into a vivid suggestion of festivities to come. One big bloom, broken from its stem, had been picked up by Hannah, the cook, and now, tucked securely into her tightly braided black hair, burned hardly more brightly than her cheeks, flushed as they were with excitement and haste.

"It's the cookin' for so many that upsets me," she averred, standing with Mary, the waitress, before a pile of plates and trying to estimate how many would be needed of that particular size. "I was brought up in a big fam'ly myself, but livin' so long in this quiet house and cookin' for one who doesn't eat what a baby would, has made me forget."

"But you wouldn't take the help he said he'd get for you," Mary reminded her.

"To be sure I wouldn't," Hannah cried, hotly. "After workin' for him all these years and gettin' such wages as he pays, would I see another come in and do for him when he has comp'ny—for once in his life? Not even from Mrs. Griggs would I take help with the cookin' and bakin'—not that she'd offer it. And I guess we've enough in the butt'ry, come there never so many extrys."

"I guess we have," Mary agreed proudly, with a glance into the stone-floor buttery, where the ample shelves were laden with food until one might well wonder if they were stoutly enough built to carry such a load. "There's nothin' stingy about him. You should see the chambers, Hannah. There's been fires burnin' in every one of the fireplaces since day before yesterd'y, because he was afraid the rooms would be damp, shut up so long. Isr'el's watched 'em like babies, too, thinkin' they might be a chimley catch fire. . . . And the sheets, Hannah, that Mrs. Griggs has brought out from the linen-closet that she always keeps locked so careful! What such an old bachelor ever wanted of so many sheets—"

"They was his mother's before him," Hannah explained. She hurried away as she spoke, a towering pile of gold-banded plates in her capable hands. "With the fam'ly she had—and not all of them livin' now to come here today—she had need of a plenty of sheets, and fine ones they was, at that. Mrs. Griggs knows just how many there is of 'em, too, I can tell you. One would think they was her own, she's that—"

The appearance of the housekeeper's face in the

doorway hushed the talk in the kitchen. Mrs. Griggs bore a message from Mr. Stephen, and to Mr. Stephen she presently returned. With all her cares on this supreme morning, Mrs. Griggs's greatest solicitude was for her master. Not that she ever thought of him by that title. If he had been her elder brother she could not have felt herself more of a sister to him, nor could she have been more anxious lest his wilfulness in the matter of the house-party prove too much for his frail strength. She had insisted with a firm hand that he remain in bed until the latest possible moment, and now that, an hour before train-time, she allowed him to get up, it was still to refuse him the trip he wanted, in his invalid chair, about the lower rooms, to see that all was as he could wish.

"You know very well," said she, "that I've not worked for three weeks getting ready, for nothing. Everything's perfect, if I do say it. You can trust me. And there's no use using up what little gimp you've got."

This was indisputable. "I suppose I haven't much 'gimp,' " Mr. Kingsley admitted, with his patient smile, "though I really feel as if I were possessed of a trifle more than usual, this morning, Mrs. Griggs."

" 'Tisn't reliable," his housekeeper responded with conviction. "It's merely excitement, Mr. Stephen, and it's likely to leave you flatter than ever if you go to counting on it."

This also being highly probable, Mr. Kingsley

submitted to her judgment, and in his own sitting-room, a large and comfortable apartment, across the wide hall from the more formal parlour, awaited his guests, himself in as festal array as he could compass. Instead of his usual dressing-gown he wore a frock-coat, of somewhat old-fashioned cut but of irreproachable freshness. (Mrs. Griggs had a method of her own for insuring the integrity of garments laid away, a method which endued them with no unpleasant preservative odours.) In his buttonhole gleamed a sprig of glossy holly, rich with berries—his hands trembled a little as he adjusted it. Unquestionably it was an exciting morning for Mr. Stephen Kingsley; he had need, as Mrs. Griggs had sagely urged, to conserve all his energies for the drafts that were to be made upon them.

From his window he watched Israel, his reliable man-of-all-work, drive off with the old family carriage and horses to the village station, two miles away, to meet the morning train, on which part of his guests were due. Others would come by trolley, still others, the most prosperous of the family, by private motor conveyance of their own, from the city, thirty miles away.

And now, in due time, the first of his Christmas guests were at his door, and Mrs. Griggs, wearing her best black-henrietta gown, her shoulders well thrown back and an expression of great dignity upon her face, was ushering them in.

———

Clara—Mrs. Pierce Wendell—caught sight of Isabel—Mrs. James Dent—before she was fairly inside brother Stephen's doors. Clara was fair and fine and impressive in elaborate widow's mourning and an air of haughtiness which became decidedly more pronounced at sight of her sister Isabel. Mrs. Dent was tall and thin, and very quietly, almost austerely, dressed. The one lived in town, the other in the country. But just why these differences in mere outward circumstance should have brought about such a breach of feeling that they could barely greet each other with courtesy was a subject to which the elder brother, who awaited them in his own room, had given much thought.

But he did not attempt to force matters. When Isabel, standing beside his chair, nodded coolly at Clara as she approached, and then moved immediately away without further greeting, Stephen took no notice. If they could have seen, his eyes took on a certain peculiar deeper shadowing which meant that his heart was intimately concerned with the matter of the sisterly estrangement. But his welcoming smile as he greeted Clara was as bright as the one he had lately turned upon Isabel, and the questions concerning her welfare with which he detained her showed as brotherly an interest as if he had not been quite sure within himself that Clara was the offender most deeply at fault.

The Christmas guests arrived in installments. By noon George's and William's families had come—on the same train, although each had taken pains to ascertain that the other was likely to await a later hour. At three in the afternoon Sylvester and Mrs. Sylvester had pulled up in a big, shiny brown limousine, accompanied by Mrs. Sylvester's maid, and driven by a chauffeur swathed in furs to the tip of his nose, as were also Mr. and Mrs. Sylvester. There were no children; it was the one childless branch of the family.

"Seems as if they might have brought somebody else in that great traveling opera-box," declared Mrs. George to Mrs. Clara from the library window. "They came straight by our house if they came the Williamsville road, as I've no doubt they did. That machine will hold seven. I shouldn't say it to Stephen, but it looks to me as if the more money Sylvester makes the closer he gets."

"That's *her* fault," responded Clara, watching between the curtains as her brother Sylvester's wife, in furs which cost several times the amount of Mrs. Clara's own, came somewhat languidly up the walk. "She's getting so exclusive she's likely to cut Sylvester's family at almost any time. Since the trouble between Sylvester and Samuel—"

"I heard through Matilda that they barely speak now," whispered Mrs. George hurriedly. The library had been invaded with a rush by seven children and a dog—the dog, Uncle Stephen's old Fido, nearly out of his head with excitement over the unexpected advent of such an army of playfellows.

"I think it's extremely improbable that Samuel will come at all," Mrs. Clara whispered back. "Mrs. Griggs admitted to me just now that it was Samuel who called her up over the 'phone. 'We expect them *all*!'—that's what she was saying. She tried to put me off with the notion that he was inquiring if the children were all here—something about presents for them—you know how generous Samuel always is with the children. But I've no doubt at all he wanted to know if Sylvester was expected. I shall be *very* much surprised if we see Samuel."

The five-o'clock train brought James Dent, Isabel's husband, and James Dent, Junior; several young people of the house of Lucas, whose mother—Marian Kingsley—was not living; and the children of Samuel, assorted ages, and accompanied by a nurse. The eldest of them, Anne, explained that her father and mother were coming in the roadster.

Mrs. Clara looked at Mrs. George. If she had shrieked at her she could not have said more plainly: "You'll see! The car will break down, they will *not* come tonight. Else why didn't they come on the train with the children?"

———

James Dent, Junior, was the last of the evening arrivals to approach his Uncle Stephen's chair. This was not from any lack of desire to greet his host, but because the instant he put his round, smiling face inside the door, he was set upon by fourteen children—this was their number now—and the dog, and pulled hither and yon and shouted at and barked at and generally given a rousing welcome. He deserved it. If ever Stevenson's description of the entrance of a happy man to a room fitted anybody it fitted James Dent, Junior.

It was, indeed, "as though another candle had been lighted," although in this young man's case a dozen candles could not have made so great a difference. And if it would be understood how impossible it was for anybody not to like Jim Dent it is only necessary to say that when he—the son of Isabel—reached Aunt Clara and kissed her heartily on her fair cheek she did not repulse him. Repulse him? One might as well try to repulse a summer breeze!

"Clear a space, all of you!" commanded James Dent, Junior. "I want a chance at Uncle Stephen. Be off! I'll not speak to any of you again till I've had ten minutes alone with him. Why, I haven't seen him for a month."

A month! Few of the others had seen him for a year. But the young man's tone expressed such hungry anticipation of a talk with the uncle whom he had not seen for a month that everybody obediently cleared out and left the two together.

Then Jim Dent sat down close beside the invalid's chair and looked straight into his uncle's gentle blue eyes with his own very brilliant blue ones—and, somehow, for all of the difference between them there was a look of the uncle about the nephew. The well-knit, sturdy young hand gripped the thin old one and held it close, and the smile the two exchanged had in it love and welcome and understanding.

"Well, you've got them all here," exulted Jim Dent. "Nobody but you could have done it. Uncle Sam's coming, Anne says. That's great, Uncle Stephen!"

"I am confidently expecting Samuel," responded the elder man. "How it will turn out I hardly dare think. They may not speak tonight. This is only Christmas Eve. But to-morrow, Jim, is Christmas Day!"

"Yes, to-morrow's Christmas Day, Uncle Steve."

"Can brothers refuse to speak—on Christmas Day, Jim?"

"I don't believe they can—under your roof, Uncle Steve."

"My roof, boy! Under God's roof!"

"It's pretty nearly the same thing," murmured Jim Dent, not irreverently.

"I may need your help, Jim."

"Sheep-dog—to bark at their heels and run them into the same pasture?"

Uncle Stephen smiled. His eyes and Jim's met with a twinkle.

"Just about that, perhaps," he admitted. "I can't tell yet. But keep your eyes open."

"I'll stand by," agreed his nephew. "It's a good thing the kiddies are here, Uncle Steve. When I came in Uncle George's children and Uncle William's were keeping more or less in separate squads, but the minute they pitched on to me the whole bunch were so tangled up I don't think they'll ever get untangled again. I had a glance at the fathers and mothers. Their faces were worth coming to see."

Mr. Kingsley looked at Jim earnestly. "I'm counting on the children, boy," said he.

"When it comes to a general mix-up," replied Jim Dent, "you can count on the youngsters every time."

The gray roadster belonging to Mr. Samuel Kingsley ran swiftly and silently through the gateway and up to the side entrance of his brother Stephen's home. Mrs. Samuel sat beside her husband; a sharp-eyed mechanician rode in the rumble behind.

"How long, Evans?" inquired Mr. Kingsley as the machine came to a standstill.

"Forty-two minutes, sir. That's pretty good time over these icy roads."

"I should say so. Came as fast as if I wanted to come," muttered the man of affairs, with his hand under his wife's arm to escort her up the steps. "As fast as if I wouldn't rather be hung, drawn and quartered than meet that skinflint Sylv—"

"Sam!" Mrs. Sam pressed his hand with her plump arm against her side. "Please be civil to Sylvester for Stephen's sake and the children's. Don't let him or them see signs of the quarrel—not at Christmas, dear."

"I won't shake hands with him," growled Samuel. "Not with Stephen himself looking on."

"Yes, you will, dear, on Christmas Eve," whispered Mrs. Sam.

By which it may be seen that the mothers of many children have large hearts, and that Mr. Stephen Kingsley had with him one more ally than he knew.

Although Mr. Samuel Kingsley may have infinitely preferred, according to his own declaration, to be hung, drawn and quartered than to enter the great, old-fashioned doorway within which somewhere awaited him an encounter with one of his own flesh and blood, nobody would have guessed it from his demeanour. Long training in what James Dent, Junior, mentally characterized, as he watched Uncle Samuel make his entrance, as the art of bluffing—acquired by men of prominence in the world everywhere—enabled that gentleman to appear upon the scene with an expression of affability mingled with pleasure on his handsome countenance, and his accustomed bearing of dignity and distinction well in evidence. As it happened, Mr. Sylvester Kingsley was at the moment close by his brother Stephen's side, although he had by no means intended to be there when his brother Samuel should arrive. How this happened it is possible that only the "sheep-dog" could have told.

"Samuel, this is giving me great happiness," said Stephen, and held his brother's strong hand for a moment in both his weak ones. Then he looked at Sylvester, who was on his farther side. Samuel also looked at Sylvester. Sylvester looked back at Samuel. Blades of steel could not have crossed with a sharper clang.

"How are you, Sylvester?" inquired Samuel, and his glance dropped to Sylvester's chin as he said it. His hand remained in Stephen's, where it received a weak pressure, a quite involuntary one, born of anxiety.

"How are you, Samuel?" inquired Sylvester in return, and his glance lowered to the expensive scarfpin in Samuel's neckwear.

Jim Dent said "Good heavens!" somewhere inside of him, and the incident was closed by his uncle Sylvester's rising and walking away out of the room. The brothers had spoken—if this were speech. They had not shaken hands. An apprehending onlooker, betting on the probabilities, would have staked a considerable sum on the proposition that they would not shake hands within the next twenty-four hours—or twenty-four years.

"Well, well—here's Anne!" cried Jim Dent joyfully. He had been looking about him for first-aid to his uncle Stephen's wounded heart. Anne was no longer of the group of children who were accustomed to leap upon Cousin Jim and demand instant sport with him. Anne, being now eighteen, and lately returned from a two-years' absence at a boarding-school somewhere abroad, had allowed James Dent, Junior, to be in the house for a full half-hour before she emerged from some upstairs retreat and came to greet him. Being Mrs. Sam's eldest daughter she was naturally extraordinarily pretty, looking much as her mother had looked twenty years before. As Mrs. Sam was still a beauty, and as she was his favourite aunt—by marriage—it will be easy to imagine that when her nephew James had greeted her he had not failed to inquire for Anne. Still, he had had no possible idea that the change in Anne was going to be so great.

Anne held out her hand with a delightful smile. But Jim Dent would have none of such a sudden accession of reserve, and promptly kissed her, as of old. Whereupon

**131**

her colour, always interesting to observe, became even more attractive, though she only said, reproachfully:

"Don't you see I'm grown up, Cousin Jim?"

Cousin Jim looked her over, from the crown of her charming dark head to the tips of her modishly shod little feet. "Bless your heart, so you are!" he exclaimed. "But will you tell me what that has to do with it?"

"Everything. I no longer can be kissed as a matter-of-course," declared Miss Anne Kingsley. "Only by special dispensation."

"Well, what do I think of that?" he demanded. "Sure, an' I don't know what I think! Still, as I see plenty of mistletoe about"—he had only to reach up a sinewy arm to secure a piece—"I can easily obtain that special dispensation."

Whereupon he kissed her again, and with appreciably more fervour than before, having discovered, between the first kiss and the second, that Anne, grown up, was unquestionably more alluring than Anne as he had last seen her, although he remembered that even then he had had premonitions as to her future which he was now not at all surprised to find had been well founded.

Feeling that nothing could be better for that heavy heart of his uncle Stephen's than the application of such balm as lay in a girl's sweetness, Jim Dent conducted his adorable cousin in to spend the next half-hour beside the invalid's chair. In this act he showed the difference between himself and the average young man—between the sheep-dog, so to speak, always under the sway of a sense of duty to keep his charges where they belong, and the sportive terrier, who thinks of nothing but his own diversion. It must be acknowledged, however, lest this young man be thought quite unnaturally altruistic, that he himself shared with his cousin Anne the pleasant task of making a dear and gentle elderly man forget for a time the load upon his breast, and that the pair of them, while they made merry for the benefit of Uncle Stephen, also laughed into each other's eyes quite as often as they did into his. Which, of course, gave him fully as much pleasure as it did themselves.

"Mother," said Jim Dent in a corner somewhere, "why not take a day off from the fuss and show Aunt Clara how to narrow, or widen, or double up, or whatever she seems to be trying to do, on that pink silk thing she's knitting? It's Christmas Eve, and she's finishing it up to give to Uncle Sam's baby, and she's all balled up. She never knit socks before. Somebody else helped her on the other one."

"James," said his mother sternly, but not as sternly as she might have spoken if her son's lips had not lightly kissed her ear before they murmured these words into it, "it is impossible to ignore your aunt's manner to me."

"It's not so awfully different, though, mother, from your manner to her. Still, let's see, how did the thing begin?" mused Jim. "She wrote that they'd all come out in July for a month, and you wrote back—"

"I said the simple truth, James, that my kitchen was quite as hot in the country as hers in the city, in July."

"It certainly was the simple truth, mother. Somewhat undecorated by a garnish of hospitality, though—eh?"

"I had not accepted your aunt's invitations to visit her in town in the winter."

"You'd had 'em, though. Don't unaccepted invitations count any?"

Isabel Dent stirred in her chair. "She had visited me time and again without invitation."

"How far back did all this happen? When I was in my cradle? I've forgotten."

"It was seven years ago last July."

"Seven years outlaws an unpaid account. Let's start another. I'll back you up if you'll go over and offer to fix up that sock. If you do, the late unpleasantness will fix itself up. It's just as easy as that. And—Uncle Steve wants it."

"James," his mother's tone was firm, "if your Aunt Clara comes to me I will not repulse her."

"She won't come. You said the last hard word."

"James!"

"All right," said Jim Dent with apparent resignation. "But even enemies declare a truce—on Christmas Eve."

Then two small boys and four girls of various sizes romped into the corner after him and he went away with them. It was difficult to do otherwise, with all six twined about his arms and pulling lustily.

" 'He that loveth not his brother whom he hath seen, how can he love God whom he hath not seen?' "

Stephen spoke the words thoughtfully.

"Steve," said Samuel, with a flushing face, "it's a mighty sight easier to love a God a fellow hasn't seen than some men he has seen. Whatever the Almighty is He's square. Sylvester isn't."

"Sam," said Stephen gently, yet with a quiet firmness which made Samuel look at him curiously, "are you absolutely certain Sylvester was not square? Admitting that his methods were peculiar, annoying, without seeming reason or justification, are you sure they were not square?"

"I'm as confident he meant to deceive me as I sit here."

"But do you *know* it? Could you prove it in a court of law?"

Samuel hesitated. That was a question not to be answered quite so easily. "I believe I could."

"But you don't *know* you could?"

"Great Caesar, Steve, I'm not omnipotent. I don't *know* I could. But—"

"Then there is a possibility—just a possibility—that you might be mistaken in your judgment of Sylvester."

"If there is it's so small that—"

"The smaller it is the more danger of losing sight of it. Yet, if it exists—"

Samuel rose abruptly. "See here, brother," he said with an effort to command his usual manner, "why not let well enough alone? I've treated Sylvester civilly here under your roof. What more can you ask? What's the use of stirring up strife on Christmas Day?"

"Am I trying to stir up strife?" breathed Stephen Kingsley, his delicate face turning even a shade paler than was its wont. "I—Sam, I'd give my right hand— not that it's worth much—to see strife end between you and Syl, here—on Christmas Day.... *What was that, Sam? What was that?*"

Samuel ran heavily to the door, opened it, looked out, glanced back, then rushed through and shut the door sharply on the outside.

"O, Lord, dear Lord, not any of the children, on Christmas Day!" pleaded a low voice inside.

It was Jim Dent who had reached young Syl first when he fell through the well from the third story to the first of Uncle Stephen's spacious old halls. Young Syl, Samuel's twelve-year-old son, named for his Uncle Sylvester at a period when the brothers had been business partners and close friends, had been having a lively scuffle with his cousin Harold, Uncle George's fourteen-year-old athlete. The set-to had raged all over the house, had reached the third story, and had arrived at a point where any means for either to get the better of the other had prevailed. Harold had succeeded in forcing his adversary into a position where he could throw him, after some schoolboy method, and, blinded by the excitement of the affair, had not realized just where he was. He had thrown Syl with such success that the younger boy had lost his clutch upon his antagonist and had gone over the low rail before Harold knew what had happened.

"Keep cool!" was Jim's first command, learned in many an emergency on school and college athletic fields. "A boy can stand a lot, and he landed on the rug."

They tried hard to obey him. His mother succeeded best, his father least. Samuel Kingsley could not wait to see his boy return to consciousness, could not wait after he had summoned a physician—two physicians—by telephone, but must needs rush out to get the gray roadster, with its sixty-horsepower cylinders, declaring that he would meet Graham on the way. Graham ran only a turtle of a forty-horsepower machine and would never get there.

His mechanician, Evans, was not on the ground. He, with Ledds, Sylvester's chauffeur, had gone off on some Christmasing of their own. With hands that trembled Samuel got his motor throbbing—it took time, because of the stiffening cold of all the mechanism. Then he leaped into his car.

"Better take time to put on your coat and gloves," said a voice behind him. "You'll drive faster, warm."

His brother Sylvester climbed in beside him, himself in fur-lined garments. He held Samuel's coat for him, and handed his brother the heavy motoring gloves of which Samuel had not stopped to think.

"I'll look out where you back; let her go," commanded Sylvester, and Samuel backed his car out of the narrow space where it had stood between Sylvester's big brown limousine and Stephen's modest phaeton. Samuel used care until he had made the curves from barn to road, between trees and hedges and the brown remains of a garden, out through the old stone-posted gateway. Then, with a straight turnpike road before him and the city only twenty miles away, Samuel opened his throttle. The slim, powerful machine, its exhaust, unmuffled, roaring a deep note of power, shot away down the road like the wind.

At a window inside Mr. William Kingsley was watching excitedly. A tall figure of the general proportions of his sister Isabel's husband, James Dent, was at his elbow. "By George!" he ejaculated, "Syl's gone with Sam!"

Mr. George Kingsley, partially deaf, caught his own first name. "What's that, Will?" he responded eagerly.

William wheeled and saw whom he was addressing. George, his anxious eyes peering down the road, was plainly not thinking of family quarrels. Why should anybody think of family quarrels with Sam's young Syl lying upstairs looking as if the life had been knocked out of him by that terrific fall? William found himself unable to answer this question.

"Sylvester's gone with Sam after Doctor Graham," he announced in George's interrogative best ear.

"You don't say!" responded George. "Well, it's a good thing."

It certainly was. Not a member of the family but would admit that. Also, if it was a good thing for Sylvester and Sam to tear down the road together in a sixty-horsepower car, after a quarrel the proportions of which anybody must concede were far more serious than those of the difficulty between George and William, it would seem rather forced, at least until the truth was known about young Syl, for two other brothers looking out of the same window to cling to outward signs of estrangement.

"Sam's got an extremely powerful machine," observed William, continuing to gaze down the road, though the aforesaid machine was already probably a mile away and far out of sight.

"I guess he has. Must go faster than Sylvester's, I should say."

"Sylvester's isn't made so much for speed as for getting about the city warm and comfortable for his wife. Syl's not much on speed, as I remember. Shouldn't wonder if Sam's pace going to meet the doctor would make Syl hang on some."

"It's Sam's boy," said George in a lower tone.

"So it is," agreed William. "Couldn't blame him if he took some chances. Don't know as he'll get Graham here more'n five minutes quicker'n he could get here with his own car, but it'll relieve the strain for Sam a little to be doing something."

"That's so," admitted George.

At this moment Harold, George's boy, with a pale, frightened face and a pair of very red eyes, came into the room and up to his father. He had no eyes for his Uncle William standing half within the long, crimson folds of the library curtains.

"Dad," said the boy, "did you know I—"

"Eh?" said his father, turning his best ear. Then

he saw his son's face. "Why, what's the matter?" he asked anxiously. "Is Syl—"

"Dad," burst out the boy, "I—I was the one that did it. *I—threw—Syl!*"

He buried his head against his father's arm.

"Why, Harry—Harry, boy—" began his father in consternation.

Uncle William came out from behind the curtain. He thought he had better get out of the room. But as he passed Harold his hand patted the young head. He stooped to the boy's ear. "We all know it was an accident," he whispered.

A nursemaid knocked upon the door of Mr. Stephen Kingsley's room. In her arms was Mrs. Sam's baby, the prettiest baby of the three who were in the house.

"Mr. Kingsley," said the maid, "Mr. Dent—the young man—said I should bring Dorothy to you and ask you to take care of her for a little while, if you didn't mind. He has something for me to do."

"Yes, yes—yes, yes," answered the invalid. "I'll keep her." He reached out his arms. "How is the boy now, do you know?" he asked. He had had a bulletin within the last five minutes, but minutes go slowly under suspense.

"They think he may not be badly hurt, sir," said the maid.

But this was what they had told him from the

beginning. He felt that they could not know. They were afraid to alarm him. Fall so far and not be badly hurt? It was not possible.

He took the baby, and laid his white cheek against hers of roseleaf pink. So Jim had sent him the baby to take up his mind. Was there anything Jim didn't think of? And one certainly cannot look after an eight-months-old baby and not give the matter considerable attention.

Young Sylvester Kingsley, Samuel's son, opened his eyes. The first thing he saw was his mother's face, which smiled at him. Mothers can always smile, if necessary, thank God! The next thing noticeable was his Cousin Jim's bright blue eyes looking rather brighter than usual. He heard a caught breath somewhere near and then a whisper: "Sh-h—don't startle him!" It sounded like his Aunt Clara's rather sibilant whisper. Aunt Clara had the tiniest sort of a lisp.

There was a strong smell of camphor in the air, and Syl's forehead seemed to be oppressed by something heavy and cold. He attempted to put up his hand to his head, but the thing didn't work, somehow. He was conscious that his arm hurt, besides. He didn't feel exactly like speaking, so he stared questioningly into his Cousin Jim's face.

"All right, old man," replied Cousin Jim instantly, in a quiet, cheerful sort of way which was most reassuring. "You've had a bit of a knockout, but we'll soon have you fixed up. Yes, I know that arm hurts—that'll be all right presently."

Out in the upper hall Aunt Clara, who had crept out of the room lest the relief of seeing the lad alive, and the wonder of watching Syl's mother smile at her boy like that, should make the sob in her own throat burst out, ran blindly into a figure at the top of the stairs.

"Oh, he's come to!" she whispered loudly.

"He has? Thank the Lord!" came back in another joyful whisper.

"But he must be awfully hurt, just the same. We can't know till the doctors come. Don't you suppose it must be time for them now?"

"I don't know. Who's with him?"

"His mother and that angel Jim. I never saw anybody like Jim Dent. He's the dearest fellow, so cool and cheerful, thinks of everything and everybody. No wonder Stephen adores him."

"Thank you, Clara," whispered the other woman. Clara hastily wiped her eyes. The hall was dim and her eyes had been thick with tears. She had been exchanging whispers with Isabel.

It didn't matter. She was glad of it. The mother of Jim Dent deserved recognition, if she *had* said her kitchen was hot in the summer. Clara put out her arms. Isabel came into them. Clara's plump cheek touched Isabel's thin shoulder. Isabel's hand patted Clara's back. Jim Dent opened the door. Seeing the affair outside he closed it again and went to find something he wanted, by a different exit. His anxiety was still great, but a side issue like this one must not be upset.

But by the second exit he found somebody else in his path. All the beautiful colour shaken out of her cheeks, her dark eyes wide with alarm, her lips pressed tight together in her effort at self-control, young Syl's sister, Anne, caught at Jim Dent's capable, blue-serge arm. She said not a word, but he answered her as if she had spoken:

"He's opened his eyes, dear. That means a good deal, I'm sure. Keep cool."

"If I could only *do* something!"

"You can—what we're all doing."

"Oh, *yes!*" breathed little Anne. "O Jim!—do you think it helps—really?"

"Know it," asserted Jim Dent, as confidently as he had ever said anything in his life. He smiled at her and hurried on. That smile of his had been known to win games for his college teams which had been all but lost—why shouldn't it cheer a frightened girl and encourage her to go on doing that one thing which was the only thing she could do, and which Jim Dent was so sure would help?

———

The gray roadster came down the road at a speed which barely allowed it to slacken in time to make the curve at the gateway. It missed the stone post on the left by the width of a tenpenny nail. Sylvester, in the rumble, turned not a hair. Thirty miles of driving, with Sam's hand on the steering-wheel, had brought Sylvester to a condition of temporary paralysis as regarded danger.

The three of them were in the house in less time than it takes to tell it, Dr. Wilford Graham propelled by a hand on each arm. It would have been difficult for him to say which of his companions seemed the more eager to get him up the stairs.

Samuel opened the door of the room where he had left young Syl, his hand shaking on the knob. A somewhat feeble but decidedly cheerful voice greeted him.

"Say, dad, you'll tell me where I tumbled from, won't you? The rest of 'em have got me stung about it."

Samuel turned around to the doctor behind him. He pushed past the doctor and bolted out into the hall. He bumped smartly into his brother Sylvester, who had stopped to wait just outside the door. Sylvester put his hand on Samuel's shoulder.

"I heard, Sam, I heard," he murmured.

Samuel nodded. He could not speak. There was no particular need that he should.

Young Syl had a broken arm. But what is a broken arm, when by acquiring it one escapes injuring some vital part of one's body? He had, also, a large-sized contusion on his head, because on the rebound he had come somewhat forcibly into contact with the newel-post. But the contusion was precisely on the spot specially fortified by Nature for such emergencies, and the doctors feared no evil results from it.

"In short," declared Doctor Graham with great satisfaction, "the boy has managed to get out of his fall easier than many a football victim who is thrown only the distance of his own height. I won't say that a Turkey carpet with a leopard-skin rug on top of it doesn't make a fairly comfortable bed to fall on. If it had been one of our modern bare floors, now!—But it wasn't."

"Mayn't I have my dinner with the rest of 'em?" begged Syl.

Dinner! The Christmas dinner! They had all forgotten it except the hero of the day. "Because I'm awfully hungry," urged Syl.

In the deserted hall downstairs Jim Dent happily encountered Anne. He seized her hand.

"Come with me to tell Uncle Stephen!" he commanded. "But—stop crying first! Uncle Steve's a pretty wise man, but he can't be expected to tell the difference between tears of sorrow and tears of crazy joy—not at first sight."

"I don't know why I'm crying," sobbed Anne, breaking down completely and burying her face on the blue-serge shoulder which conveniently offered itself at the moment, just as she had done many times since she was a baby. Even when she was eight and Cousin Jim was fifteen, that shoulder of his had been one to hide one's unhappy eyes upon. "I didn't cry a drop—till I knew Syl was s-safe!"

"I know. Queer, isn't it? It always works that way. I confess I had some difficulty in seeing the way across the room myself, a few minutes ago. But wipe 'em away and come on! Uncle Stephen mustn't have to wait for his news. Look up here. Smile! Here—maybe this will help—" and for the third time within twenty-four hours he stooped and kissed her.

The tremulous lips broke suddenly into the smile he sued for. Through the tears shone a sudden mischievous light. "Cousin Jim," she observed, "you seem to have changed your methods a good deal. Always before it was chocolates. Are you out of chocolates?"

"No, I'm not out of chocolates." James Dent, Junior put his hand into his blue-serge pocket and produced a small box. "But you're too old for 'em," he explained, and put the box back.

He hurried her past the threshold of Mr. Stephen Kingsley's room. Across the baby's golden head Uncle Stephen looked tensely up at them. It needed but one look. Then his nephew sprang forward and took Anne's baby sister from a grasp which had grown suddenly nerveless, and his niece, stooping over her uncle's chair, gently patted a white cheek down which the first tear of relief was slowly trickling.

It seems to "work that way" with the whole human race. Except, perhaps, with mothers. Upstairs, Mrs. Sam sat beside her boy's bed, and his keen young eyes saw no tears upon her lovely, radiant face. If she cried at all it was only in her heart—her happy heart—which ached yet with the agony of what might have been—on Christmas Day.

It was a good thing that the dining-room in the old house was a big one. Mr. Kingsley had specially decreed that everybody—everybody—should be seated at one great table. There was to be no compromise effected by having the children wait for the "second table"—has any one who has ever waited for that "second table" at a family gathering forgotten what an ordeal it is, or how interminably long the old folks are about it? There were twenty-nine of them, including the three babies, but by some marvel of arrangement Mrs. Griggs had managed to make a place for every one.

"But you'll have to say how we're to seat them," said Mrs. Griggs, anxiously invading Mr. Stephen Kingsley's room. "With all our planning we've forgot that part. You'd better make me out a list, so I can lay those holly cards you've written the names on."

"Bless my soul," murmured Mr. Kingsley, "must they be specially arranged? Of course they must. I had forgotten. Clara"—he turned to his sister who came in at the moment—"help me with this, will you?"

"Give me the cards, Mrs. Griggs," requested Mrs.

Clara capably. She swept a clear space on the table at her brother's elbow as she spoke.

"What's all this?" asked Jim Dent at the door five minutes later. "Card games?"

"Do come and help me, Jim," cried his aunt. "I thought this would be easy, but it's not. I can't keep George's and William's families apart," she explained in a lower tone. "There are so many of them."

"Don't try."

"Oh, but I must. They—you know that old—"

"It seems to be a thing of the past. I met Uncle George's boy Harold and Uncle William coming downstairs hand in hand just now. They'd been up to see Syl together."

"Jim!" His uncle's face lighted as if the sunlight had struck it. "But the fathers?"

Jim put his head out of the door and took a survey of the room beyond. "Sitting on opposite sides of the fireplace," he announced.

"That's pretty near," admitted Mr. Kingsley. "That's certainly pretty near. With a fire between them. I wonder what—"

"Syl's tumble did it. It made the mix-up we were looking for. Not exactly as we would have planned it, but rather more effectively, I should say."

"Stephen," said Mrs. Clara, moving the cards about in an absent sort of way, "Stephen and Jim, I want to tell you that—well—Isabel and I—"

"Yes," helped Stephen eagerly.

"Good for you!" encouraged her nephew.

"We couldn't seem to keep it up—not here—on Christmas Day—after Syl—" Tears were suddenly threatening the holly cards. Mrs. Clara rose quickly. "I think they're all right now, Stephen," she said, indicating the cards and clearing her eyes with a touch of a lace-bordered handkerchief. "I've put Sam and Syl at the far ends of the table."

"I want them near together."

"But—had you better?"

"I'm going to risk it."

"Risk it, Uncle Steve," advised Jim. "Everybody's taking chances to-day."

"But—Sam and Sylvester!" persisted Clara doubtfully.

"It's Christmas Day with them, too," argued Jim.

Mrs. Clara went out with the cards and laid them down at the proper places. She had arranged them as nearly as possible in approved dinner style, a man next a woman, then a boy, then a girl, then another man, another woman, and so on.

When she had gone Jim sneaked out and scrutinized this arrangement. Laughing to himself he picked up the cards and juggled with them. About his uncle Stephen he grouped the cards of his three brothers and their wives. At the other end of the table he put all the children together.

"There, that's better," said Jim with conviction, to himself.

Mrs. Griggs announced dinner. Jim Dent brought Uncle Stephen out first in his wheel-chair and placed him at the head of the table. Then came the rest, Samuel Kingsley carrying his son Syl, looking very hero-like indeed, with his bandaged head and his arm in a sling. All the children's eyes were riveted fascinatedly on Syl as he was placed in a special easy chair at the foot of the table, where nobody could possibly by any chance hit the injured arm.

On one side of Mr. Stephen Kingsley, Mrs. Samuel found her place; on the other side, Mrs. Sylvester. Sylvester was next Mrs. Sam, Sam beyond Mrs. Syl. How he dared, everyone wondered, thinking it Uncle Stephen's plan. Uncle Stephen himself turned a little pale as he saw them standing behind their chairs. Only Jim Dent, whose wide-awake eyes had been seeing things all day, felt at all cool about it. And even he was not quite as cool as he looked.

There was a moment's hushed silence before they sat down, even the children fluttering into quiet. Then, just as everybody laid hands on chairback, Samuel Kingsley spoke.

"Steve," he said, looking at his brother, "I want to make a little speech."

Everybody was at attention. Stephen Kingsley looked up, wondering. He smiled at his brother, but his heart was making riot in his feeble breast. What was Sam going to do?

"I want to say," said Samuel—then he stopped. He was an accomplished after-dinner speaker, was Samuel Kingsley, but he had never had a speech to make like this one. He had thought he had it ready on his tongue, but it stuck in his throat. He turned and looked down the table at his boy Syl. Syl nodded at him, comprehending in a boyish way that his father was having some sort of difficulty with his speaking apparatus. Then Samuel looked at Mrs. Samuel, who smiled at him. She was a little pale yet, but her smile was bright as ever. Yet still Samuel could not make his speech.

The silence grew tense. Jim Dent, leaning forward and watching his uncle eagerly, felt that it must be relieved. He lifted his glass. "Here's to Uncle Sam's speech!" he cried.

The tension broke. Everybody laughed—a little agitatedly, and Uncle Sam's firm lips, under the close-cut, gray moustache, wavered, then set themselves. He looked at his nephew, and something about the sympathetic affection in the bright blue eyes steadied him.

"I'm afraid I can't make it, after all, Jim," said Samuel. "But perhaps I can act it."

And he stretched his hand across the table toward his brother Sylvester, who grasped it, as everybody could see, with a grip that stung.

Jim Dent's eyes flew to his Uncle Stephen's face. He saw it like that of Saint Stephen's of old, *"as it had been the face of an angel."*

To young Sylvester Kingsley, hero of the day, was destined to come still further distinction. It was all of a chance observation of his, made just before his removal to bed—at the same hour as his baby sister, much to his disgust. But, resigning himself to his fate, as Cousin Jim stooped to bear him away he gave one last look about the pleasant, holly-hung room.

Although their elders had kept as many of the family differences from their children's ears as was possible, they had not been able to forestall the use of the children's sharp eyes, and the sight Syl now saw struck him as unusual. It was nothing more than the gathering of five brothers, of varying ages, about the chair of one of their number, in front of the great fireplace where roared and crackled a mighty fire of logs. But the expressions of geniality and cordial interest upon the five faces indicated such good fellowship that the young son of Samuel Kingsley was moved to say to his cousin Jim:

"What a lot of brothers there are in this house! Dad's got four, and I've three and Harold's two, and they're all in this room. This ought to be called 'Brotherly House.'"

153

"So it ought," agreed Jim Dent, smiling at the thought. "It would be a fine name, and true, too."

He carried the boy away, and stopped to tell him a story after he was in bed—a football story, such as only Cousin Jim could tell, because he knew all about it from the inside. But when Jim came back to the fireside he told them of young Syl's idea. "And a jolly idea I call it, don't you?" he added.

Uncle Stephen looked from one to another of the four men around him, and saw the assenting smiles upon their faces—a bit shamefaced, perhaps, yet genuine.

Samuel Kingsley rose to his feet. "I could make my speech now," he said, with a happy laugh, his hands shoved well down into his pockets, where they jingled some loose change there in a boyish fashion. "But I don't want to. I'm only going to say that as long as I have a brother in the world like Stephen Kingsley I'm coming to see him as often as he'll have me. And the more of you boys I meet here the better I'll be pleased—particularly if the boy I meet here happens to be—" he glanced, smiling, across the little circle—"my brother Syl!"

"Hear, hear!" answered Sylvester Kingsley's deep voice.

So, to Stephen Kingsley's intense delight, *"Brotherly House"* it was—and has been ever since.

# The Romance *of*

## *a* Christmas Card

*by*
Kate
Douglas
Wiggin

## 1

It was Christmas Eve and a Saturday night when Mrs. Larrabee, the Beulah minister's wife, opened the door of the study where her husband was deep in the revision of his next day's sermon, and thrust in her comely head framed in a knitted rigolette.

"Luther, I'm going to run down to Letty's. We think the twins are going to have measles; it's the only thing they haven't had, and Letty's spirits are not up to concert pitch. You look like a blessed old prophet to-night, my dear! What's the text?"

The minister pushed back his spectacles and ruffled his gray hair.

"Isaiah VI, 8: *'And I heard the voice of the Lord, saying whom shall I send? . . . Then said I, Here am I, send me!'*"

**157**

"It doesn't sound a bit like Christmas, some-how."

"It has the spirit, if it hasn't the sound," said the minister. "There is always so little spare money in the village that we get less and less accustomed to sharing what we have with others. I want to remind the people that there are different ways of giving, and that the bestowing of one's self in service and good deeds can be the best of all gifts. Letty Boynton won't need the sermon!—Don't be late, Reba."

"Of course not. When was I ever late? It has just struck seven and I'll be back by eight to choose the hymns. And oh! Luther, I have some fresh ideas for Christmas cards and I am going to try my luck with them in the marts of trade. There are hundreds of thousands of such things sold nowadays; and if the 'Boston Banner' likes my verses well enough to send me the paper regularly, why shouldn't the people who make cards like them too, especially when I can draw and paint my own pictures?"

"I've no doubt they'll like them; who wouldn't? If the parish knew what a ready pen you have, they'd suspect that you help me in my sermons! The question is, will the publishers send you a check, or only a copy of your card?"

"I should relish a check, I confess; but oh! I should like almost as well a beautifully colored card, Luther, with a picture of my own inventing on it, my own verse, and R. L. in tiny letters somewhere in the corner! It would make such a lovely Christmas present! And I should be so proud; inside of course, not outside! I would cover my halo with my hat so that nobody in the congregation would ever notice it!"

The minister laughed.

"Consult Letty, my dear. David used to be in some sort of picture business in Boston. She will know, perhaps, where to offer your card!"

At the introduction of a new theme into the conversation Mrs. Larrabee slipped into a chair by the door, her lantern swinging in her hand.

"David can't be as near as Boston or we should hear of him sometimes. A pretty sort of brother to be meandering foot-loose over the earth, and Letty working her fingers to the bone to support his children—twins at that! It was just like David Gilman to have twins! Doesn't it seem incredible that he can let Christmas go by without a message? I dare say he doesn't even remember that his babies were born on Christmas eve. To be sure he is only Letty's half-brother, but after all they grew up together and are nearly the same age."

"You always judged David a little severely, Reba. Don't despair of reforming any man till you see the grass growing over his bare bones. I always have a soft spot in my heart for him when I remember his friendship for my Dick; but that was before your time.—Oh!

these boys, these boys!" The minister's voice quavered. "We give them our very life-blood. We love them, cherish them, pray over them, do our best to guide them, yet they take the path that leads from home. In some way, God knows how, we fail to call out the return love, or even the filial duty and respect!—Well, we won't talk about it, Reba; my business is to breathe the breath of life into my text: 'Here am I, Lord, send me!' Letty certainly continues to say it heroically, whatever her troubles."

"Yes, Letty is so ready for service that she will always be sent, till the end of time; but if David ever has an interview with his Creator I can hear him say: "Here am I, Lord; send Letty!'"

The minister laughed again. He laughed freely and easily nowadays. His first wife had been a sort of understudy for a saint, and after a brief but depressing connubial experience she had died, leaving him with a boy of six; a boy who already, at that tender age, seemed to cherish a passionate aversion to virtue in any form—the result, perhaps, of daily doses of the catechism administered by an abnormally pious mother.

The minister had struggled valiantly with his paternal and parochial cares for twelve lonely years when he met, wooed, and won (very much to his astonishment and exaltation) Reba Crosby. There never was a better bargain driven! She was forty-five by the family Bible but twenty-five in face, heart, and mind, while he would have been printed as sixty in "Who's Who in New Hampshire" although he was far older in patience and experience and wisdom. The minister was spiritual, frail, and a trifle prone to self-deprecation; the minister's new wife was spirited, vigorous, courageous, and clever. She was also Western-born, college-bred, good as gold, and invincibly, incurably gay. The minister grew younger every year, for Reba doubled his joys and halved his burdens, tossing them from one of her fine shoulders to the other as if they were feathers. She swept into the quiet village life of Beulah like a salt sea breeze. She infused a new spirit into the bleak church "sociables" and made them positively agreeable functions. The choir ceased from wrangling, the Sunday-School plucked up courage and flourished like a green bay tree. She managed the deacons, she braced up the missionary societies, she captivated the parish, she cheered the depressed and depressing old ladies and cracked jokes with the invalids.

"Ain't she a little mite too jolly for a minister's wife?" questioned Mrs. Ossian Popham, who was a professional pessimist.

"If this world is a place of want, woe, wantonness, an' wickedness, same as you claim, Maria, I don't see how a minister's wife *can* be too jolly!" was her husband's cheerful reply. "Look how she's melted up the ice in both congregations, so't the other church is most willin' we should prosper, so long as Mis' Lar-

**161**

rabee stays here an' we don't get too fur ahead of 'em in attendance. Me for the smiles, Maria!''

And Osh Popham was right; for Reba Larrabee convinced the members of the rival church (the rivalry between the two being in rigidity of creed, not in persistency in good works) that there was room in heaven for at least two denominations; and said that if they couldn't unite in this world, perhaps they'd get round to it in the next. Finally, she saved Letitia Boynton's soul alive by giving her a warm, understanding friendship, and she even contracted to win back the minister's absent son some time or other, and convince him of the error of his ways.

"Let Dick alone a little longer, Luther," she would say; "don't hurry him, for he won't come home so long as he's a failure; it would please the village too much, and Dick hates the village. He doesn't accept our point of view, that we must love our enemies and bless them that despitefully use us. The village did despitefully use Dick, and for that matter, David Gilman too. They were criticized, gossiped about, judged without mercy. Nobody believed in them, nobody ever praised them;—and what is that about praise being the fructifying sun in which our virtues ripen, or something like that? I'm not quoting it right, but I wish I'd said it. They were called wild when most of their wildness was exuberant vitality; their mistakes were magnified, their mad pranks exaggerated. If I'd been married to you, my dear, while Dick was growing up, I wouldn't have let you keep him here in this little backwater of life; he needed more room, more movement. They wouldn't have been so down on him in Racine, Wisconsin!"

Mrs. Larrabee lighted her lantern, closed the door behind her, and walked briskly down the lonely road that led from the parsonage at Beulah Corner to Letitia Boynton's house. It was bright moonlight and the ground was covered with light-fallen snow, but the lantern habit was a fixed one among Beulah ladies, who, even when they were not widows or spinsters, made their evening calls mostly without escort. The light of a lantern not only enabled one to pick the better side of a bad road, but would illuminate the face of any male stranger who might be of a burglarious or murderous disposition. Reba Larrabee was not a timid person; indeed, she was wont to say that men were so scarce in Beulah that unless they were out-and-out ruffians it would be an inspiration to meet a few, even if it were only to pass them in the middle of the road.

There was a light in the meeting-house as she passed, and then there was a long stretch of shining white silence unmarked by any human habitation till she came to the tumble-down black cottage inhabited by "Door-Button" Davis, as the little old man was called in the village. In the distance she could see Osh Popham's two-story house brilliantly illuminated by kerosene lamps, and as she drew nearer she even descried Ossian himself, seated at the cabinet organ in his shirt-sleeves, practicing the Christmas anthem, his daughter holding a candle to the page while she struggled to adjust a circuitous alto to her father's tenor. On the hither side of the Popham house, and quite obscured by it, stood Letitia Boynton's one-story gray cottage. It had a clump of tall cedar trees for background and the bare branches of the elms in front were hung lightly with snow garlands. As Mrs. Larrabee came closer, she set down her lantern and looked fixedly at the familiar house as if something new arrested her gaze.

"It looks like a little night-light!" she thought. "And how queer of Letty to be sitting at the open window!"

Nearer still she crept, yet not so near as to startle her friend. A tall brass candlestick, with a lighted tallow candle in it, stood on the table in the parlor window; but the room in which Letty sat was unlighted save by the fire on the hearth, which gleamed brightly behind the quaint andirons—Hessian soldiers of iron, painted in gay colors. Over the mantel hung the portrait of Letty's mother, a benign figure clad in black silk, the handsome head topped by a snowy muslin cap with floating strings. Just round the corner of the fireplace was a half-open door leading into a tiny bedroom, and the flickering flame lighted the heads of two

164

sleeping children, arms interlocked, bright tangled curls flowing over one pillow.

Letty herself sat in a low chair by the open window wrapped in an old cape of ruddy brown homespun, from the folds of which her delicate head rose like a flower in a bouquet of autumn leaves. One elbow rested on the table; her chin in the cup of her hand. Her head was turned away a little so that one could see only the knot of bronze hair, the curve of a cheek, and the sweep of an eyelash.

"What a picture!" thought Reba. "The very thing for my Christmas card! It would do almost without a change, if only she is willing to let me use her."

"Wake up, Letty!" she called. "Come and let me in!—Why, your front door isn't closed!"

"The fire smoked a little when I first lighted it," said Letty, rising when her friend entered, and then softly shutting the bedroom door that the children might not waken. "The night is so mild and the room so warm, I couldn't help opening the window to look at the moon on the snow. Sit down, Reba! How good of you to come when you've been rehearsing for the Christmas Tree exercises all the afternoon."

## 2

t's never 'good' of me to come to talk with you, Letty!" And the minister's wife sank into a comfortable seat and took off her rigolette. "Enough virtue has gone out of me to-day to Christianize an entire heathen nation! Oh! how I wish Luther would go and preach to a tribe of cannibals somewhere, and make me superintendent of the Sabbath-School! How I should like to deal, just for a change, with some simple problem like the undesirability and indigestibility involved in devouring your next-door neighbor! Now I pass my life in saying, 'Love your neighbor as yourself'; which is far more difficult than to say, 'Don't *eat* your neighbor, it's such a disgusting habit,—and wrong besides,'—though I dare say they do it half the time because the market is bad. The first thing I'd do would

166

be to get my cannibals to raise sheep. If they ate more mutton, they wouldn't eat so many missionaries."

Letty laughed. "You're so funny, Reba dear, and I was so sad before you came in. Don't let the minister take you to the cannibals until after I die!"

"No danger!—Letty, do you remember I told you I'd been trying my hand on some verses for a Christmas card?"

"Yes; have you sent them anywhere?"

"Not yet. I couldn't think of the right decoration and color scheme and was afraid to trust it all to the publishers. Now I've found just what I need for one of them, and you gave it to me, Letty!"

"I?"

"Yes, you; to-night, as I came down the road. The house looked so quaint, backed by the dark cedars, and the moon and the snow made everything dazzling. I could see the firelight through the open window, the Hessian soldier andirons, your mother's portrait, the children asleep in the next room, and you, wrapped in your cape waiting or watching for something or somebody."

"I wasn't watching or waiting! I was dreaming," said Letty hurriedly.

"You looked as if you were watching, anyway, and I thought if I were painting the picture I would call it 'Expectancy,' or 'The Vigil,' or 'Sentry Duty.'

However, when I make you into a card, Letty, nobody will know what the figure at the window means, till they read my verses."

"I'll give you the house, the room, the andirons, and even mother's portrait, but you don't mean that you want to put *me* on the card?" And Letty turned like a startled deer as she rose and brushed a spark from the hearth-rug.

"No, not the whole of you, of course, though I'm not clever enough to get a likeness even if I wished. I merely want to make a color sketch of your red-brown cape, your hair that matches it, your ear, an inch of cheek, and the eyelashes of one eye, if you please, ma'am."

"That doesn't sound quite so terrifying." And Letty looked more manageable.

"Nobody'll ever know that a real person sat at a real window and that I saw her there; but when I send the card with a finished picture, and my verses beautifully lettered on it, the printing people will be more likely to accept it."

"And if they do, shall I have a dozen to give to my Bible-class?" asked Letty in a wheedling voice.

"You shall have more than that! I'm willing to divide my magnificent profits with you. You will have furnished the picture and I the verses. It's wonderful, Letty,—it's providential! You just *are* a Christmas card to-night! It seems so strange that you even put the lighted candle in the window when you never heard my verse. The candle caught my eye first, and I remembered the Christmas customs we studied for the church festival,—the light to guide the Christ Child as he walks through the dark streets on the Eve of Mary."

"Yes, I thought of that," said Letty, flushing a little. "I put the candle there first so that the house shouldn't be all dark when the Pophams went by to choir-meeting, and just then I—I remembered, and was glad I did it!"

"These are my verses, Letty." And Reba's voice was soft as she turned her face away and looked at the flames mounting upward in the chimney:—

My door is on the latch to-night,
    The hearth fire is aglow.
I seem to hear swift passing feet,—
    The Christ Child in the snow.

My heart is open wide to-night
    For stranger, kith or kin.
I would not bar a single door
    Where Love might enter in!

There was a moment's silence and Letty broke it. "It means the sort of love the Christ Child brings, with peace and goodwill in it. I'm glad to be a part of that card, Reba, so long as nobody knows me, and—"

Here she made an impetuous movement and, covering her eyes with her hands, burst into a despairing flood of confidence, the words crowding each other and tumbling out of her mouth as if they feared to be stopped.

"After I put the candle on the table . . . I could not rest for thinking . . . I wasn't ready in my soul to light the Christ Child on his way . . . I was bitter and unresigned . . . It is three years to-night since the children were born . . . and each year I have hoped and waited and waited and hoped, thinking that David might remember. David! my brother, their father! Then the fire on the hearth, the moon and the snow quieted me, and I felt that I wanted to open the door, just a little. No one will notice that it's ajar, I thought, but there's a touch of welcome in it, anyway. And after a few minutes I said to myself: 'It's no use, David won't come; but I'm glad the firelight shines on mother's picture, for he loved mother, and if she hadn't died when he was scarcely more than a boy, things might have been different. . . . The reason I opened the bedroom door—something I never do when the babies are asleep—was because I needed a sight of their faces to reconcile me to my duty and take the resentment out of my heart . . . and it did flow out, Reba,—out into the stillness. It is so dazzling white outside, I couldn't bear my heart to be shrouded in gloom!"

"Poor Letty!" And Mrs. Larrabee furtively wiped

away a tear. "How long since you have heard? I didn't dare ask."

"Not a word, not a line for nearly three months, and for the half-year before that it was nothing but a note, sometimes with a five-dollar bill enclosed. David seems to think it the natural thing for me to look after his children; as if there could be no question of any life of my own."

"You began wrong, Letty. You were born a prop and you've been propping somebody ever since."

"I've done nothing but my plain duty. When my mother died there was my stepfather to nurse, but I was young and strong; I didn't mind; and he wasn't a burden long, poor father. Then, after four years came the shock of David's reckless marriage. When he asked if he might bring that girl here until her time of trial was over, it seemed to me I could never endure it! But there were only two of us left, David and I; I thought of mother and said yes."

"I remember, Letty; I had come to Beulah then."

"Yes, and you know what Eva was. How David, how anybody, could have loved her, I cannot think! Well, he brought her, and you know how it turned out. David never saw her alive again, nor ever saw his babies after they were three days old. Still, what can you expect of a father who is barely twenty-one?"

"If he's old enough to have children, he's old enough to notice them," said Mrs. Larrabee with her accustomed spirit. "Somebody ought to jog his sense of responsibility. It's wrong for women to assume men's burdens beyond a certain point; it only makes them more selfish. If you only knew where David is, you ought to bundle the children up and express them to his address. Not a word of explanation or apology; simply tie a tag on them, saying, 'Here's your Twins!' "

"But I love the babies," said Letty smiling through her tears, "and David may not be in a position to keep them."

"Then he shouldn't have had them," retorted Reba promptly; "especially not two of them. There's such a thing as a man's being too lavish with babies when he has no intention of doing anything for them but bring them into the world. If you had a living income, it would be one thing, but it makes me burn to have you stitching on coats to feed and clothe your half-brother's children!"

"Perhaps it doesn't make any difference—now!" sighed Letty, pushing back her hair with an abstracted gesture. "I gave up a good deal for the darlings once, but that's past and gone. Now, after all, they're the only life I have, and I'd rather make coats for them than for myself."

Letty Boynton had never said so much as this to Mrs. Larrabee in the three years of their friendship, and on her way back to the parsonage, the minister's wife puzzled a little over the look in Letty's face when she said, "David seemed to think there could be no question of any life of my own"; and again, "I gave up a good deal for the darlings once!"

"Luther," she said to the minister, when the hymns had been chosen, the sermon pronounced excellent, and they were toasting their toes over the sitting-room fire,—"Luther, do you suppose there ever was anything between Letty Boynton and your Dick?"

"No," he answered reflectively, "I don't think so. Dick always admired Letty and went to the house a great deal, but I imagine that was chiefly for David's sake, for they were as like as peas in a pod in the matter of mischief. If there had been more than friendship between Dick and Letty, Dick would never have gone away from Beulah, or if he had gone, he surely would have come back to see how Letty fared. A fellow yearns for news of the girl he loves even when he is content to let silence reign between him and his old father.— What makes you think there was anything particular, Reba?"

"What makes anybody think anything!—I wonder why some people are born props, and others leaners or twiners? I believe the very nursing-bottle leaned heavily against Letty when she lay on her infant pillow. I didn't know her when she was a child, but I believe that when she was eight all the other children of three and five in the village looked to her for support and guidance!"

"It's a great vocation—that of being a prop," smiled the minister, as he peeled a red Baldwin apple, carefully preserving the spiral and eating it first.

"I suppose the wobbly vine thinks it's grand to be a stout trellis when it needs one to climb on, but doesn't the trellis ever want to twine, I wonder?" And Reba's tone was doubtful.

"Even the trellis leans against the house, Reba."

"Well, Letty never gets a chance either to lean or to twine! Her family, her friends, her acquaintances, even the stranger within her gates, will pass trees, barber poles, telephone and telegraph poles, convenient corners of buildings, fence posts, ladders, and lightning rods for the sake of winding their weakness around her strength. When she sits down from sheer exhaustion, they come and prop themselves against her back. If she goes to bed, they climb up on the footboard, hang a drooping head, and look her wistfully in the eye for sympathy. Prop on, prop ever, seems to be the underlying law of the universe!"

"Poor Reba! She is talking of Letty and thinking of herself!" And the minister's eye twinkled.

"Well, a little!" admitted his wife; "but I'm only a village prop, not a family one. Where you are concerned"—and she administered an affectionate pat to his cheek as she rose from her chair—"I'm a trellis that leans against a rock!"

*3*

**L**etitia Boynton's life had been rather a drab one as seen through other people's eyes, but it had never seemed so to her till within the last few years. Her own father had been the village doctor, but of him she had no memory. Her mother's second marriage to a venerable country lawyer, John Gilman, had brought a kindly, inefficient stepfather into the family, a man who speedily became an invalid needing constant nursing. The birth of David when Letty was three years old brought a new interest into the household, and the two children grew to be fast friends; but when Mrs. Gilman died, and Letty found herself at eighteen the mistress of the house, the nurse of her aged stepfather, and the only guardian of a boy of fifteen, life became difficult. More difficult still it became when the old lawyer died, for he at least had been a sort of fictitious

175

head of the family and his mere existence kept David within bounds.

David was a lively, harum-scarum, handsome youth, good at lessons, popular with his companions, always in a scrape, into which he was generally drawn by the minister's son, so the neighbors thought. At any rate, Dick Larrabee, as David's senior, received the lion's share of the blame when mischief was abroad. If Parson Larrabee's boy couldn't behave any better than an unbelieving blacksmith's, a Methodist farmer's, or a Baptist storekeeper's, what was the use of claiming superior efficacy for the Congregational form of belief?

"Dick's father's never succeeded in bringing him into the church, though he's worked on him from the time he was knee-high to a toad," said Mrs. Popham.

"P'raps his mother kind o' vaccinated him with religion 'stid o' leavin' him to take it the natural way, as the ol' sayin' is," was her husband's response. "The first Mis' Larrabee was as good as gold, but she may have overdone the trick a little mite, mebbe; and what's more, I kind o' suspicion the parson thinks so himself. He ain't never been quite the same sence Dick left home, 'cept in preachin'; an' I tell you, Maria, his high-water mark there is higher'n ever. Abel Dunn o' Boston walked home from meetin' with me Thanksgivin', an', says he, takin' off his hat an' moppin' his forehead, 'Osh,' says he, 'does your minister preach like that every Sunday?' 'No,' says I, 'he don't. If he did we couldn't stan' it! He preaches like that about once a month, an' we don't care what he says the rest o' the time.' "

"Well, so far as boys are concerned, preachin' ain't so reliable, for behavin' purposes, as a good young alder switch," was the opinion of Mrs. Popham, her children being of the comatose kind, whose minds had never been illuminated by the dazzling idea of disobedience.

"Land sakes, Maria! There ain't alders enough on the river-bank to switch religion into a boy like Dick Larrabee. It's got to come like a thief in the night, as the ol' sayin' is, but I guess I don't mean thief, I guess I mean star: it's got to come kind o' like a star in a dark night. If the whole village, 'generate an' onregenerate, hadn't 'a' kep' on naggin' an' hectorin' an' criticizin' them two boys, Dick an' Dave,—carryin' tales an' multiplyin' of 'em by two, '*ong root,*' as the ol' sayin' is,—I dare say they'd 'a' both been here yet; 'stid o' roamin' roun' the earth seekin' whom they may devour."

There was considerable truth in Ossian Popham's remark, as Letty could have testified; for the conduct of the Boynton-Gilman household, as well as that of the minister, had been continually under inspection and discussion.

Nothing could remain long hidden in Beulah. Nobody spied, nobody pried, nobody listened at doors or windows, nobody owned a microscope, nobody took any particular notice of events, or if they did they preserved an attitude of profound indifference while doing it,—yet everything was known sooner or later. The amount of the fish and meat bill, the precise extent of credit, the number of letters in the post, the amount of fuel burned, the number of absences from church and prayer-meeting, the calls or visits made and received, the hours of arrival or departure, the source of all incomes,—these details were the common property of the village. It even took cognizance of more subtle things; for it observed and recorded the fluctuations of all love affairs, and the fluctuations also in the religious experiences of various persons not always in spiritual equilibrium; for the soul was an object of scrutiny in Beulah, as well as mind, body, and estate.

Letty Boynton used to feel that nothing was exclusively her own; that she belonged to Beulah part and parcel; but Dick Larrabee was far more restive under the village espionage than were she and David.

It was natural that David should want to leave Beulah and make his way in the world, and his sister did not oppose it. Dick's circumstances were different. He had inherited a small house and farm from his mother, had enjoyed a college education, and had been offered a share in a good business in a city twelve miles away. He left Beulah because he hated it. He left because he could not endure his father's gentle remonstrances or the bewilderment in his stepmother's eyes. She was a newcomer in the household and her glance seemed to say: "Why on earth do you behave so badly to your father when you're such a delightful chap?" He left because Deacon Todd had prayed for him publicly at a Christian Endeavor meeting; because Mrs. Popham had circulated a wholly baseless scandal about him; and finally because in his young misery the only being who could have comforted him by joining her hapless fortunes to his had refused to do so. He didn't know why. He had always counted on Letty when the time should come to speak the word. He had shown his heart in everything but words; what more did a girl want? Of course, if anyone preferred a purely fantastic duty to a man's love, and allowed a scapegrace brother to foist two red-faced, squalling babies on her, there was nothing to be said. So, in this frame of mind he had had one flaming, passionate, wrongheaded scene with his father, and strode out of Beulah with dramatic gestures of shaking its dust off his feet. His father, roused for once from his lifelong patience, had been rather terrible in that last scene; so terrible that he had never forgiven himself, or really believed himself fully forgiven by God, though his son had alienated half the village and nearly rent the parish in twain by his conduct.

As for Letty, she held her peace. She could only hope that the minister and his wife suspected nothing, and she was sure of Beulah's point of view. That a girl would never give up a suitor, if she had any hope of tying him to her for life, was a popular form of belief in the community; and strangely enough it was chiefly the women, not the men, who made it current. Now and then a soft-hearted and chivalrous male would observe indulgently of some village beauty, "I shouldn't wonder a mite if she could 'a' had Bill for the askin' ''; but this opinion would be met by such a chorus of feminine incredulity that its author generally withdrew it as unsound and untenable.

It was then, when Dick had gone away, that the days had grown drab and long, but the twins kept Letty's inexperienced hands busy, though in the first year she had the help of old Miss Clarissa Perry, a childless expert in the bringing-up of babies.

The friendship of Reba Larrabee, so bright and cheery and comprehending, was a never-ending solace. There was nothing of the martyr about Letty. She was not wholly resigned to her lot, and to tell the truth she did not intend to be, for a good many years yet.

"I'm not a minister, but I'm the wife of a minister, which is the next best thing," Mrs. Larrabee used to say. "I tell you, Letty, there's no use in human creatures being resigned till their bodies are fairly worn out with fighting. When you can't think of another mortal thing to do, be resigned; but I'm convinced that the

Lord is ashamed of us when we fold our hands too soon!"

"You were born courageous, Reba!" And Letty would look admiringly at the rosy cheeks and bright eyes of her friend.

"My blood circulates freely; that helps me a lot. Everybody's blood circulates in Racine, Wisconsin."— And the minister's wife laughed genially. "Yours, hereabouts, freezes up in your six months of cold weather, and when it begins to thaw out the snow is ready to fall again. That sort of thing induces depression, although no mere climate would account for Mrs. Popham.—Ossian said to Luther the other day: 'Maria ain't hardly to blame, parson. She come from a gloomy stock. The Ladds was all gloomy, root and branch. They say that the Ladd babies was always discouraged two days after they was born.' "

The cause of Letty's chief heartache, the one that she could reveal to nobody, was that her brother should leave her nowadays so completely to her own resources. She recalled the time when he came home from Boston, pale, haggard, ashamed, and told her of his marriage, months before. She could read in his lacklustre eyes, and hear in his voice, the absence of love, the fear of the future. That was bad enough, but presently he said: "Letty, there's more to tell. I've no money, and no place to put my wife, but there's a child coming. Can I bring her here till—afterwards? You won't like her, but she's so ailing and despondent just now that I think she'll behave herself, and I'll take her away as soon as she's able to travel. She would never stay here in the country, anyway; you couldn't hire her to do it."

She came: black-haired, sullen-faced Eva, with a vulgar beauty of her own, much damaged by bad temper, discontent, and illness. Oh, those terrible weeks for Letty, hiding her own misery, putting on a brave face with the neighbors, keeping the unwelcome sister-in-law in the background.

It was bitterly cold, and Eva raged against the climate, the house, the lack of a servant, the absence of gayety, and above all at the prospect of motherhood. Her resentment against David, for some reason unknown to Letty, was deep and profound and she made no secret of it; until the outraged Letty, goaded into speech one day, said: "Listen, Eva! David brought you here because his sister's house was the proper place for you just now. I don't know why you married each other, but you did, and it's evidently a failure. I'm going to stand by David and see you through this trouble, but while you're under my roof you'll have to speak respectfully of my brother; not so much because he's my brother, but because he's your husband and the father of the child that's coming:—do you understand?"

Letty had a good deal of red in her bronze hair and her brown eyes were as capable of flashing fire as Eva's black ones; so the girl not only refrained from venting her spleen upon the absent David, but ceased to talk altogether, and the gloom in the house was as black as if Mrs. Popham and all her despondent ancestors were living under its roof.

The good doctor called often and did his best, shrugging his shoulders and lifting his eyebrows as he said: "Let her work out her own salvation. I doubt if she can, but we'll give her the chance. If the problem can be solved, the child will do it."

 ell, the problem never was solved, never in this world, at least; and those who were in the sitting-room chamber when Eva was shown her two babies lying side by side on a pillow, never forgot the quick glance of horrified incredulity, or the shriek of aversion with which she greeted them.

Letty had a sense of humor, and it must be confessed that when the scorned and discarded babies were returned to her, and she sat by the kitchen stove trying to plan a second bottle, a second cradle, and see how far the expected baby could divide its modest outfit with the unexpected one, she burst into a fit of hysterical laughter mingled with an outpour of tears.

The doctor came in from the sick-room puzzled and crestfallen from his interview with an entirely new specimen of womankind. He had brought Letty and

David into the world and soothed the last days of all her family, and now in this tragedy—for tragedy it was—he was her only confidant and adviser.

Letty looked at him, the tears streaming from her eyes.

"Oh, Doctor Lee, Doctor Lee! If an overruling Providence could smile, wouldn't He smile now? David and Eva never wanted to marry each other, I'm sure of it, and the last thing they desired was a child. Now there are two of them. Their father is away, their mother won't look at them! What will become of me until Eva gets well and behaves like a human being? I never promised to be an aunt to twins; I never did like twins; I think they're downright vulgar!"

> "Waly waly! bairns are bonny:
> One's enough and twa's ower mony,"

quoted the doctor. "It's worse even than you think, my poor Letty, for the girl can't get well, because she won't! She has gritted her teeth, turned her face to the wall, and refused her food. It's the beginning of the end. You are far likelier to be a foster mother than an aunt!"

Letty's face changed and softened and her color rose. She leaned over the two pink, crumpled creatures, still twitching nervously with the amazement and discomfort of being alive.

185

"Come to your Aunt Letty then and be mothered!" she sobbed, lifting the pillow and taking it, with its double burden, into her arms. "You shan't suffer, poor innocent darlings, even if those who brought you into the world turn away from you! Come to your Aunt Letty and be mothered!"

"That's right, that's right," said the doctor over a lump in his throat. "We mustn't let the babies pay the penalty of their parents' sins; and there's one thing that may soften your anger a little, Letty: Eva's not right; she's not quite responsible. There are cases where motherhood, that should be a joy, brings nothing but mental torture and perversion of instinct. Try and remember that, if it helps you any. I'll drop in every two or three hours and I'll write David to come at once. He must take his share of the burden."

Well, David came, but Eva was in her coffin. He was grave and silent, and it could not be said that he showed a trace of fatherly pride. He was very young, it is true, thoroughly ashamed of himself, very unhappy, and anxious about his new cares; but Letty could not help thinking that he regarded the twins as a sort of personal insult,—perhaps not on their own part, nor on Eva's, but as an accident that might have been prevented by a competent Providence. At any rate, he carried himself as a man with a grievance, and when he looked at his offspring, which was seldom, it seemed to Letty that he regarded the second one as an

186

unnecessary intruder and cherished a secret resentment at its audacity in coming to this planet uninvited. He went back to his work in Boston without its having crossed his mind that anybody but his sister could take care of his children. He didn't really regard them as children or human beings; it takes a woman's vision to make that sort of leap into the future. Until a newborn baby can show some personal beauty, evince some intellect, stop squirming and squealing, and exhibit enough self-control to let people sleep at night, it is not, as a rule, *persona grata* to anyone but its mother.

David did say vaguely to Letty when he was leaving, that he hoped "they would be good," the screams that rent the air at the precise moment of farewell rather giving the lie to his hopes.

Letty was struggling to end the interview without breaking down, for she was worn out nervously as well as physically, and thought if she could only be alone with her problems and her cares she would rather write to David than tell him her mind face to face.

Brother and sister held each other tightly for a moment, kissed each other good-bye, and then Letty watched Osh Popham's sleigh slipping off with David into the snowy distance, the merry tinkle of the bells adding to the sadness in her dreary heart. Dick gone yesterday, Dave to-day; Beulah without Dick and Dave! The two joys of her life were missing and in their places two unknown babies whose digestive systems were going to need constant watching, according to Dr. Lee. Then she went about with set lips, doing the last sordid things that death brings in its wake; doing them as she had seen her mother do before her. She threw away the husks in Eva's under mattress and put fresh ones in; she emptied the feathers from the feather bed and pillows and aired them in the sun while she washed the ticking; she scrubbed the paint in the sickroom, and in between her tasks learned from Clarissa Perry the whole process of bringing up babies by hand.

That was three years ago. At first David had sent ten dollars a month from his slender earnings, never omitting it save for urgent reasons. He evidently thought of the twins as "company" for his sister and their care a pleasant occupation, since she had "almost" a living income; taking in a few coats to make, just to add an occasional luxury to the bare necessities of life provided by her mother's will.

His letters were brief, dispirited, and infrequent, but they had not ceased altogether till within the last few months, during which Letty's to him had been returned from Boston with "Not found" scribbled on the envelopes.

The firm in whose care Letty had latterly addressed him simply wrote, in answer to her inquiries, that Mr. Gilman had not been in their employ for some time and they had no idea of his whereabouts.

The rest was silence.

# 5

**A** good deal of water had run under Beulah Bridge since Letty Boynton had sat at her window on a December evening unconsciously furnishing copy and illustration for a Christmas card; yet there had been very few outward changes in the village. Winter had melted into spring, burst into summer, faded into autumn, lapsed into winter again,—the same old, ever-recurring pageant in the world of Nature, and the same procession of incidents in the neighborhood life.

The harvest moon and the hunter's moon had come and gone; the first frost, the family dinners and reunions at Thanksgiving, the first snowfall; and now, as Christmas approached, the same holiday spirit was abroad in the air, slightly modified as it passed by Mrs. Popham's mournful visage.

One or two babies had swelled the census, giving the minister hope of a larger Sunday School; one or two of the very aged neighbors had passed into the beyond; and a few romantic and enterprising young farmers had espoused wives, among them Osh Popham's son.

The manner of their choice was not entirely to the liking of the village. Digby Popham had married into the rival church and as his betrothed was a masterful young lady it was feared that Digby would leave Mr. Larrabee's flock to worship with his wife. Another had married without visible means of support, a proceeding always to be regretted by thoroughly prudent persons over fifty; and the third, Deacon Todd's eldest son, had somehow or other met a siren from Vermont and insisted on wedding her when there were plenty of marriageable girls in Beulah.

"I've no patience with such actions!" grumbled Mrs. Popham. "Young folks are so full of notions nowadays that they look for change and excitement everywheres. I s'pose James Todd thinks it's a decent, respectable way of actin', to turn his back on the girls he's been brought up an' gone to school with, and court somebody he never laid eyes on till a year ago. It's a free country, but I must say I don't think it's very refined for a man to go clear off somewheres and marry a perfect stranger!"

Births, marriages, and deaths, however, paled into

insignificance compared with the spectacular début of the minister's wife as a writer and embellisher of Christmas cards, two at least having been seen at the local milliner's store. How many she had composed, and how many of them (said Mrs. Popham) might have been rejected, nobody knew, though there was much speculation; and more than one citizen remarked on the size of the daily package of mail matter handed out by the rural delivery man at the parsonage gate.

No one but Mrs. Larrabee and Letty Boynton were in possession of all the thrilling details attending the public appearance of these works of art; the words and letters of appreciation, the commendation, and the occasional blows to pride that attended their acceptance and publication.

Mrs. Larrabee's first attempt, with the sketch of Letty at the window on Christmas Eve, her hearth-fire aglow, her heart and her door open that Love might enter in if the Christ Child came down the snowy street,—this went to the Excelsior Card Company in a large Western city, and the following correspondence ensued:

Mrs. Luther Larrabee,
*Beulah, N.H.*
Dear Madam:—
    Your letter bears a well-known post-mark, for my father and my grandfather

were born and lived in New Hampshire, "up Beulah way." I accept your verses because of the beauty of the picture that accompanied them, and because Christmas means more than holly and plum pudding and gift-laden trees to me, for I am a religious man,—a ministerial father and three family deacons saw to that, though it doesn't always work that way!—Frankly, I do not expect your card to have a wide appeal, so I offer you only five dollars.

A Christmas card, my dear madam, must have a greeting, and yours has none. If the pictured room were a real room, and someone who had seen or lived in it should recognize it, it would attract his eye, but we cannot manufacture cards to meet such romantic improbabilities. I am emboldened to ask you (because you live in Beulah) if you will not paint the outside of some lonely, little New Hampshire cottage, as humble as you like, and make me some more verses; something, say, about "the folks back home."

Sincerely yours,
REUBEN SMALL.

BEULAH, N.H.

DEAR MR. SMALL:—

I accept your offer of five dollars for my maiden effort in Christmas cards with thanks, and will try my hand at something more popular. I am not above liking to make a "wide appeal," but the subject you propose is rather a staggering one, because you accompany it with a phrase lacking rhythm, and difficult to rhyme. You will at once see, by running through the alphabet, that "roam" is the only serviceable rhyme for *"home,"* but the union of the two suggests jingle or doggerel. I defy any minor poet when furnished with such a phrase, to refrain from bursting at once into:—

No matter where you travel, no matter
  where you roam,
You'll never dum-di-dum-di-dee
  The folks back home.

     Sincerely yours,

      REBA LARRABEE.

P.S. On second thought I believe James Whitcomb Riley could do it and overcome the difficulties, but alas! I have not his touch!

Dear Mrs. Larrabee:—

We never refuse verses because they are too good for the public. Nothing is too good for the public, but the public must be the judge of what pleases it.

"The folks back home" is a phrase that will strike the eye and ear of thousands of wandering sons and daughters. They will choose that card from the heaped-up masses on the counters and send it to every State in the Union. If you will glance at your first card you will see that though people may read it they will always leave it on the counter. I want my cards on counters, by the thousand, but I don't intend that they should be left there!

Make an effort, dear Mrs. Larrabee! I could get "the folks back home" done here in the office in half an hour, but I'm giving you the chance because you live in Beulah, New Hampshire, and because you make beautiful pictures.

Sincerely yours,
Reuben Small.

Dear Mr. Small:—

I enclose a colored sketch of the out-side of the cottage whose living-room I used in my first card. I chose it because I love the person who lives in it; because it always looks beautiful in the snow, and because the tree is so picturesque. The fact that it is gray for lack of paint may remind a casual wanderer that there is something to do, now and then, for the "folks back home." The verse is just as bad as I thought it would be. It seems incredible that anyone should buy it, but ours is a big country and there are many kinds of people living in it, so who knows? Why don't you accept my picture and then you write the card? I could not put my initials on this! They are unknown, to be sure, and I should want them to be, if you use it!

Sincerely yours,
REBA LARRABEE.

Now here's a Christmas greeting
   To the "folks back home."
It comes to you across the space,
   Dear folks back home!
I've searched the wide world over,
   But no matter where I roam,
No friends are like the old friends,
   No folks like those back home!

Dear Mrs. Larrabee:—

I gave you five dollars for the first picture and verses, which you, as a writer, regard more highly than I, who am merely a manufacturer. Please accept twenty dollars for "The Folks Back Home," on which I hope to make up my loss on the first card! I insist on signing the despised verse with your initials. In case R. L. should later come to mean something, you will be glad that a few thousand people have seen it.

Sincerely,

Reuben Small.


The Hessian soldier andirons, the portrait over the Boynton mantel, and even Letty Boynton's cape were identified on the first card, sooner or later, but it was obvious that Mrs. Larrabee had to have a picture for her verses and couldn't be supposed to make one up "out of her head"; though Osh Popham declared it had been done again and again in other parts of the world. Also it was agreed that, as Letty's face was not distinguishable, nobody outside of Beulah could recognize her by her cape; and that anyhow it couldn't make much difference, for if anybody wanted to spend fifteen cents on a card he would certainly buy the one about "the folks back home." The popularity of this was established by the fact that it was selling, not only in Beulah and Greentown, but in Boston, and in Racine, Wisconsin, and, it was rumored, even in Chicago. The village milliner in Beulah had disposed of twenty-seven copies in thirteen days and the minister's wife was universally conceded to be the most celebrated person in the State of New Hampshire.

Letty Boynton had an uncomfortable moment when she saw the first card, but common sense assured her that outside of a handful of neighbors no one would identify her home surroundings; meantime she was proud of Reba's financial and artistic triumph in "The Folks Back Home" and generously glad that she had no share in it.

Twice during the autumn David had broken his silence, but only to send her a postal from some Western town, telling her that he should have no regular address for a time; that he was traveling for a publishing firm and felt ill-adapted to the business. He hoped that she and the children were well, for he himself was not; etc., etc.

The twins had been photographed by Osh Popham, who was Jack of all trades and master of many, and a sight of their dimpled charms, curly heads, and straight little bodies would have gladdened any father's heart, Letty thought. However, she scorned to win David back by any such specious means. If he didn't care to know whether his children were humpbacked, bow-legged, cross-eyed, club-footed, or feeble-minded, why should she enlighten him? This was her usual frame of mind, but in these last days of the year how she longed to pop the bewitching photographs and Reba's Christmas cards into an envelope and send them to David.

But where? No word at all for weeks and weeks, and then only a postal from St. Joseph, saying that he had given up his position on account of poor health. Nothing in all this to keep Christmas on, thought Letty, and she knitted and crocheted and sewed with extra ardor that the twins' stockings might be filled with bright things of her own making.

*6*

On the afternoon before Christmas of that year, the North Station in Boston was filled with hurrying throngs on the way home for the holidays. Everybody looked tired and excited, but most of them had happy faces, and men and women alike had as many bundles as they could carry; bundles and boxes quite unlike the brown paper ones with which commuters are laden on ordinary days. These were white packages, beribboned and beflowered and behollied and bemistletoed, to be gently carried and protected from crushing.

The train was filled to overflowing and many stood in the aisles until Latham Junction was reached and the overflow alighted to change cars for Greentown and way stations.

Among the crowd were two men with suit-cases who hurried into the way train and, entering the smoking car from opposite ends, met in the middle of the aisle, dropped their encumbrances, stretched out a hand and ejaculated in the same breath:

"Dick Larrabee, upon my word!"

"Dave Gilman, by all that's great!—Here, let's turn over a seat for our baggage and sit together. Going home, I s'pose?"

The men had not met for some years, but each knew something of the other's circumstances and hoped that the other didn't know too much. They scanned each other's faces, Dick thinking that David looked pinched and pale, David half-heartedly registering the quick impression that Dick was prosperous.

"Yes," David answered; "I'm going home for a couple of days. It's such a confounded journey to that one-horse village that a business man can't get there but once in a generation!"

"Awful hole!" confirmed Dick. "Simply awful hole! I didn't get it out of my system for years."

"Married?" asked David.

"No; rather think I'm not the marrying kind, though the fact is I've had no time for love affairs— too busy. Let's see, you have a child, haven't you?"

"Yes; Letty has seen to all that business for me since my wife died." (Wild horses couldn't have dragged the information from him that the "child" was "twins," and Dick didn't need it anyway, for he had heard the news the morning he left Beulah.) "Wonder if there have been many changes in the village?"

"Don't know; there never used to be! Mrs. Popham has been ailing for years,—she couldn't die; and Deacon Todd wouldn't!" Dick's old animosities still lingered faintly in his memory, though his laughing voice and the twinkle in his eyes showed plainly that no bitterness was left. "How's business with you, David?"

"Only so-so. I've had the devil's own luck lately. Can't get anything that suits me or that pays a decent income. I formed a new connection the other day, but I can't say yet what there is in it. I'm just out of hospital; operation; they cut out the wrong thing first, I believe, sewed me up absent-mindedly, then remembered it was the other thing, and did it over again. At any rate, that's the only way I can account for their mewing me up there for two months."

"Well, well, that is hard luck! I'm sorry, old boy! Things didn't begin to go my way either till within the last few months. I've always made a fair living and saved a little money, but never gained any real headway. Now I've got a first-rate start and the future looks pretty favorable, and best of all, pretty safe.—No trouble at home calls you back to Beulah? I hope Letty is all right?" Dick cast an anxious side glance at David, though he spoke carelessly.

"Oh, no! Everything's serene, so far as I know. I'm a poor correspondent, especially when I've no good news to tell; and anyway, the mere sight of a pen ties my tongue. I'm just running down to surprise Letty."

Dick looked at David again. He began to think he didn't like him. He used to, when they were boys, but when he brought that unaccountable wife home and foisted her and her babies on Letty, he rather turned against him. David was younger than himself, four or five years younger, but he looked as if he hadn't grown up. Surely his boyhood chum hadn't used to be so pale and thin-chested or his mouth so ladylike and pretty. A good face, though; straight and clean, with honest eyes and a likeable smile. Lack of will, perhaps, or a persistent run of ill luck. Letty had always kept him stiffened up in the old days. Dick recalled one of his father's phrases to the effect that Dave Gilman would spin on a very small biscuit, and wondered if it were still true.

"And you, Dick? Your father's still living? You see I haven't kept up with Beulah lately."

"Keeping up with Beulah! It sounds like the title of a novel, but the hero would have to be a snail or he'd pass Beulah in the first chapter!—Yes, father's hale and hearty, I believe."

"You come home every Christmas, I s'pose?" inquired David.

"No; as a matter of fact this is my first visit since I left for good."

"That's about my case." And David hung his head a little, unconsciously.

"That so? Well, I was a hot-headed fool when I said good-bye to Beulah, and it's taken me all this time to cool off and make up my mind to apologize to the dad. There's—there's rather a queer coincidence about my visit just at this time."

"Speaking of coincidences," said David, "I can beat yours, whatever it is. If the thought of your father brought you back, my mother drew me—this way!" And he took something from his inside coat pocket.— "Do you see that?"

Dick regarded the object blankly, then with a quick gesture dived into his pocket and brought forth another of the same general character. "How about this?" he asked.

Each had one of Reba Larrabee's Christmas cards but David had the first unsuccessful one and Dick the popular one with the lonely little gray house and the verse about the folks back home.

The men looked at each other in astonishment and Dick gave a low whistle. Then they bent over the cards together.

"It was mother's picture that pulled me back to Beulah, I don't mind telling you," said David, his mouth twitching. "Don't you see it?"

"Oh! Is that your mother?" And Dick scanned the card closely.

"Don't you remember her portrait that always hung there after she died?"

"Yes, of course!" And Dick's tone was apologetic. "You see the face is so small I didn't notice it, but I recognize it now and remember the portrait."

"Then the old sitting-room!" exclaimed David. "Look at the rag carpet and the blessed old andirons! Gracious! I've crawled round those Hessian soldiers, burned my fingers and cracked my skull on 'em, often enough when I was a kid! When I'd studied the card five minutes, I bought a ticket and started for home."

David's eyes were suffused and his lip trembled.

"I don't wonder," said Dick. "I recognize the dear old room right enough, and of course I should know Letty."

"It didn't occur to me that it *was* Letty for some time," said her brother. "There's just the glimpse of a face shown, and no real likeness."

"Perhaps not," agreed Dick. "A stranger wouldn't have known it for Letty, but if it had been only that cape I should have guessed. It's as familiar as Mrs. Popham's bugle bonnet, and much prettier. She wore it every winter,—skating, you know,—and it's just the color of her hair."

"Letty has a good-shaped head," said David judicially. "It shows, even in the card."

"And a remarkable ear," added Dick, "so small and so close to her head."

"I never notice people's ears," confessed David.

"Don't you? I do, and eyelashes, too. Mother's got Letty's eyelashes down fine.—She's changed, Dave, Letty has! That hurts me. She was always so gay and chirpy. In this picture she has a sad, faraway, listening look, but mother may have put that in just to make it interesting."

Or perhaps I've had something to do with the change of expression! thought David. "What attracted me first," he added, "was your mother's verses. She always had a knack of being pious without cramming piety down your throat. I liked that open door. It meant welcome, no matter how little you'd deserved it."

"Where'd you get your card, Dave?" asked Dick. "It's prettier than mine."

"A nurse brought it to me in the hospital just because she took a fancy to it. She didn't know it would mean anything to me, but it did—a relapse!" And David laughed shamedfacedly. "I guess she'll confine herself to beef tea after this!—Where'd you get yours?"

"Picked it up on a dentist's mantelpiece when I was waiting for an appointment. I was traveling round the room, hands in my pockets, when suddenly I saw this card standing up against an hour-glass. The color caught me. I took it to the window, and at first I was puzzled. It certainly was Letty's house. The door's open you see and there's somebody in the window. I knew it was Letty, but how could any card publisher have found the way to Beulah? Then I discovered mother's initials snarled up in holly, and remembered that she was always painting and illuminating."

"Queer job, life is!" said David, putting his card back in his pocket and wishing there were a little more time, or that he had a little more courage, so that he might confide in Dick Larrabee. He felt a desire to tell him some of the wretchedness he had lived through. It would be a comfort just to hint that his unhappiness had made him a coward, so that the very responsibilities that serve as a spur to some men had left him until now cold, unstirred, unvitalized.

"You're right!" Dick answered. "Life is a queer job and it doesn't do to shirk it. And just as queer as anything in life is the way that mother's Christmas cards brought us back to Beulah! They acted as a sort of magic, didn't they?—Jiminy! I believe the next station is Beulah. I hope the depot team will be hitched up."

"Yes, here we are; seven o'clock and the train only thirty-five minutes late. It always made a point of that on holidays!"

"Never mind!" And Dick's tone was as gay as David's was sober. "The beanpot will have gone back to the cellarway and the doughnuts to the crock, but the 'folks back home' 'll get 'em out for us, and a mince pie, too, and a cut of sage cheese."

"There won't be any 'folks back home,' we're so late, I'm thinking. There's always a Christmas Eve festival at the church, you know. They never change—in Beulah."

"Then, by George, they can have me for Santa Claus!" said Dick as they stepped out on the platform. "Why, it doesn't seem cold at all; yet look at the ice on the river! What skating, and what a moon! My blood's up, and if I find the parsonage closed, I'll follow on to the church and make my peace with the members. There's a kind of spell on me! For the first time in years I feel as though I could shake hands with Deacon Todd."

"Well, Merry Christmas to you, Dick,—I'm going to walk. Good gracious! Have you come to spend the winter?" For various bags and parcels were being flung out on the platform with that indifference and irresponsibility that bespeak the touch of the seasoned baggage-handler.

"You didn't suppose I was coming back to Beulah empty-handed, on Christmas Eve, did you? If I'm in time for the tree, I'm going to give those blue-nosed, frost-bitten little youngsters something to remember! Jump in, Dave, and ride as far as the turn of the road."

In a few minutes the tottering old signboard that

marked the way to Beulah Center hove in sight, and David jumped from the sleigh to take his homeward path.

"Merry Christmas again, Dick!" he waved.

"Same to you, Dave! I'll come myself to say it to Letty the first minute I see smoke coming from your chimney tomorrow morning. Tell her you met me, will you, and that my visit is partly for her, only that father had to have his turn first. She'll know why. Tell her mother's card had Christmas magic in it, tell—"

"Say, tell her the rest yourself, will you, Dick?" And Dave broke into a run down the hill road that led to Letty.

"I will, indeed!" breathed Dick into his muffler.

7

**R**epeating history, Letty was again at her open window. She had been half-ashamed to reproduce the card, as it were, but something impelled her. She was safe from scrutiny, too, for everybody had gone to the tree—the Pophams, Mr. Davis, Clarissa Perry, everybody for a quarter of a mile up and down the street, and by now the company would be gathered and the tree lighted. She could keep watch alone, the only sound being that of the children's soft breathing in the next room.

Letty had longed to go to the festival herself, but old Clarissa Perry, who cared for the twins now and then in Letty's few absences, had a niece who was going to "speak a piece," and she yearned to be present and share in the glory; so Letty was kept at home as she had been numberless other times during the three years of her vicarious motherhood.

The night was mild again, as in the year before. The snow lay like white powder on the hard earth; the moon was full, and the street was a length of dazzling silence. The lighted candle was in the parlor window, shining toward the meeting-house, the fire burned brightly on the hearth, the front door was ajar. Letty wrapped her old cape round her shoulders, drew her hood over her head, and seating herself at the window repeated under her breath:—

"My door is on the latch to-night,
    The hearth-fire is aglow.
I seem to hear swift passing feet,—
    The Christ Child in the snow.

"My heart is open wide to-night
    For stranger, kith, or kin;
I would not bar a single door
    Where Love might enter in!"

And then a footstep, drawing ever nearer, sounded crunch, crunch, in the snow. Letty pushed her chair back into the shadow. The footstep halted at the gate, came falteringly up the path, turned aside, and came nearer the window. Then a voice said: "Don't be frightened Letty, it's David! Can I come in? I haven't any right to, except that it's Christmas Eve."

That, indeed, was the magic, the all-comprehending phrase that swept the past out of mind with one swift stroke: the acknowledgment of unworthiness, the childlike claim on the forgiving love that should be in every heart on such a night as this. Resentment melted away like mist before the sun. Her deep grievance—where had it gone? How could she speak anything but welcome? For what was the window open, the fire lighted, the door ajar, the guiding candle-flame, but that Love, and David, might enter in?

There were few words at first; nothing but close-locked hands and wet cheeks pressed together. Then Letty sent David into the children's room by himself. If the twins were bewitching when awake, they were nothing short of angelic when asleep.

David came out a little later, his eyes reddened with tears, his hair rumpled, his face flushed. He seemed like a man awed by an entirely new experience. He could not speak, he could only stammer brokenly:—

"As God is my witness, Letty, there's been something wrong with me up to this moment. I never thought of them as my children before, and I can't believe that such as they can belong to me. They were never wanted, and I've never had any interest in them.

**211**

I owe them to you, Letty; you've made them what they are; you, and no one else."

"If there hadn't been something there to build on, my love and care wouldn't have counted for much. They're just like dear mother's people for good looks and brains and pretty manners: they're pure Shirley all the way through, the twinnies are."

"It's lucky for me that they are!" said David humbly. "You see, Letty, I married Eva to keep my promise. If I was old enough to make it, I was old enough to keep it, so I thought. She never loved me, and when she found out that I didn't love her any longer she turned against me. Our life together was awful, from beginning to end, but she's in her grave, and nobody'll ever hear my side, now that she can't tell hers. When I looked at those two babies the day I left you, I thought of them only as retribution; and the vision of them—ugly, wrinkled, writhing little creatures—has been in my mind ever since."

"They were compensation, not retribution, David. I ought to have told you how clever and beautiful they were, but you never asked and my pride was up in arms. A man should stand by his own flesh and blood, even if it isn't attractive; that's what I believe."

"I know, I know! But I've had no feeling for three years. I've been like a frozen man, just drifting, trying to make both ends meet, my heart dead and my body full of pain. I'm just out of a hospital—two months in all."

"David! Why didn't you let me know, or send for me?"

"Oh, it was way out in Missouri. I was taken ill very suddenly at the hotel in St. Joseph and they moved me at once. There were two operations first and last, and I didn't know enough to feed myself most of the time."

"Poor, poor Buddy! Did you have good care?"

"The best. I had more than care. Ruth Bentley, the nurse that brought me back to life, made me see what a useless creature I was."

Some woman's instinct stirred in Letty at a new note in her brother's voice and a new look in his face. She braced herself for his next words, sure that they would open a fresh chapter. The door and the window were closed now, the shades pulled down, the fire low; the hour was ripe for confidences.

"You see, Letty,"—and David cleared his throat nervously, and looked at the coals gleaming behind the Hessian soldiers,—"it's a time for a thorough house-cleaning, body, mind, and soul, a long illness is; and Miss Bentley knew well enough that all was wrong with me. I mentioned my unhappy marriage and told her all about you, but I said nothing about the children."

"Why should you?" asked Letty, although her mind had leaped to the reason already.

"Well, I was a poor patient in one of the cheapest rooms; broken in health, without any present means of support. I wanted to stand well with her, she had been so good to me, and I thought if she knew about the twins she wouldn't believe I could ever make a living for three."

"Still less for *four*!" put in Letty, with an irrepressible note of teasing in her tone.

She had broken the ice. Like a torrent set free, David dashed into the story of the last two months and Ruth Bentley's wonderful influence. How she had recreated him within as well as without. How she was the best and noblest of women, willing to take a pauper by the hand and brace him up for a new battle with life.

"Strength appeals to me," confessed David. "Perhaps it's because I am weak; for I'm afraid I am, a little!"

"Be careful, Davy! Eva was strong!"

David shuddered. He remembered a strength that lashed and buffeted and struck and overpowered.

"Ruth is different," he said. " 'Out of the strong came forth sweetness' used to be one of Parson Larrabee's texts. That's Ruth's kind of strength.—Can I— will you let me bring her here to see you, Letty,—say for New Year's? It's all so different from the last time

I asked you. Then I knew I was bringing you nothing but sorrow and pain, but Ruth carries her welcome in her face."

The prop inside of Letty wavered unsteadily for a moment and then stood in its accustomed upright position.

"Why not?" she asked. "It's the right thing to do; but you must tell her about the children first."

"Oh! I did that long ago, after I found out that she cared. It was only at first that I didn't dare. I haven't told you, but she went out for her daily walk and brought me home a Christmas card, the prettiest one she could find, she said. I was propped up on pillows, as weak as a kitten. I looked at it and looked at it, and when I saw that it was this room, the old fireplace and mother's picture, and the Hessian soldier andirons, when I realized there was a face at the window and that the door was ajar,—everything just swam before me and I fainted dead away. I had a relapse, and when I was better again I told her everything. She's fond of children. It didn't make any difference, except for her to say that the more she had to do for me, the more she wanted to do it."

"Well," said Letty with a break in her voice, "that's love, so far as I can see, and if you've been lucky enough to win it, take it and be thankful, and above all, nurse and keep it.—So one of Reba's cards, the one the publisher thought would never sell, found

**215**

you and brought you back! How wonderful! We little thought of that, Reba and I!"

"Reba's work didn't stop there, Letty! There was so much that had to be said between you and me, just now, that I couldn't let another subject creep in till it was finished and we were friends;—but Dick Larrabee saw Reba's card about 'the folks back home' in Chicago and he bought a ticket for Beulah just as I did. We met in the train and compared notes."

"Dick Larrabee home?"

The blood started in Letty's heart and sped hither and thither, warming her from head to foot.

"Yes, looking as fit as a fiddle; the way a man looks when things are coming his way."

"But what did the card mean to him? Did he seem to like Reba's verses?"

"Yes, but I guess the card just spelled home to him; and he recognized this house in a minute, of course. I showed him my card and he said: 'That's Letty fast enough: I know the cape.' He recognized you in a minute, he said."

He knew the cape! Yes, the old cape had been close to his shoulder many a time. He liked it and said it matched her hair.

"He was awfully funny about your ear, too! I told him I never noticed women's ears, and he said he did, when they were pretty, and their eyelashes, too.—Anything remarkable about your eyelashes, Letty?"

"Nothing that I'm aware of!" said Letty laughingly, although she was fibbing and she knew it.

"And he said he'd call and say 'Merry Christmas' to you the first thing tomorrow; that he would have been here to-night but you'd know his father had to come first. You don't mind being second to the parson, do you?"

No, Letty didn't mind. Her heart was unaccountably light and glad, like a girl's heart. It was the Eve of Mary when all women are blest because of one. The Wise Men brought gifts to the Child; Letty had often brought hers timidly, devoutly, trustfully, and perhaps to-night they were coming back to her!

## 8

**P**ut the things down on the front steps," said Dick to the driver as he neared the parsonage. "If there's nobody at home I'll go on up to the church after I've got this stuff inside."

"Got a key?"

"No, don't need one. I've picked all the locks with a penknife many a time. Besides, the key is sure to be under the doormat. Yes, here it is! Of all the unaccountable customs I ever knew, that's the most laughable!"

"Works all right for you!"

"Yes, and for all the other tramps,"—and Dick opened the door and lifted in his belongings. "Goodnight," he called to the driver; "I'll walk up to the church after I've found out whether mother keeps the mince pie and cider apple sauce in the same old place."

218

A few minutes later, his hunger partially stayed, Dick Larrabee locked the parsonage door and took the well-trodden path across the church common. It was his father's feet, he knew, that had worn the shoveled path so smooth; his kind, faithful feet that had sped to and fro on errands of mercy, never faltering in all the years.

It was nearly eight o'clock. The sound of the melodeon, with children's voices, floated out from the white-painted meeting-house, all ablaze with light; or as much ablaze as a kerosene chandelier and six side lamps could make it. The horse sheds were crowded with teams of various sorts, the horses well blanketed and standing comfortably in straw; and the last straggler was entering the right-hand door of the church as Dick neared the steps. Simultaneously the left-hand door opened, and on the background of the light inside appeared the figure of Mrs. Todd, the wife of his ancient enemy, the senior deacon. Dick could see that a sort of dressing-room had been curtained off in the little entry, as it had often been in former times of tableaux and concerts and what not. Valor, not discretion, was the better policy, and walking boldly up to the steps Dick took off his fur cap and said, "Good evening, Mrs. Todd!"

"Good gracious me! Where under the canopy did you hail from, Dick Larrabee? Was your folks lookin' for you? They ain't breathed a word to none of us."

"No, I'm a surprise, Mrs. Todd."

"Well, I know you've given me one! Will you wait a spell till the recitations is over? You'd scare the children so, if you go in now, that they'd forget their pieces more'n they gen'ally do."

"I can endure the loss of the 'pieces,' " said Dick with a twinkle in his eye.

At which Mrs. Todd laughed comprehendingly, and said: "Isaac'll get a stool or a box or something; there ain't a vacant seat in the church. I wish we could say the same o' Sundays!—Isaac! Isaac! Come out and see who's here," she called under her breath. "He won't be long. He's tendin' John Trimble in the dressin'-room. He was the only one in the village that was willin' to be Santa Claus an' he wa'n't over-willin'. Now he's et something for supper that disagrees with him awfully and he's all doubled up with colic. We can't have the tree till the exercises is over, but that won't be mor'n fifteen minutes, so I sent Isaac home to make a mustard plaster. He's puttin' it on John now. John's dreadful solemn and unamusin' when he's well, and I can't think how he'll act when he's all crumpled up with stomach-ache, an' the mustard plaster drawin' like fire."

Dick threw back his head and laughed. He had forgotten just how unexpected Beulah's point of view always was.

Deacon Todd now came out cautiously.

"I've got it on him, mother, tho' he's terrible unresigned to it; an' I've given him a stiff dose o' Jamaica Ginger. We can tell pretty soon whether he can take his part."

"Here's Dick Larrabee come back, Isaac, just when we thought he had given up Beulah for good an' all!" said Mrs. Todd.

The Deacon stood on the top step, his gaunt, grizzled face peering above the collar of his great coat; not a man to eat his words very often, Deacon Isaac Todd.

"Well, young man," he said, "you've found your way home, have you? It's about time, if you want to see your father alive!"

"If it hadn't been for you and others like you, men who had forgotten what it was to be young, I should never have gone away," said Dick hotly. "What had I done worse than a dozen others, only that I happened to be the minister's son?"

"That's just it; you were bringin' trouble on the parish, makin' talk that reflected on your father. Folks said if he couldn't control his own son, he wa'n't fit to manage a church. You played cards, you danced, you drove a fast horse."

"I never did a thing I'm ashamed of but one,"— and Dick's voice was firm. "My misdeeds were nothing but boyish nonsense, but the village never gave me credit for a single virtue. I ought to have remembered father's position, but whatever I was or whatever I did,

**221**

you had no right to pray for me openly for full five minutes at a public meeting. That galled me worse than anything!"

"Now, Isaac," interrupted Mrs. Todd. "I hope you'll believe me! I've told you once a week, on an average, these last three years, that you might have chastened Dick some other way besides prayin' for him in meetin'!"

The Deacon smiled grimly. "You both talk as if prayin' was one of the seven deadly sins," he said.

"I'm not objecting to your prayers," agreed Dick, "but there were plenty of closets in your house where you might have gone and told the Lord your opinion of me; only that wasn't good enough for you; you must needs tell the whole village!"

"There, father, that's what I always said," agreed Mrs. Todd.

"Well, I ain't one that can't yield when the majority's against me," said the Deacon, "particularly when I'm treatin' John Trimble for the colic. If you'll stop actin' so you threaten to split the church, Dick Larrabee, I'll stop prayin' for you. The Lord knows how I feel about it now, so I needn't keep on remindin' Him."

9

"That's a bargain and here's my hand on it," cried Dick. "Now, what do you say to letting me be Santa Claus? Come on in and let's look at John Trimble. He'd make a splendid Job or Jeremiah, but I wouldn't let him spoil a Christmas festival!"

"Do let Dick take the part, father,"—and Mrs. Todd's tone was most ingratiating. "John's terrible dull and bashful anyway, an' mebbe he'd have a pain he couldn't stan' jest when he's givin' out the presents. An' Dick is always so amusin'."

Deacon Todd led the way into the improvised dressing-room. He had removed John's gala costume in order to apply the mustard faithfully and he lay in a crumpled heap in the corner. The plaster itself adorned a stool near by.

"Now, John! John! That plaster won't do you no

**223**

good on the stool. It ain't the stool that needs drawin'; it's your stomach," argued Mrs. Todd.

"I'm drawed pretty nigh to death a'ready," moaned John. "I'm rore, that's what I am,—rore! An' I won't be Santa Claus neither. I want to go home."

"Wrop him up and get him into your sleigh, father, and take him home; then come right back. Bed's the place for him. Keep that hot flat-iron on his stomach, if he'd rather have it than the mustard. Men-folks are such cowards. I'll dress Dick while you're gone. Mebbe it's a Providence!"

On the whole, Dick agreed with Mrs. Todd as he stood ready to make his entrance. The School Committee was in the church and he had had much to do with its members in former days. The Selectmen of the village were present, and he had made their acquaintance once, in an executive session. The deacons were all there and the pillars of the church and the choir and the organist—a spinster who had actively disapproved when he had put beans in the melodeon one Sunday. Yes, it was best to meet them in a body on a festive occasion like this, when the rigors of the village point of view were relaxed. It would relieve him of several dozen private visits of apology, and altogether he felt that his courage would have wavered had he not been disguised as another person altogether: a popular favorite; a fat, jolly, rollicking dispenser of bounties to the general public. When he finally discarded his cos-

tume, would it not be easier, too, to meet his father
first before the church full of people and have the solemn hour with him alone, later at night? Yes, as Mrs.
Todd said, "Mebbe 't was a Providence!"

There was never such a merry Christmas festival in the
Orthodox church of Beulah; everybody was of one
mind as to that. There was a momentary fear that John
Trimble, a pillar of prohibition, might have imbibed
hard cider; so gay, so nimble, so mirth-provoking was
Santa Claus. When was John Trimble ever known to
unbend sufficiently to romp up the side aisle jingling
his sleigh bells, and leap over a front pew stuffed with
presents, to gain the vantage-ground he needed for the
distribution of his pack? The wing pews on one side
of the pulpit had been floored over and the Christmas
Tree stood there, triumphant in beauty, while the gifts
strewed the green-covered platform at its feet.

How gay, how audacious, how witty was Santa
Claus! How the village had always misjudged John
Trimble, and how completely had John Trimble hitherto obscured his light under a bushel. In his own
proper person children avoided him, but they crowded
about this Santa Claus, encircling his legs, gurgling with
joy when they were lifted to his shoulder, their laughter ringing through the church at his droll antics. A
sense of mystery grew when he opened a pack on the

pulpit stairs, a pack unfamiliar in its outward aspect to the Committee on Entertainment. Every girl had a little doll dressed in fashionable attire, and every boy a brilliantly colored, splendidly noisy, tin trumpet; but hanging to every toy by a red ribbon was Mrs. Larrabee's Christmas card; her despised one about the "folks back home."

The publishers' check to the minister's wife had been accompanied by a dozen complimentary copies, but these had been sent to Reba's Western friends and relations; and although the card was on many a marble-topped table in Beulah, it had not been bought by all the inhabitants, by any means. Fifteen cents would purchase something useful, and Beulah did not contain many Crœsuses. Still, here the cards were,—enough of them for everybody,—with a linen handkerchief for every woman and every man in the meeting-house, and a dozen more sticking out of the pack, as the people in the front pews could plainly see. Modest gifts, but plenty of them, and nobody knew from whence they came! There was a buzzing in the church, a buzzing that grew louder and more persistent when Santa Claus threw a lace scarf around Mrs. Larrabee's shoulders and approached her husband with a fine beaver collar in his hands: hands that trembled, as everybody could see, when he buttoned the piece of fur around the old minister's neck.

And the minister? He had been half in, and half

out of, a puzzling dream for ten minutes, and when those hands of Santa Claus touched him, his flesh quivered. They reminded him of baby fingers that had crept around his neck years ago when he patiently walked the parsonage floor at night with his ailing child in his arms. Every drop of blood in his veins called out for answer. He looked above the white cotton beard and mustache to a pair of dark eyes; merry, mischievous, yet tender and soft; at a brown wavy lock escaping from the home-made wig. Then those who were near heard a weak voice say, "My son!" and those who were far away observed Santa Claus tear off his wig and beard, heard him cry, "Father!"—and, as Mrs. Todd said afterwards, saw him "fall on to the minister's neck right there before the whole caboodle, an' cling to him for all the world like an engaged couple, only they wouldn't 'a' made so free in public."

No ice but would have thawed in such an atmosphere! Grown-up Beulah forgot how much trouble Dick Larrabee had caused in other days, and the children had found a friend for all time. The extraordinary number of dolls, trumpets, handkerchiefs, and Christmas cards circulating in the meeting-house raised the temperature considerably, and induced a general feeling that if Dick Larrabee had really ever been a bit wild and reckless, he had evidently reformed, and prospered, besides.

Yes, no one but a kind and omniscient Provi-

dence could have so beautifully arranged Dick Larrabee's homecoming, and so wisely superintended his
complete reinstatement in the good graces of Beulah
village. A few maiden ladies felt that he had been a
trifle immodest in embracing, and especially in kissing,
his father in front of the congregation; venturing the
conviction that kissing, an indecorous custom in any
event, was especially lamentable in public.

"Pity Letty Boynton missed this evenin'," said
Mrs. Todd. "Her an' Dick allers had a fancy for each
other, so I've heard, though I don't know how true.
Clarissa Perry might jest as well have stayed with the
twins as not, for her niece that spoke a piece forgot
'bout half of it an' Clarissa was in a cold sweat every
minute. Then the niece had a fit o' cryin', she was so
ashamed at failin', an' Clarissa had to take her home.
So they both missed the tree, an' Letty might 'a' been
here as well as not an' got her handkerchief an' her
card. I sent John Trimble's to him by the doctor, but
he didn't take no notice, Isaac said, for the doctor was
liftin' off the hot flatiron an' puttin' turpentine on the
spot where I'd had my mustard.—Anyway, if John had
to have the colic he couldn't 'a' chosen a better time,
an' if he gets over it, I shall be real glad he had it; for
nobody ever seen sech a Santa Claus as Dick Larrabee
made, an' there never was, an' never will be, sech a
lively, an' amusin' an' free-an'-easy evenin' in the Orthodox church."

*10*

**B**less the card!" sighed David thankfully as he sat down to smoke a good-night pipe and propped his feet contentedly against the little Hessian soldiers. The blaze of the logs on his own family hearthstone, after many months of steam heaters in the hall bedrooms of cheap hotels, how it soothed his tired heart and gave it visions of happiness to come! The card was on his knee, where he could look from its pictured scene to the real one of which he was again a glad and grateful part.

"Bless the card!" whispered Letty Boynton to herself as she went to her moonlit bedroom. Her eyes searched the snowy landscape and found the parsonage, "over the hills and far away." Then her heart flew like a bird across the distance and beat its wings in gladness, for a faint light streamed from the parson's study windows and she knew that father and son were together. That, in itself, was enough, with David sleeping under the home roof; but to-morrow was coming and to-morrow might be hers—her very own!

"Bless the card!" said Reba Larrabee, the tears shining in her eyes as she left the minister alone with his son. "Bless everybody and everything! Above all, bless God, 'from whom all blessings flow.'"

"Bless the card," said Dick Larrabee when he went up the narrow parsonage stairs to the room of his boyhood and found everything as it had been years ago. He leaned the little piece of paper magic against the mantel clock, threw it a kiss, and then, opening his pocket-book, he went nearer to the lamp and took out the faded tintype of a brown-haired girl in a brown cape. "Bless the card!" he said again, with a new note in his voice: "Bless the girl! And bless to-morrow if it brings me what I want most in all the world!"

# A
# Christmas Carol
## by
## Charles
## Dickens

# *Marley's Ghost*

 arley was dead, to begin with. There is no doubt whatever about that. The register of his burial was signed by the clergyman, the clerk, the undertaker, and the chief mourner. Scrooge signed it. And Scrooge's name was good upon 'Change for anything he chose to put his hand to. Old Marley was as dead as a doornail.

Mind! I don't mean to say that I know of my own knowledge, what there is particularly dead about a door-nail. I might have been inclined, myself, to regard a coffin-nail as the deadest piece of ironmongery in the trade. But the wisdom of our ancestors is in the simile; and my unhallowed hands shall not disturb it, or the country's done for. You will, therefore, permit me to repeat, emphatically, that Marley was as dead as a door-nail.

Scrooge knew he was dead? Of course he did. How could it be otherwise? Scrooge and he were partners for I don't know how many years. Scrooge was his sole executor, his sole administrator, his sole assign, his sole residuary legatee, his sole friend, and sole mourner. And even Scrooge was not so dreadfully cut up by the sad event but that he was an excellent man of business on the very day of the funeral, and solemnised it with an undoubted bargain.

The mention of Marley's funeral brings me back to the point I started from. There is no doubt that Marley was dead. This must be distinctly understood, or nothing wonderful can come of the story I am going to relate. If we were not perfectly convinced that Hamlet's father died before the play began, there would be nothing more remarkable in his taking a stroll at night, in an easterly wind, upon his own ramparts, than there would be in any other middle-aged gentleman rashly turning out after dark in a breezy spot—say St. Paul's Churchyard, for instance—literally to astonish his son's weak mind.

Scrooge never painted out Old Marley's name. There it stood, years afterwards, above the warehouse door: Scrooge and Marley. The firm was known as Scrooge and Marley. Sometimes people new to the business called Scrooge Scrooge, and sometimes Marley, but he answered to both names. It was all the same to him.

Oh! but he was a tight-fisted hand at the grind-stone, Scrooge! a squeezing, wrenching, grasping, scraping, clutching, covetous old sinner! Hard and sharp as flint, from which no steel had ever struck out generous fire; secret, and self-contained, and solitary as an oyster. The cold within him froze his old features, nipped his pointed nose, shrivelled his cheek, stiffened his gait; made his eyes red, his thin lips blue; and spoke out shrewdly in his grating voice. A frosty rime was on his head, and on his eyebrows, and his wiry chin. He carried his own low temperature always about with him; he iced his office in the dog-days, and didn't thaw it one degree at Christmas.

External heat and cold had little influence on Scrooge. No warmth could warm, no wintry weather chill him. No wind that blew was bitterer than he, no falling snow was more intent upon its purpose, no pelting rain less open to entreaty. Foul weather didn't know where to have him. The heaviest rain, and snow, and hail, and sleet could boast of the advantage over him in only one respect. They often 'came down' handsomely, and Scrooge never did.

Nobody ever stopped him in the street to say, with gladsome looks, 'My dear Scrooge, how are you? When will you come to see me?' No beggars implored him to bestow a trifle, no children asked him what it was o'clock, no man or woman ever once in all his life inquired the way to such and such a place, of Scrooge.

Even the blind men's dogs appeared to know him; and, when they saw him coming on, would tug their owners into doorways and up courts; and then would wag their tails as though they said, 'No eye at all is better than an evil eye, dark master!'

But what did Scrooge care? It was the very thing he liked. To edge his way along the crowded paths of life, warning all human sympathy to keep its distance, was what the knowing ones call 'nuts' to Scrooge.

Once upon a time—of all the good days in the year, on Christmas Eve—old Scrooge sat busy in his counting-house. It was cold, bleak, biting weather; foggy withal; and he could hear the people in the court outside go wheezing up and down, beating their hands upon their breasts, and stamping their feet upon the pavement stones to warm them. The City clocks had only just gone three, but it was quite dark already—it had not been light all day—and candles were flaring in the windows of the neighbouring offices, like ruddy smears upon the palpable brown air. The fog came pouring in at every chink and keyhole, and was so dense without, that, although the court was of the narrowest, the houses opposite were mere phantoms. To see the dingy cloud come drooping down, obscuring everything, one might have thought that nature lived hard by, and was brewing on a large scale.

The door of Scrooge's counting-house was open,

that he might keep his eye upon his clerk, who in a dismal little cell beyond, a sort of tank, was copying letters. Scrooge had a very small fire, but the clerk's fire was so very much smaller that it looked like one coal. But he couldn't replenish it, for Scrooge kept the coal-box in his own room; and so surely as the clerk came in with the shovel, the master predicted that it would be necessary for them to part. Wherefore the clerk put on his white comforter, and tried to warm himself at the candle; in which effort, not being a man of strong imagination, he failed.

'A merry Christmas, uncle! God save you!' cried a cheerful voice. It was the voice of Scrooge's nephew, who came upon him so quickly that this was the first intimation he had of his approach.

'Bah!' said Scrooge. 'Humbug!'

He had so heated himself with rapid walking in the fog and frost, this nephew of Scrooge's, that he was all in a glow; his face was ruddy and handsome; his eyes sparkled, and his breath smoked again.

'Christmas a humbug, uncle!' said Scrooge's nephew. 'You don't mean that, I am sure?'

'I do,' said Scrooge. 'Merry Christmas! What right have you to be merry? What reason have you to be merry? You're poor enough.'

'Come, then,' returned the nephew gaily. 'What right have you to be dismal? What reason have you to be morose? You're rich enough.'

Scrooge, having no better answer ready on the spur of the moment, said, 'Bah!' again; and followed it up with 'Humbug!'

'Don't be cross, uncle!' said the nephew.

'What else can I be,' returned the uncle, 'when I live in such a world of fools as this? Merry Christmas! Out upon merry Christmas! What's Christmas-time to you but a time for paying bills without money; a time for finding yourself a year older, and not an hour richer; a time for balancing your books, and having every item in 'em through a round dozen of months presented dead against you? If I could work my will,' said Scrooge indignantly, 'every idiot who goes about with "Merry Christmas" on his lips should be boiled with his own pudding, and buried with a stake of holly through his heart. He should!'

'Uncle!' pleaded the nephew.

'Nephew!' returned the uncle sternly, 'keep Christmas in your own way, and let me keep it in mine.'

'Keep it!' repeated Scrooge's nephew. 'But you don't keep it.'

'Let me leave it alone, then,' said Scrooge. 'Much good may it do you! Much good it has ever done you!'

'There are many things from which I might have derived good, by which I have not profited, I dare say,' returned the nephew; 'Christmas among the rest. But I am sure I have always thought of Christmas-time, when it has come round—apart from the veneration due to its sacred name and origin, if anything belonging to it can be apart from that—as a good time; a kind, forgiving, charitable, pleasant time; the only time I know of, in the long calendar of the year, when men and women seem by one consent to open their shut-up hearts freely, and to think of people below them as if they really were fellow-passengers to the grave, and not another race of creatures bound on other journeys. And therefore, uncle, though it has never put a scrap of gold or silver in my pocket, I believe that it *has* done me good and *will* do me good; and I say, God bless it!'

The clerk in the tank involuntarily applauded. Becoming immediately sensible of the impropriety, he poked the fire, and extinguished the last frail spark for ever.

'Let me hear another sound from *you*,' said Scrooge, 'and you'll keep your Christmas by losing your situation! You're quite a powerful speaker, sir,' he added, turning to his nephew. 'I wonder you don't go into Parliament.'

'Don't be angry, uncle. Come! Dine with us to-morrow.'

Scrooge said that he would see him— Yes, indeed he did. He went the whole length of the expression, and said that he would see him in that extremity first.

'But why?' cried Scrooge's nephew. 'Why?'

'Why did you get married?' said Scrooge.

'Because I fell in love.'

'Because you fell in love!' growled Scrooge, as if that were the only one thing in the world more ridiculous than a merry Christmas. 'Good afternoon!'

'Nay, uncle, but you never came to see me before that happened. Why give it as a reason for not coming now?'

'Good afternoon,' said Scrooge.

'I want nothing from you; I ask nothing of you; why cannot we be friends?'

'Good afternoon!' said Scrooge.

'I am sorry, with all my heart, to find you so resolute. We have never had any quarrel to which I have been a party. But I have made the trial in homage to Christmas, and I'll keep my Christmas humour to the last. So A Merry Christmas, uncle!'

'Good afternoon,' said Scrooge.

'And A Happy New Year!'

'Good afternoon!' said Scrooge.

His nephew left the room without an angry word, notwithstanding. He stopped at the outer door to bestow the greetings of the season on the clerk, who, cold as he was, was warmer than Scrooge; for he returned them cordially.

'There's another fellow,' muttered Scrooge, who overheard him: 'my clerk, with fifteen shillings a week, and a wife and family, talking about a merry Christmas. I'll retire to Bedlam.'

This lunatic, in letting Scrooge's nephew out, had let two other people in. They were portly gentlemen, pleasant to behold, and now stood, with their hats off, in Scrooge's office. They had books and papers in their hands, and bowed to him.

'Scrooge and Marley's, I believe,' said one of the gentlemen, referring to his list. 'Have I the pleasure of addressing Mr. Scrooge, or Mr. Marley?'

'Mr. Marley has been dead these seven years,' Scrooge replied. 'He died seven years ago, this very night.'

'We have no doubt his liberality is well represented by his surviving partner,' said the gentleman, presenting his credentials.

It certainly was; for they had been two kindred spirits. At the ominous word 'liberality' Scrooge frowned, and shook his head, and handed the credentials back.

'At this festive season of the year, Mr. Scrooge,' said the gentleman, taking up a pen, 'it is more than usually desirable that we should make some slight provision for the poor and destitute, who suffer greatly at the present time. Many thousands are in want of common necessaries; hundreds of thousands are in want of common comforts, sir.'

'Are there no prisons?' asked Scrooge.

'Plenty of prisons,' said the gentleman, laying down the pen again.

'And the Union workhouses?' demanded Scrooge. 'Are they still in operation?'

'They are. Still,' returned the gentleman, 'I wish I could say they were not.'

'The Treadmill and the Poor Law are in full vigour, then?' said Scrooge.

'Both very busy, sir.'

'Oh! I was afraid, from what you said at first, that something had occurred to stop them in their useful course,' said Scrooge. 'I am very glad to hear it.'

'Under the impression that they scarcely furnish Christian cheer of mind or body to the multitude,' returned the gentleman, 'a few of us are endeavouring to raise a fund to buy the Poor some meat and drink, and means of warmth. We choose this time, because it is a time, of all others, when Want is keenly felt, and Abundance rejoices. What shall I put you down for?'

'Nothing!' Scrooge replied.

'You wish to be anonymous?'

'I wish to be left alone,' said Scrooge. 'Since you ask me what I wish, gentlemen, that is my answer. I don't make merry myself at Christmas, and I can't afford to make idle people merry. I help to support the establishments I have mentioned—they cost enough: and those who are badly off must go there.'

'Many can't go there; and many would rather die.'

'If they would rather die,' said Scrooge, 'they had

better do it, and decrease the surplus population. Be-sides—excuse me—I don't know that.'

'But you might know it,' observed the gentleman.

'It's not my business,' Scrooge returned. 'It's enough for a man to understand his own business, and not to interfere with other people's. Mine occupies me constantly. Good afternoon, gentlemen!'

Seeing clearly that it would be useless to pursue their point, the gentlemen withdrew. Scrooge resumed his labours with an improved opinion of himself, and in a more facetious temper than was usual with him.

Meanwhile the fog and darkness thickened so, that people ran about with flaring links, proffering their services to go before horses in carriages, and conduct them on their way. The ancient tower of a church, whose gruff old bell was always peeping slily down at Scrooge out of a Gothic window in the wall, became invisible, and struck the hours and quarters in the clouds, with tremulous vibrations afterwards, as if its teeth were chattering in its frozen head up there. The cold became intense. In the main street, at the corner of the court, some labourers were repairing the gas-pipes, and had lighted a great fire in a brazier, round which a party of ragged men and boys were gathered: warming their hands and winking their eyes before the blaze in rapture. The water-plug being left in solitude, its overflowings suddenly congealed, and turned to misanthropic ice. The brightness of the shops, where holly sprigs and berries crackled in the lamp heat of the windows, made pale faces ruddy as they passed. Poulterers' and grocers' trades became a splendid joke: a glorious pageant, with which it was next to impossible to believe that such dull principles as bargain and sale had anything to do. The Lord Mayor, in the stronghold of the mighty Mansion House, gave orders to his fifty cooks and butlers to keep Christmas as a Lord Mayor's household should; and even the little tailor, whom he had fined five shillings on the previous Monday for being drunk and bloodthirsty in the streets, stirred up to-morrow's pudding in his garret, while his lean wife and the baby sallied out to buy the beef.

Foggier yet, and colder! Piercing, searching, biting cold. If the good St. Dunstan had but nipped the Evil Spirit's nose with a touch of such weather as that, instead of using his familiar weapons, then indeed he would have roared to lusty purpose. The owner of one scant young nose, gnawed and mumbled by the hungry cold as bones are gnawed by dogs, stooped down at Scrooge's keyhole to regale him with a Christmas carol; but, at the first sound of

'God bless you, merry gentleman,
May nothing you dismay!'

Scrooge seized the ruler with such energy of action that the singer fled in terror, leaving the keyhole to the fog, and even more congenial frost.

At length the hour of shutting up the counting-house arrived. With an ill-will Scrooge dismounted from his stool, and tacitly admitted the fact to the expectant clerk in the tank, who instantly snuffed his candle out, and put on his hat.

'You'll want all day to-morrow, I suppose?' said Scrooge.

'If quite convenient, sir.'

'It's not convenient,' said Scrooge, 'and it's not fair. If I was to stop half-a-crown for it, you'd think yourself ill used, I'll be bound?'

The clerk smiled faintly.

'And yet,' said Scrooge, 'you don't think *me* ill used when I pay a day's wages for no work.'

The clerk observed that it was only once a year.

'A poor excuse for picking a man's pocket every twenty-fifth of December!' said Scrooge, buttoning his greatcoat to the chin. 'But I suppose you must have the whole day. Be here all the earlier next morning.'

The clerk promised that he would; and Scrooge walked out with a growl. The office was closed in a twinkling, and the clerk, with the long ends of his white comforter dangling below his waist (for he boasted no greatcoat), went down a slide on Cornhill, at the end of a lane of boys, twenty times, in honour of its being Christmas Eve, and then ran home to Camden Town as hard as he could pelt, to play at blindman's-bluff.

Scrooge took his melancholy dinner in his usual melancholy tavern; and having read all the newspapers, and beguiled the rest of the evening with his banker's book, went home to bed. He lived in chambers which had once belonged to his deceased partner. They were a gloomy suite of rooms, in a lowering pile of building up a yard, where it had so little business to be, that one could scarcely help fancying it must have run there when it was a young house, playing at hide-and-seek with other houses, and have forgotten the way out again. It was old enough now, and dreary enough; for nobody lived in it but Scrooge, the other rooms being all let out as offices. The yard was so dark that even Scrooge, who knew its every stone, was fain to grope with his hands. The fog and frost so hung about the black old gateway of the house, that it seemed as if the Genius of the Weather sat in mournful meditation on the threshold.

Now, it is a fact that there was nothing at all particular about the knocker on the door, except that it was very large. It is also a fact that Scrooge had seen it, night and morning, during his whole residence in that place; also that Scrooge had as little of what is called fancy about him as any man in the City of London, even including—which is a bold word—the cor-

246

poration, aldermen, and livery. Let it also be borne in mind that Scrooge had not bestowed one thought on Marley since his last mention of his seven-years'-dead partner that afternoon. And then let any man explain to me, if he can, how it happened that Scrooge, having his key in the lock of the door, saw in the knocker, without its undergoing any intermediate process of change—not a knocker, but Marley's face.

Marley's face. It was not in impenetrable shadow, as the other objects in the yard were, but had a dismal light about it, like a bad lobster in a dark cellar. It was not angry or ferocious, but looked at Scrooge as Marley used to look; with ghostly spectacles turned up on its ghostly forehead. The hair was curiously stirred, as if by breath or hot air; and, though the eyes were wide open, they were perfectly motionless. That, and its livid colour, made it horrible; but its horror seemed to be in spite of the face, and beyond its control, rather than a part of its own expression.

As Scrooge looked fixedly at this phenomenon, it was a knocker again.

To say that he was not startled, or that his blood was not conscious of a terrible sensation to which it had been a stranger from infancy, would be untrue. But he put his hand upon the key he had relinquished, turned it sturdily, walked in, and lighted his candle.

He *did* pause, with a moment's irresolution, before he shut the door; and he *did* look cautiously behind it first, as if he half expected to be terrified with the sight of Marley's pigtail sticking out into the hall. But there was nothing on the back of the door, except the screws and nuts that held the knocker on, so he said, 'Pooh, pooh!' and closed it with a bang.

The sound resounded through the house like thunder. Every room above, and every cask in the wine-merchant's cellars below, appeared to have a separate peal of echoes of its own. Scrooge was not a man to be frightened by echoes. He fastened the door, and walked across the hall, and up the stairs: slowly, too: trimming his candle as he went.

You may talk vaguely about driving a coach and six up a good old flight of stairs, or through a bad young Act of Parliament; but I mean to say you might have got a hearse up that staircase, and taken it broadwise, with the splinter-bar towards the wall, and the door towards the balustrades: and done it easy. There was plenty of width for that, and room to spare; which is perhaps the reason why Scrooge thought he saw a locomotive hearse going on before him in the gloom. Half-a-dozen gas-lamps out of the street wouldn't have lighted the entry too well, so you may suppose that it was pretty dark with Scrooge's dip.

Up Scrooge went, not caring a button for that. Darkness is cheap, and Scrooge liked it. But, before he shut his heavy door, he walked through his rooms to see that all was right. He had just enough recollection of the face to desire to do that.

Sitting-room, bedroom, lumber-room. All as they should be. Nobody under the table, nobody under the sofa; a small fire in the grate; spoon and basin ready; and the little saucepan of gruel (Scrooge had a cold in his head) upon the hob. Nobody under the bed; nobody in the closet; nobody in his dressing-gown, which was hanging up in a suspicious attitude against the wall. Lumber-room as usual. Old fireguard, old shoes, two fish baskets, washing-stand on three legs, and a poker.

Quite satisfied, he closed his door, and locked himself in; double locked himself in, which was not his custom. Thus secured against surprise, he took off his cravat; put on his dressing-gown and slippers, and his nightcap; and sat down before the fire to take his gruel.

It was a very low fire indeed; nothing on such a bitter night. He was obliged to sit close to it, and brood over it, before he could extract the least sensation of warmth from such a handful of fuel. The fireplace was an old one, built by some Dutch merchant long ago, and paved all round with quaint Dutch tiles, designed to illustrate the Scriptures. There were Cains and Abels, Pharaoh's daughters, Queens of Sheba, Angelic messengers descending through the air on clouds like featherbeds, Abrahams, Belshazzars, Apostles putting off to sea in butter-boats, hundreds of figures to attract his thoughts; and yet that face of Marley, seven years dead, came like the ancient Prophet's rod, and swallowed up the whole. If each smooth tile had been a blank at first, with power to shape some picture on its surface from the disjointed fragments of his thoughts, there would have been a copy of old Marley's head on every one.

'Humbug!' said Scrooge; and walked across the room.

After several turns he sat down again. As he threw his head back in the chair, his glance happened to rest upon a bell, a disused bell, that hung in the room, and communicated, for some purpose now forgotten, with a chamber in the highest storey of the building. It was with great astonishment, and with a strange, inexplicable dread, that, as he looked, he saw this bell begin to swing. It swung so softly in the outset that it scarcely made a sound; but soon it rang out loudly, and so did every bell in the house.

This might have lasted half a minute, or a minute, but it seemed an hour. The bells ceased, as they had begun, together. They were succeeded by a clanking noise deep down below as if some person were dragging a heavy chain over the casks in the wine-merchant's cellar. Scrooge then remembered to have heard that ghosts in haunted houses were described as dragging chains.

The cellar door flew open with a booming sound,

and then he heard the noise much louder on the floors below; then coming up the stairs; then coming straight towards his door.

'It's humbug still!' said Scrooge. 'I won't believe it.'

His colour changed, though, when, without a pause, it came on through the heavy door and passed into the room before his eyes. Upon its coming in, the dying flame leaped up, as though it cried, 'I know him! Marley's Ghost!' and fell again.

The same face: the very same. Marley in his pigtail, usual waistcoat, tights, and boots; the tassels on the latter bristling, like his pigtail, and his coat-skirts, and the hair upon his head. The chain he drew was clasped about his middle. It was long, and wound about him like a tail; and it was made (for Scrooge observed it closely) of cash-boxes, keys, padlocks, ledgers, deeds, and heavy purses wrought in steel. His body was transparent: so that Scrooge, observing him, and looking through his waistcoat, could see the two buttons on his coat behind.

Scrooge had often heard it said that Marley had no bowels, but he had never believed it until now.

No, nor did he believe it even now. Though he looked the phantom through and through, and saw it standing before him; though he felt the chilling influence of its death-cold eyes, and marked the very texture of the folded kerchief bound about its head and chin, which wrapper he had not observed before, he was still incredulous, and fought against his senses.

'How now!' said Scrooge, caustic and cold as ever. 'What do you want with me?'

'Much!'—Marley's voice; no doubt about it.

'Who are you?'

'Ask me who I *was*.'

'Who *were* you, then?' said Scrooge, raising his voice. 'You're particular, for a shade.' He was going to say '*to* a shade,' but substituted this, as more appropriate.

'In life I was your partner, Jacob Marley.'

'Can you—can you sit down?' asked Scrooge, looking doubtfully at him.

'I can.'

'Do it, then.'

Scrooge asked the question, because he didn't know whether a ghost so transparent might find himself in a condition to take a chair; and felt that in the event of its being impossible, it might involve the necessity of an embarrassing explanation. But the Ghost sat down on the opposite side of the fireplace, as if he were quite used to it.

'You don't believe in me,' observed the Ghost.

'I don't,' said Scrooge.

'What evidence would you have of my reality beyond that of your own senses?'

'I don't know,' said Scrooge.

'Why do you doubt your senses?'

'Because,' said Scrooge, 'a little thing affects them. A slight disorder of the stomach makes them cheats. You may be an undigested bit of beef, a blot of mustard, a crumb of cheese, a fragment of an underdone potato. There's more of gravy than of grave about you, whatever you are!'

Scrooge was not much in the habit of cracking jokes, nor did he feel in his heart by any means waggish then. The truth is, that he tried to be smart, as a means of distracting his own attention, and keeping down his terror; for the spectre's voice disturbed the very marrow in his bones.

To sit staring at those fixed, glazed eyes in silence, for a moment, would play, Scrooge felt, the very deuce with him. There was something very awful, too, in the spectre's being provided with an infernal atmosphere of his own. Scrooge could not feel it himself, but this was clearly the case; for though the Ghost sat perfectly motionless, its hair, and skirts, and tassels were still agitated as by the hot vapour from an oven.

'You see this toothpick?' said Scrooge, returning quickly to the charge, for the reason just assigned; and wishing, though it were only for a second, to divert the vision's stony gaze from himself.

'I do,' replied the Ghost.

'You are not looking at it,' said Scrooge.

'But I see it,' said the Ghost, 'notwithstanding.'

'Well!' returned Scrooge, 'I have but to swallow this, and be for the rest of my days persecuted by a legion of goblins, all of my own creation. Humbug, I tell you: humbug!'

At this the spirit raised a frightful cry, and shook its chain with such a dismal and appalling noise, that Scrooge held on tight to his chair, to save himself from falling in a swoon. But how much greater was his horror when the phantom, taking off the bandage round his head, as if it were too warm to wear indoors, its lower jaw dropped down upon its breast!

Scrooge fell upon his knees, and clasped his hands before his face.

'Mercy!' he said. 'Dreadful apparition, why do you trouble me?'

'Man of the worldly mind!' replied the Ghost, 'do you believe in me or not?'

'I do,' said Scrooge; 'I must. But why do spirits walk the earth, and why do they come to me?'

'It is required of every man,' the Ghost returned, 'that the spirit within him should walk abroad among his fellow-men, and travel far and wide; and, if that spirit goes not forth in life, it is condemned to do so after death. It is doomed to wander through the world—oh, woe is me!—and witness what it cannot share, but might have shared on earth, and turned to happiness!'

Again the spectre raised a cry, and shook its chain and wrung its shadowy hands.

'You are fettered,' said Scrooge, trembling. 'Tell me why?'

'I wear the chain I forged in life,' replied the Ghost. 'I made it link by link, and yard by yard; I girded it on of my own free will, and of my own free will I wore it. Is its pattern strange to *you*?'

Scrooge trembled more and more.

'Or would you know,' pursued the Ghost, 'the weight and length of the strong coil you bear yourself? It was full as heavy and as long as this seven Christmas Eves ago. You have laboured on it since. It is a ponderous chain!'

Scrooge glanced about him on the floor, in the expectation of finding himself surrounded by some fifty or sixty fathoms of iron cable; but he could see nothing.

'Jacob!' he said imploringly. 'Old Jacob Marley, tell me more! Speak comfort to me, Jacob!'

'I have none to give,' the Ghost replied. 'It comes from other regions, Ebenezer Scrooge, and is conveyed by other ministers, to other kinds of men. Nor can I tell you what I would. A very little more is all permitted to me. I cannot rest, I cannot stay, I cannot linger anywhere. My spirit never walked beyond our counting-house—mark me;—in life my spirit never roved beyond the narrow limits of our money-changing hole; and weary journeys lie before me!'

It was a habit with Scrooge, whenever he became thoughtful, to put his hands in his breeches pockets. Pondering on what the Ghost had said, he did so now, but without lifting up his eyes, or getting off his knees.

'You must have been very slow about it, Jacob,' Scrooge observed in a business-like manner, though with humility and deference.

'Slow!' the Ghost repeated.

'Seven years dead,' mused Scrooge. 'And travelling all the time?'

'The whole time,' said the Ghost. 'No rest, no peace. Incessant torture of remorse.'

'You travel fast?' said Scrooge.

'On the wings of the wind,' replied the Ghost.

'You might have got over a great quantity of ground in seven years,' said Scrooge.

The Ghost, on hearing this, set up another cry, and clanked its chain so hideously in the dead silence of the night, that the Ward would have been justified in indicting it for a nuisance.

'Oh! captive, bound, and double-ironed,' cried the phantom, 'not to know that ages of incessant labour, by immortal creatures, for this earth must pass into eternity before the good of which it is susceptible is all developed! Not to know that any Christian spirit working kindly in its little sphere, whatever it may be, will find its mortal life too short for its vast means of usefulness! Not to know that no space of regret can make amends for one life's opportunities misused! Yet such was I! Oh, such was I!'

'But you were always a good man of business, Jacob,' faltered Scrooge, who now began to apply this to himself.

'Business!' cried the Ghost, wringing its hands again. 'Mankind was my business. The common welfare was my business; charity, mercy, forbearance, and benevolence were, all, my business. The dealings of my trade were but a drop of water in the comprehensive ocean of my business!'

It held up its chain at arm's-length, as if that were the cause of all its unavailing grief, and flung it heavily upon the ground again.

'At this time of the rolling year,' the spectre said, 'I suffer most. Why did I walk through crowds of fellow-beings with my eyes turned down, and never raise them to that blessed Star which led the Wise Men to a poor abode? Were there no poor homes to which its light would have conducted *me*?'

Scrooge was very much dismayed to hear the spectre going on at this rate, and began to quake exceedingly.

'Hear me!' cried the Ghost. 'My time is nearly gone.'

'I will,' said Scrooge. 'But don't be hard upon me! Don't be flowery, Jacob! Pray!'

'How it is that I appear before you in a shape that you can see, I may not tell. I have sat invisible beside you many and many a day.'

It was not an agreeable idea. Scrooge shivered, and wiped the perspiration from his brow.

'That is no light part of my penance,' pursued the Ghost. 'I am here to-night to warn you that you have yet a chance and hope of escaping my fate. A chance and hope of my procuring, Ebenezer.'

'You were always a good friend to me,' said Scrooge. 'Thankee!'

'You will be haunted,' resumed the Ghost, 'by Three Spirits.'

Scrooge's countenance fell almost as low as the Ghost's had done.

'Is that the chance and hope you mentioned, Jacob?' he demanded in a faltering voice.

'It is.'

'I—I think I'd rather not,' said Scrooge.

'Without their visits,' said the Ghost, 'you cannot hope to shun the path I tread. Expect the first tomorrow when the bell tolls One.'

'Couldn't I take 'em all at once, and have it over, Jacob?' hinted Scrooge.

'Expect the second on the next night at the same hour. The third, upon the next night when the last stroke of Twelve has ceased to vibrate. Look to see me

no more; and look that, for your own sake, you remember what has passed between us!'

When it had said these words, the spectre took its
wrapper from the table, and bound it round its head
as before. Scrooge knew this by the smart sound its
teeth made when the jaws were brought together by
the bandage. He ventured to raise his eyes again, and
found his supernatural visitor confronting him in an
erect attitude, with its chain wound over and about its
arm.

The apparition walked backward from him; and,
at every step it took, the window raised itself a little,
so that, when the spectre reached it, it was wide open.
It beckoned Scrooge to approach, which he did. When
they were within two paces of each other, Marley's
Ghost held up its hand, warning him to come no
nearer. Scrooge stopped.

Not so much in obedience as in surprise and fear;
for, on the raising of the hand, he became sensible of
confused noises in the air; incoherent sounds of lam-
entation and regret; wailings inexpressibly sorrowful
and self-accusatory. The spectre, after listening for a
moment, joined in the mournful dirge; and floated out
upon the bleak, dark night.

Scrooge followed to the window: desperate in his
curiosity. He looked out.

The air was filled with phantoms, wandering

hither and thither in restless haste, and moaning as they went. Every one of them wore chains like Marley's Ghost; some few (they might be guilty governments) were linked together; none were free. Many had been personally known to Scrooge in their lives. He had been quite familiar with one old ghost in a white waistcoat, with a monstrous iron safe attached to its ankle, who cried piteously at being unable to assist a wretched woman with an infant, whom it saw below upon a doorstep. The misery with them all was clearly, that they sought to interfere, for good, in human matters, and had lost the power for ever.

Whether these creatures faded into mist, or mist enshrouded them, he could not tell. But they and their spirit voices faded together; and the night became as it had been when he walked home.

Scrooge closed the window, and examined the door by which the Ghost had entered. It was double locked, as he had locked it with his own hands, and the bolts were undisturbed. He tried to say 'Humbug!' but stopped at the first syllable. And being, from the emotions he had undergone, or the fatigues of the day, or his glimpse of the Invisible World, or the dull conversation of the Ghost, or the lateness of the hour, much in need of repose, went straight to bed without undressing, and fell asleep upon the instant.

*Stave Two:*

## The First of the Three Spirits

**W**hen Scrooge awoke it was so dark, that, looking out of bed, he could scarcely distinguish the transparent window from the opaque walls of his chamber. He was endeavouring to pierce the darkness with his ferret eyes, when the chimes of a neighbouring church struck the four quarters. So he listened for the hour.

To his great astonishment, the heavy bell went on from six to seven, and from seven to eight, and regularly up to twelve; then stopped. Twelve! It was past two when he went to bed. The clock was wrong. An icicle must have got into the works. Twelve!

He touched the spring of his repeater, to correct this most preposterous clock. Its rapid little pulse beat twelve, and stopped.

'Why, it isn't possible,' said Scrooge, 'that I can have slept through a whole day and far into another night. It isn't possible that anything has happened to the sun, and this is twelve at noon!'

The idea being an alarming one, he scrambled out of bed, and groped his way to the window. He was obliged to rub the frost off with the sleeve of his dressing-gown before he could see anything; and could see very little then. All he could make out was, that it was still very foggy and extremely cold, and that there was no noise of people running to and fro, and making a great stir, as there unquestionably would have been if night had beaten off bright day, and taken possession of the world. This was a great relief, because 'Three days after sight of this First of Exchange pay to Mr. Ebenezer Scrooge or his order,' and so forth, would have become a mere United States security if there were no days to count by.

Scrooge went to bed again, and thought, and thought, and thought it over and over, and could make nothing of it. The more he thought, the more perplexed he was; and, the more he endeavoured not to think, the more he thought.

Marley's Ghost bothered him exceedingly. Every time he resolved within himself, after mature inquiry, that it was all a dream, his mind flew back again, like a strong spring released, to its first position, and presented the same problem to be worked all through, 'Was it a dream or not?'

Scrooge lay in this state until the chime had gone

three-quarters more, when he remembered, on a sudden, that the Ghost had warned him of a visitation when the bell tolled one. He resolved to lie awake until the hour was passed; and, considering that he could no more go to sleep than go to heaven, this was, perhaps, the wisest resolution in his power.

The quarter was so long, that he was more than once convinced he must have sunk into a doze unconsciously, and missed the clock. At length it broke upon his listening ear.

'Ding, dong!'

'A quarter past,' said Scrooge, counting.

'Ding, dong!'

'Half past,' said Scrooge.

'Ding, dong!'

'A quarter to it,' said Scrooge.

'Ding, dong!'

'The hour itself,' said Scrooge triumphantly, 'and nothing else!'

He spoke before the hour bell sounded, which it now did with a deep, dull, hollow, melancholy ONE. Light flashed up in the room upon the instant, and the curtains of his bed were drawn.

The curtains of his bed were drawn aside, I tell you, by a hand. Not the curtains at his feet, nor the curtains at his back, but those to which his face was addressed. The curtains of his bed were drawn aside; and Scrooge, starting up into a half-recumbent attitude, found himself face to face with the unearthly visitor who drew them: as close to it as I am now to you, and I am standing in the spirit at your elbow.

It was a strange figure—like a child; yet not so like a child as like an old man, viewed through some supernatural medium, which gave him the appearance of having receded from the view, and being diminished to a child's proportions. Its hair, which hung about its neck and down its back, was white, as if with age; and yet the face had not a wrinkle in it, and the tenderest bloom was on the skin. The arms were very long and muscular; the hands the same, as if its hold were of uncommon strength. Its legs and feet, most delicately formed, were, like those upper members, bare. It wore a tunic of the purest white; and round its waist was bound a lustrous belt, the sheen of which was beautiful. It held a branch of fresh green holly in its hand; and, in singular contradiction of that wintry emblem, had its dress trimmed with summer flowers. But the strangest thing about it was, that from the crown of its head there sprang a bright clear jet of light, by which all this was visible; and which was doubtless the occasion of its using, in its duller moments, a great extinguisher for a cap, which it now held under its arm.

Even this, though, when Scrooge looked at it with increasing steadiness, was *not* its strangest quality. For, as its belt sparkled and glittered, now in one part and now in another, and what was light one instant at another time was dark, so the figure itself fluctuated in its distinctness; being now a thing with one arm, now with one leg, now with twenty legs, now a pair of legs without a head, now a head without a body: of which dissolving parts no outline would be visible in the dense gloom wherein they melted away. And, in the very wonder of this, it would be itself again; distinct and clear as ever.

'Are you the Spirit, sir, whose coming was foretold to me?' asked Scrooge.

'I am!'

The voice was soft and gentle. Singularly low, as if, instead of being so close behind him, it were at a distance.

'Who and what are you?' Scrooge demanded.

'I am the Ghost of Christmas Past.'

'Long Past?' inquired Scrooge, observant of its dwarfish stature.

'No. Your past.'

Perhaps Scrooge could not have told anybody why, if anybody could have asked him; but he had a special desire to see the Spirit in his cap, and begged him to be covered.

'What!' exclaimed the Ghost, 'would you so soon put out, with worldly hands, the light I give? Is it not enough that you are one of those whose passions made this cap, and force me through whole trains of years to wear it low upon my brow?'

Scrooge reverently disclaimed all intention to offend or any knowledge of having wilfully 'bonneted' the Spirit at any period of his life. He then made bold to inquire what business brought him there.

'Your welfare!' said the Ghost.

Scrooge expressed himself much obliged, but could not help thinking that a night of unbroken rest would have been more conducive to that end. The Spirit must have heard him thinking, for it said immediately—

'Your reclamation, then. Take heed!'

It put out its strong hand as it spoke, and clasped him gently by the arm.

'Rise! and walk with me!'

It would have been in vain for Scrooge to plead that the weather and the hour were not adapted to pedestrian purposes; that bed was warm, and the thermometer a long way below freezing; that he was clad but lightly in his slippers, dressing-gown, and nightcap; and that he had a cold upon him at that time. The grasp, though gentle as a woman's hand, was not to be resisted. He rose; but, finding that the Spirit made towards the window, clasped its robe in supplication.

'I am a mortal,' Scrooge remonstrated, 'and liable to fall.'

'Bear but a touch of my hand *there*,' said the Spirit, laying it upon his heart, 'and you shall be upheld in more than this!'

266

As the words were spoken, they passed through the wall, and stood upon an open country road, with fields on either hand. The city had entirely vanished. Not a vestige of it was to be seen. The darkness and the mist had vanished with it, for it was a clear, cold, winter day, with snow upon the ground.

'Good Heaven!' said Scrooge, clasping his hands together, as he looked about him. 'I was bred in this place. I was a boy here!'

The Spirit gazed upon him mildly. Its gentle touch, though it had been light and instantaneous, appeared still present to the old man's sense of feeling. He was conscious of a thousand odours floating in the air, each one connected with a thousand thoughts, and hopes, and joys, and cares long, long forgotten!

'Your lip is trembling,' said the Ghost. 'And what is that upon your cheek?'

Scrooge muttered, with an unusual catching in his voice, that it was a pimple; and begged the Ghost to lead him where he would.

'You recollect the way?' inquired the Spirit.

'Remember it!' cried Scrooge with fervour; 'I could walk it blindfold.'

'Strange to have forgotten it for so many years!' observed the Ghost. 'Let us go on.'

They walked along the road, Scrooge recognising every gate, and post, and tree, until a little market-town appeared in the distance, with its bridge, its church, and winding river. Some shaggy ponies now were seen trotting towards them with boys upon their backs, who called to other boys in country gigs and carts, driven by farmers. All these boys were in great spirits, and shouted to each other, until the broad fields were so full of merry music, that the crisp air laughed to hear it.

'These are but shadows of the things that have been,' said the Ghost. 'They have no consciousness of us.'

The jocund travellers came on; and as they came, Scrooge knew and named them every one. Why was he rejoiced beyond all bounds to see them? Why did his cold eye glisten, and his heart leap up as they went past? Why was he filled with gladness when he heard them give each other Merry Christmas, as they parted at cross-roads and by-ways for their several homes? What was merry Christmas to Scrooge? Out upon merry Christmas! What good had it ever done to him?

'The school is not quite deserted,' said the Ghost. 'A solitary child, neglected by his friends, is left there still.'

Scrooge said he knew it. And he sobbed.

They left the high-road by a well-remembered lane and soon approached a mansion of dull red brick, with a little weather-cock surmounted cupola on the roof, and a bell hanging in it. It was a large house, but one of broken fortunes; for the spacious offices were little used, their walls were damp and mossy, their windows broken, and their gates decayed. Fowls clucked and strutted in the stables; and the coach-houses and sheds were overrun with grass. Nor was it more retentive of its ancient state within; for, entering the dreary hall, and glancing through the open doors of many rooms, they found them poorly furnished, cold, and vast. There was an earthy savour in the air, a chilly bareness in the place, which associated itself somehow with too much getting up by candle light and not too much to eat.

They went, the Ghost and Scrooge, across the hall, to a door at the back of the house. It opened before them, and disclosed a long, bare, melancholy room, made barer still by lines of plain deal forms and desks. At one of these a lonely boy was reading near a feeble fire; and Scrooge sat down upon a form, and wept to see his poor forgotten self as he had used to be.

Not a latent echo in the house, not a squeak and scuffle from the mice behind the panelling, not a drip from the half-thawed waterspout in the dull yard behind, not a sigh among the leafless boughs of one despondent poplar, not the idle swinging of an empty storehouse door, no, not a clicking in the fire, but fell upon the heart of Scrooge with softening influence, and gave a freer passage to his tears.

The Spirit touched him on the arm, and pointed

to his younger self, intent upon his reading. Suddenly a man in foreign garments, wonderfully real and distinct to look at, stood outside the window, with an axe stuck in his belt, and leading by the bridle an ass laden with wood.

'Why, it's Ali Baba!' Scrooge exclaimed in ecstasy. 'It's dear old honest Ali Baba! Yes, yes, I know. One Christmas-time, when yonder solitary child was left here all alone, he *did* come, for the first time, just like that. Poor boy! And Valentine,' said Scrooge, 'and his wild brother, Orson; there they go! And what's his name, who was put down in his drawers, asleep, at the gate of Damascus; don't you see him? And the Sultan's Groom turned upside down by the Genii; there he is upon his head! Serve him right! I'm glad of it. What business had he to be married to the Princess?'

To hear Scrooge expending all the earnestness of his nature on such subjects, in a most extraordinary voice between laughing and crying; and to see his heightened and excited face; would have been a surprise to his business friends in the City, indeed.

'There's the Parrot!' cried Scrooge. 'Green body and yellow tail, with a thing like a lettuce growing out of the top of his head; there he is! Poor Robin Crusoe he called him, when he came home again after sailing round the island. "Poor Robin Crusoe, where have you been, Robin Crusoe?" The man thought he was dreaming, but he wasn't. It was the Parrot, you know. There goes Friday, running for his life to the little creek! Halloa! Hoop! Halloo!'

Then, with a rapidity of transition very foreign to his usual character, he said, in pity for his former self, 'Poor boy!' and cried again.

'I wish,' Scrooge muttered, putting his hand in his pocket, and looking about him, after drying his eyes with his cuff; 'but it's too late now.'

'What is the matter?' asked the Spirit.

'Nothing,' said Scrooge. 'Nothing. There was a boy singing a Christmas carol at my door last night. I should like to have given him something: that's all.'

The Ghost smiled thoughtfully, and waved its hand, saying as it did so, 'Let us see another Christmas!'

Scrooge's former self grew larger at the words, and the room became a little darker and more dirty. The panels shrunk, the windows cracked; fragments of plaster fell out of the ceiling, and the naked laths were shown instead; but how all this was brought about Scrooge knew no more than you do. He only knew that it was quite correct; that everything had happened so; that there he was, alone again, when all the other boys had gone home for the jolly holidays.

He was not reading now, but walking up and down despairingly. Scrooge looked at the Ghost, and, with a mournful shaking of his head, glanced anxiously towards the door.

It opened; and a little girl, much younger than the boy, came darting in, and, putting her arms about his neck, and often kissing him, addressed him as her 'dear, dear brother.'

'I have come to bring you home, dear brother!' said the child, clapping her tiny hands, and bending down to laugh. 'To bring you home, home, home!'

'Home, little Fan?' returned the boy.

'Yes!' said the child, brimful of glee. 'Home for good and all. Home for ever and ever. Father is so much kinder than he used to be, that home's like heaven! He spoke so gently to me one dear night when I was going to bed, that I was not afraid to ask him once more if you might come home; and he said Yes, you should; and sent me in a coach to bring you. And you're to be a man!' said the child, opening her eyes; 'and are never to come back here; but first we're to be together all the Christmas long, and have the merriest time in all the world.'

'You are quite a woman, little Fan!' exclaimed the boy.

She clapped her hands and laughed, and tried to touch his head; but, being too little laughed again, and stood on tiptoe to embrace him. Then she began to drag him, in her childish eagerness, towards the door; and he, nothing loath to go, accompanied her.

A terrible voice in the hall cried, 'Bring down Master Scrooge's box, there!' and in the hall appeared

the schoolmaster himself, who glared on Master
Scrooge with a ferocious condescension, and threw him
into a dreadful state of mind by shaking hands with
him. He then conveyed him and his sister into the
veriest old well of a shivering best parlour that ever
was seen, where the maps upon the wall, and the ce-
lestial and terrestrial globes in the windows, were waxy
with cold. Here he produced a decanter of curiously
light wine, and a block of curiously heavy cake, and
administered instalments of those dainties to the young
people; at the same time sending out a meagre servant
to offer a glass of 'something' to the postboy, who
answered that he thanked the gentleman, but, if it was
the same tap as he had tasted before, he had rather not.
Master Scrooge's trunk being by this time tied on to
the top of the chaise, the children bade the schoolmaster good-bye right willingly; and, getting into it, drove
gaily down the garden sweep; the quick wheels dashing
the hoar-frost and snow from off the dark leaves of the
evergreens like spray.

'Always a delicate creature, whom a breath might
have withered,' said the Ghost. 'But she had a large
heart!'

'So she had,' cried Scrooge. 'You're right. I will
not gainsay it, Spirit. God forbid!'

'She died a woman,' said the Ghost, 'and had, as
I think, children.'

'One child,' Scrooge returned.

'True,' said the Ghost. 'Your nephew!'

Scrooge seemed uneasy in his mind, and answered briefly, 'Yes.'

Although they had but that moment left the school behind them, they were now in the busy thoroughfares of a city, where shadowy passengers passed and repassed; where shadowy carts and coaches battled for the way, and all the strife and tumult of a real city were. It was made plain enough, by the dressing of the shops, that here, too, it was Christmas-time again; but it was evening, and the streets were lighted up.

The Ghost stopped at a certain warehouse door, and asked Scrooge if he knew it.

'Know it!' said Scrooge. 'Was I apprenticed here?'

They went in. At sight of an old gentleman in a Welsh wig, sitting behind such a high desk, that if he had been two inches taller, he must have knocked his head against the ceiling, Scrooge cried in great excitement—

'Why, it's old Fezziwig! Bless his heart, it's Fezziwig alive again!'

Old Fezziwig laid down his pen, and looked up at the clock, which pointed to the hour of seven. He rubbed his hands; adjusted his capacious waistcoat; laughed all over himself, from his shoes to his organ of benevolence; and called out, in a comfortable, oily, rich, fat, jovial voice—

'Yo ho, there! Ebenezer! Dick!'

Scrooge's former self, now grown a young man, came briskly in, accompanied by his fellow-'prentice.

'Dick Wilkins, to be sure!' said Scrooge to the Ghost. 'Bless me, yes. There he is. He was very much attached to me, was Dick. Poor Dick! Dear, dear!'

'Yo ho, my boys!' said Fezziwig. 'No more work to-night. Christmas Eve, Dick. Christmas, Ebenezer! Let's have the shutters up,' cried old Fezziwig, with a sharp clap of his hands, 'before a man can say Jack Robinson!'

You wouldn't believe how those two fellows went at it! They charged into the street with the shutters— one, two, three—had 'em up in their places—four, five, six—barred 'em and pinned 'em—seven, eight, nine— and came back before you could have got to twelve, panting like racehorses.

'Hilli-ho!' cried old Fezziwig, skipping down from the high desk with wonderful agility. 'Clear away, my lads, and let's have lots of room here! Hilli-ho, Dick! Chirrup, Ebenezer!'

Clear away! There was nothing they wouldn't have cleared away, or couldn't have cleared away, with old Fezziwig looking on. It was done in a minute. Every movable was packed off, as if it were dismissed from public life for evermore; the floor was swept and watered, the lamps were trimmed, fuel was heaped upon the fire; and the warehouse was as snug, and warm, and dry, and bright a ball-room as you would desire to see upon a winter's night.

In came a fiddler with a music-book, and went up to the lofty desk, and made an orchestra of it, and tuned like fifty stomach-aches. In came Mrs. Fezziwig, one vast substantial smile. In came the three Miss Fezziwigs, beaming and lovable. In came the six young followers whose hearts they broke. In came all the young men and women employed in the business. In came the housemaid, with her cousin the baker. In came the cook with her brother's particular friend the milkman. In came the boy from over the way, who was suspected of not having board enough from his master; trying to hide himself behind the girl from next door but one, who was proved to have had her ears pulled by her mistress. In they all came, one after another; some shyly, some boldly, some gracefully, some awkwardly, some pushing, some pulling; in they all came, any how and every how. Away they all went, twenty couple at once; hands half round and back again the other way; down the middle and up again; round and round in various stages of affectionate grouping; old top couple always turning up in the wrong place; new top couple starting off again as soon as they got there; all top couples at last, and not a bottom one to help them! When this result was brought about, old Fezziwig, clapping his hands to stop the dance, cried out, 'Well done!' and the fiddler plunged his hot face into a pot of porter, especially provided for that purpose. But, scorning rest upon his reappearance, he instantly began again, though there were no dancers yet, as if the other fiddler had been carried home, exhausted, on a shutter, and he were a brand-new man resolved to beat him out of sight, or perish.

There were more dances, and there were forfeits, and more dances, and there was cake, and there was negus, and there was a great piece of Cold Roast, and there was a great piece of Cold Boiled, and there were mincepies, and plenty of beer. But the great effect of the evening came after the Roast and Boiled, when the fiddler (an artful dog, mind! The sort of man who knew his business better than you or I could have told it him!) struck up 'Sir Roger de Coverley.' Then old Fezziwig stood out to dance with Mrs. Fezziwig. Top couple, too; with a good stiff piece of work cut out for them; three or four and twenty pair of partners; people who were not to be trifled with; people who would dance, and had no notion of walking.

But if they had been twice as many—ah! four times—old Fezziwig would have been a match for them, and so would Mrs. Fezziwig. As to *her*, she was worthy to be his partner in every sense of the term. If that's not high praise, tell me higher, and I'll use it. A positive light appeared to issue from Fezziwig's calves. They shone in every part of the dance like moons. You couldn't have predicted, at any given time, what would become of them next. And when old Fezziwig and Mrs. Fezziwig had gone all through the dance; advance and retire, both hands to your partner, bow and curtsy, cork-screw, thread-the-needle, and back again to your place: Fezziwig 'cut'—cut so deftly, that he appeared to wink with his legs, and came upon his feet again without a stagger.

When the clock struck eleven, this domestic ball broke up. Mr. and Mrs. Fezziwig took their stations, one on either side the door, and, shaking hands with every person individually as he or she went out, wished him or her a Merry Christmas. When everybody had retired but the two 'prentices, they did the same to them; and thus the cheerful voices died away, and the lads were left to their beds; which were under a counter in the back-shop.

During the whole of this time Scrooge had acted like a man out of his wits. His heart and soul were in the scene, and with his former self. He corroborated everything, remembered everything, enjoyed everything, and underwent the strangest agitation. It was not until now, when the bright faces of his former self and Dick were turned from them, that he remembered the Ghost, and became conscious that it was looking full upon him, while the light upon its head burnt very clear.

'A small matter,' said the Ghost, 'to make these silly folks so full of gratitude.'

'Small!' echoed Scrooge.

The Spirit signed to him to listen to the two apprentices, who were pouring out their hearts in praise of Fezziwig; and when he had done so, said:

'Why! Is it not? He has spent but a few pounds of your mortal money: three or four, perhaps. Is that so much that he deserves this praise?'

'It isn't that,' said Scrooge, heated by the remark, and speaking unconsciously like his former, not his latter self. 'It isn't that, Spirit. He has the power to render us happy or unhappy; to make our service light or burdensome; a pleasure or a toil. Say that his power lies in words and looks; in things so slight and insignificant that it is impossible to add and count 'em up: what then? The happiness he gives is quite as great as if it cost a fortune.'

He felt the Spirit's glance, and stopped.

'What is the matter?' asked the Ghost.

'Nothing particular,' said Scrooge.

'Something, I think?' the Ghost insisted.

'No,' said Scrooge, 'no. I should like to be able to say a word or two to my clerk just now. That's all.'

His former self turned down the lamps as he gave utterance to the wish; and Scrooge and the Ghost again stood side by side in the open air.

'My time grows short,' observed the Spirit. 'Quick!'

This was not addressed to Scrooge, or to any one whom he could see, but it produced an immediate effect. For again Scrooge saw himself. He was older now; a man in the prime of life. His face had not the harsh and rigid lines of later years; but it had begun to wear the signs of care and avarice. There was an eager, greedy, restless motion in the eye, which showed the passion that had taken root, and where the shadow of the growing tree would fall.

He was not alone, but sat by the side of a fair young girl in a mourning dress: in whose eyes there were tears, which sparkled in the light that shone out of the Ghost of Christmas Past.

'It matters little,' she said softly. 'To you, very little. Another idol has displaced me; and, if it can cheer and comfort you in time to come as I would have tried to do, I have no just cause to grieve.'

'What Idol has displaced you?' he rejoined.

'A golden one.'

'This is the even-handed dealing of the world!' he said. 'There is nothing on which it is so hard as poverty; and there is nothing it professes to condemn with such severity as the pursuit of wealth!'

'You fear the world too much,' she answered gently. 'All your other hopes have merged into the hope of being beyond the chance of its sordid reproach. I have seen your nobler aspirations fall off one by one, until the master passion, Gain, engrosses you. Have I not?'

'What then?' he retorted. 'Even if I have grown so much wiser, what then? I am not changed towards you.'

She shook her head.

'Am I?'

'Our contract is an old one. It was made when we were both poor, and content to be so, until, in good season, we would improve our worldly fortune by our patient industry. You *are* changed. When it was made you were another man.'

'I was a boy,' he said impatiently.

'Your own feeling tells you that you were not what you are,' she returned. 'I am. That which promised happiness when we were one in heart is fraught with misery now that we are two. How often and how keenly I have thought of this I will not say. It is enough that I *have* thought of it, and can release you.'

'Have I ever sought release?'

'In words. No. Never.'

'In what, then?'

'In a changed nature; in an altered spirit; in another atmosphere of life; another Hope as its great end. In everything that made my love of any worth or value in your sight. If this had never been between us,' said the girl, looking mildly, but with steadiness, upon him;

'tell me, would you seek me out and try to win me now? Ah, no!'

He seemed to yield to the justice of this supposition in spite of himself. But he said, with a struggle, 'You think not.'

'I would gladly think otherwise if I could,' she answered. 'Heaven knows! When *I* have learned a Truth like this, I know how strong and irresistible it must be. But if you were free to-day, to-morrow, yesterday, can even I believe that you would choose a dowerless girl—you who, in your very confidence with her, weigh everything by Gain: or, choosing her, if for a moment you were false enough to your one guiding principle to do so, do I not know that your repentance and regret would surely follow? I do; and I release you. With a full heart, for the love of him you once were.'

He was about to speak; but, with her head turned from him, she resumed:

'You may—the memory of what is past half makes me hope you will—have pain in this. A very, very brief time, and you will dismiss the recollection of it gladly, as an unprofitable dream, from which it happened well that you awoke. May you be happy in the life you have chosen!'

She left him, and they parted.

'Spirit!' said Scrooge, 'show me no more! Conduct me home. Why do you delight to torture me?'

'One shadow more!' exclaimed the Ghost.

'No more!' cried Scrooge. 'No more! I don't wish to see it. Show me no more!'

But the relentless Ghost pinioned him in both his arms, and forced him to observe what happened next.

They were in another scene and place; a room, not very large or handsome, but full of comfort. Near to the winter fire sat a beautiful young girl, so like that last that Scrooge believed it was the same, until he saw *her*, now a comely matron, sitting opposite her daughter. The noise in this room was perfectly tumultuous, for there were more children there than Scrooge in his agitated state of mind could count; and, unlike the celebrated herd in the poem, they were not forty children conducting themselves like one, but every child was conducting itself like forty. The consequences were uproarious beyond belief; but no one seemed to care; on the contrary, the mother and daughter laughed heartily, and enjoyed it very much; and the latter, soon beginning to mingle in the sports, got pillaged by the young brigands most ruthlessly. What would I not have given to be one of them! Though I never could have been so rude, no, no! I wouldn't for the wealth of all the world have crushed that braided hair, and torn it down; and for the precious little shoe, I wouldn't have plucked it off, God bless my soul! to save my life. As to measuring her waist in sport, as they did, bold young brood, I couldn't have done it; I should have expected my arm to have grown round it for a punishment, and never come straight again. And yet I should have dearly liked, I own, to have touched her lips; to have questioned her, that she might have opened them; to have looked upon the lashes of her downcast eyes, and never raised a blush; to have let loose waves of hair, an inch of which would be a keepsake beyond price: in short, I should have liked, I do confess, to have had the lightest license of a child, and yet to have been man enough to know its value.

But now a knocking at the door was heard, and such a rush immediately ensued that she, with laughing face and plundered dress, was borne towards it the centre of a flushed and boisterous group, just in time to greet the father, who came home attended by a man laden with Christmas toys and presents. Then the shouting and the struggling, and the onslaught that was made on the defenceless porter! The scaling him, with chairs for ladders, to dive into his pockets, despoil him of brown-paper parcels, hold on tight by his cravat, hug him round his neck, pummel his back, and kick his legs in irrepressible affection! The shouts of wonder and delight with which the development of every package was received! The terrible announcement that the baby had been taken in the act of putting a doll's frying pan into his mouth, and was more than suspected of having swallowed a fictitious turkey, glued on a wooden platter! The immense relief of finding this a false alarm! The joy, and gratitude, and ecstasy! They are all indescribable alike. It is enough that, by degrees, the children and their emotions got out of the parlour, and, by one stair at a time, up to the top of the house, where they went to bed, and so subsided.

And now Scrooge looked on more attentively than ever, when the master of the house, having his daughter leaning fondly on him, sat down with her and her mother at his own fireside; and when he thought that such another creature, quite as graceful and as full of promise, might have called him father, and been a spring-time in the haggard winter of his life, his sight grew very dim indeed.

'Belle,' said the husband, turning to his wife with a smile, 'I saw an old friend of yours this afternoon.'

'Who was it?'

'Guess!'

'How can I? Tut, don't I know?' she added in the same breath, laughing as he laughed. 'Mr. Scrooge.'

'Mr. Scrooge it was. I passed his office window; and as it was not shut up, and he had a candle inside, I could scarcely help seeing him. His partner lies upon the point of death, I hear; and there he sat alone. Quite alone in the world, I do believe.'

'Spirit!' said Scrooge in a broken voice, 'remove me from this place.'

'I told you these were shadows of the things that have been,' said the Ghost. 'That they are what they are do not blame me!'

'Remove me!' Scrooge exclaimed, 'I cannot bear it!'

He turned upon the Ghost, and seeing that it looked upon him with a face, in which in some strange way there were fragments of all the faces it had shown him, wrestled with it.

'Leave me! Take me back. Haunt me no longer!'

In the struggle, if that can be called a struggle in which the Ghost with no visible resistance on its own part was undisturbed by any effort of its adversary, Scrooge observed that its light was burning high and bright; and dimly connecting that with its influence over him, he seized the extinguisher-cap, and by a sudden action pressed it down upon its head.

The Spirit dropped beneath it, so that the extinguisher covered its whole form; but though Scrooge pressed it down with all his force, he could not hide the light, which streamed from under it, in an unbroken flood upon the ground.

He was conscious of being exhausted, and overcome by an irresistible drowsiness; and, further, of being in his own bedroom. He gave the cap a parting squeeze, in which his hand relaxed; and had barely time to reel to bed, before he sank into a heavy sleep.

# Stave Three:

## The Second of the Three Spirits

waking in the middle of a prodigiously tough snore, and sitting up in bed to get his thoughts together, Scrooge had no occasion to be told that the bell was again upon the stroke of One. He felt that he was restored to consciousness in the right nick of time, for the especial purpose of holding a conference with the second messenger despatched to him through Jacob Marley's intervention. But finding that he turned uncomfortably cold when he began to wonder which of his curtains this new spectre would draw back, he put them every one aside with his own hands, and, lying down again, established a sharp look-out all round the bed. For he wished to challenge the Spirit on the moment of its appearance, and did not wish to be taken by surprise and made nervous.

Gentlemen of the free-and-easy sort, who plume

themselves on being acquainted with a move or two, and being usually equal to the time of day, express the wide range of their capacity for adventure by observing that they are good for anything from pitch-and-toss to manslaughter; between which opposite extremes, no doubt, there lies a tolerably wide and comprehensive range of subjects. Without venturing for Scrooge quite as hardily as this, I don't mind calling on you to believe that he was ready for a good broad field of strange appearances, and that nothing between a baby and a rhinoceros would have astonished him very much.

Now, being prepared for almost anything, he was not by any means prepared for nothing; and consequently, when the bell struck One, and no shape appeared, he was taken with a violent fit of trembling. Five minutes, ten minutes, a quarter of an hour went by, yet nothing came. All this time he lay upon his bed, the very core and centre of a blaze of ruddy light, which streamed upon it when the clock proclaimed the hour; and which, being only light, was more alarming than a dozen ghosts, as he was powerless to make out what it meant, or would be at; and was sometimes apprehensive that he might be at that very moment an interesting case of spontaneous combustion, without having the consolation of knowing it. At last, however, he began to think—as you or I would have thought at first; for it is always the person not in the predicament who knows what ought to have been done in it, and would unquestionably have done it too—at last, I say, he began to think that the source and secret of this ghostly light might be in the adjoining room, from whence, on further tracing it, it seemed to shine. This idea taking full possession of his mind, he got up softly, and shuffled in his slippers to the door.

The moment Scrooge's hand was on the lock a strange voice called him by his name, and bade him enter. He obeyed.

It was his own room. There was no doubt about that. But it had undergone a surprising transformation. The walls and ceiling were so hung with living green, that it looked a perfect grove; from every part of which bright gleaming berries glistened. The crisp leaves of holly, mistletoe, and ivy reflected back the light, as if so many little mirrors had been scattered there; and such a mighty blaze went roaring up the chimney as that dull petrification of a hearth had never known in Scrooge's time, or Marley's, or for many and many a winter season gone. Heaped up on the floor, to form a kind of throne, were turkeys, geese, game, poultry, brawn, great joints of meat, sucking-pigs, long wreaths of sausages, mince-pies, plum-puddings, barrels of oysters, red-hot chestnuts, cherry-cheeked apples, juicy oranges, luscious pears, immense twelfth-cakes, and seething bowls of punch, that made the chamber dim with their delicious steam. In easy state upon this couch there sat a jolly Giant, glorious to see; who bore a glowing torch, in shape not unlike Plenty's horn, and held it up, high up, to shed its light on Scrooge as he came peeping round the door.

'Come in!' exclaimed the Ghost. 'Come in! and know me better, man!'

Scrooge entered timidly, and hung his head before this Spirit. He was not the dogged Scrooge he had been; and though the Spirit's eyes were clear and kind, he did not like to meet them.

'I am the Ghost of Christmas Present,' said the Spirit. 'Look upon me!'

Scrooge reverently did so. It was clothed in one simple deep green robe, or mantle, bordered with white fur. This garment hung so loosely on the figure, that its capacious breast was bare, as if disdaining to be warded or concealed by any artifice. Its feet, observable beneath the ample folds of the garment, were also bare; and on its head it wore no other covering than a holly wreath, set here and there with shining icicles. Its dark-brown curls were long and free; free as its genial face, its sparkling eye, its open hand, its cheery voice, its unconstrained demeanour, and its joyful air. Girded round its middle was an antique scabbard; but no sword was in it, and the ancient sheath was eaten up with rust.

'You have never seen the like of me before!' exclaimed the Spirit.

'Never,' Scrooge made answer to it.

'Have never walked forth with the younger members of my family; meaning (for I am very young) my elder brothers born in these later years?' pursued the Phantom.

'I don't think I have,' said Scrooge. 'I am afraid I have not. Have you had many brothers, Spirit?'

'More than eighteen hundred,' said the Ghost.

'A tremendous family to provide for,' muttered Scrooge.

The Ghost of Christmas Present rose.

'Spirit,' said Scrooge submissively, 'conduct me where you will. I went forth last night on compulsion, and I learned a lesson which is working now. Tonight if you have aught to teach me, let me profit by it.'

'Touch my robe!'

Scrooge did as he was told, and held it fast.

Holly, mistletoe, red berries, ivy, turkeys, geese, game, poultry, brawn, meat, pigs, sausages, oysters, pies, puddings, fruit, and punch, all vanished instantly. So did the room, the fire, the ruddy glow, the hour of night, and they stood in the city streets on Christmas morning, where (for the weather was severe) the people made a rough, but brisk and not unpleasant kind of music, in scraping the snow from the pavement in front of their dwellings, and from the tops of their houses, whence it was mad delight to the boys to see it come plumping down into the road below, and splitting into artificial little snowstorms.

The house-fronts looked black enough, and the windows blacker, contrasting with the smooth white sheet of snow upon the roofs, and with the dirtier snow upon the ground; which last deposit had been ploughed up in deep furrows by the heavy wheels of carts and waggons: furrows that crossed and recrossed each other hundreds of times where the great streets branched off; and made intricate channels, hard to trace in the thick yellow mud and icy water. The sky was gloomy, and the shortest streets were choked up with a dingy mist, half thawed, half frozen, whose heavier particles descended in a shower of sooty atoms, as if all the chimneys in Great Britain had, by one consent, caught fire, and were blazing away to their dear heart's content. There was nothing very cheerful in the climate or the town, and yet was there an air of cheerfulness abroad that the clearest summer air and brightest summer sun might have endeavoured to diffuse in vain.

For the people who were shovelling away on the house-tops were jovial and full of glee; calling out to one another from the parapets, and now and then exchanging a facetious snowball—better-natured missile far than many a wordy jest—laughing heartily if it went right, and not less heartily if it went wrong. The poulterers' shops were still half open, and the fruiterers' were radiant in their glory. There were great, round, pot-bellied baskets of chestnuts, shaped like the waistcoats of jolly old gentlemen, lolling at the doors, and tumbling out into the street in their apoplectic opulence. There were ruddy, brown-faced, broad-girthed Spanish onions, shining in the fatness of their growth like Spanish friars, and winking from their shelves in wanton slyness at the girls as they went by, and glanced demurely at the hung-up mistletoe. There were pears and apples clustered high in blooming pyramids; there were bunches of grapes, made, in the shopkeepers' benevolence, to dangle from conspicuous hooks that people's mouths might water gratis as they passed; there were piles of filberts, mossy and brown, recalling, in their fragrance, ancient walks among the woods, and pleasant shufflings ankle deep through withered leaves; there were Norfolk Biffins, squab and swarthy, setting off the yellow of the oranges and lemons, and, in the great compactness of their juicy persons, urgently entreating and beseeching to be carried home in paper bags and eaten after dinner. The very gold and silver fish, set forth among these choice fruits in a bowl, though members of a dull and stagnant-blooded race, appeared to know that there was something going on; and, to a fish, went gasping round and round their little world in slow and passionless excitement.

The Grocers'! oh, the Grocers'! nearly closed, with perhaps two shutters down, or one; but through those gaps such glimpses! It was not alone that the scales descending on the counter made a merry sound, or that the twine and roller parted company so briskly, or that the canisters were rattled up and down like juggling tricks, or even that the blended scents of tea and coffee were so grateful to the nose, or even that the raisins were so plentiful and rare, the almonds so extremely white, the sticks of cinnamon so long and straight, the other spices so delicious, the candied fruits so caked and spotted with molten sugar as to make the coldest lookers-on feel faint, and subsequently bilious. Nor was it that the figs were moist and pulpy, or that the French plums blushed in modest tartness from their highly-decorated boxes, or that everything was good to eat and in its Christmas dress; but the customers were all so hurried and so eager in the hopeful promise of the day, that they tumbled up against each other at the door, crashing their wicker baskets wildly, and left their purchases upon the counter, and came running back to fetch them, and committed hundreds of the like mistakes, in the best humour possible; while the grocer and his people were so frank and fresh, that the polished hearts with which they fastened their aprons behind might have been their own, worn out-side for general inspection, and for Christmas daws to peck at if they chose.

But soon the steeples called good people all to church and chapel, and away they came, flocking through the streets in their best clothes and with their gayest faces. And at the same time there emerged, from scores of by-streets, lanes, and nameless turnings, innumerable people, carrying their dinners to the bakers' shops. The sight of these poor revellers appeared to interest the Spirit very much, for he stood with Scrooge beside him in a baker's doorway, and, taking off the covers as their bearers passed, sprinkled incense on their dinners from his torch. And it was a very uncommon kind of torch, for once or twice, when there were angry words between some dinner-carriers who had jostled each other, he shed a few drops of water on them from it, and their good-humour was restored directly. For they said, it was a shame to quarrel upon Christmas Day. And so it was! God love it, so it was!

In time the bells ceased, and the bakers were shut up; and yet there was a genial shadowing forth of all these dinners, and the progress of their cooking, in the thawed blotch of wet above each bakers' oven, where the pavement smoked as if its stones were cooking too.

'Is there a peculiar flavour in what you sprinkle from your torch?' asked Scrooge.

'There is. My own.'

'Would it apply to any kind of dinner on this day?' asked Scrooge.

'To any kindly given. To a poor one most.'

'Why to a poor one most?' asked Scrooge.

'Because it needs it most.'

'Spirit!' said Scrooge, after a moment's thought,

'I wonder you, of all the beings in the many worlds about us, should desire to cramp these people's opportunities of innocent enjoyment.'

'I!' cried the Spirit.

'You would deprive them of their means of dining every seventh day, often the only day on which they can be said to dine at all,' said Scrooge; 'wouldn't you?'

'I!' cried the Spirit.

'You seek to close these places on the Seventh Day,' said Scrooge. 'And it comes to the same thing.'

'I seek!' exclaimed the Spirit.

'Forgive me if I am wrong. It has been done in your name, or at least in that of your family,' said Scrooge.

'There are some upon this earth of yours,' returned the Spirit, 'who lay claim to know us, and who do their deeds of passion, pride, ill-will, hatred, envy, bigotry, and selfishness in our name, who are as strange to us, and all our kith and kin, as if they had never lived. Remember that, and charge their doings on themselves, not us.'

Scrooge promised that he would; and they went on, invisible, as they had been before, into the suburbs of the town. It was a remarkable quality of the Ghost (which Scrooge had observed at the baker's), that notwithstanding his gigantic size, he could accommodate himself to any place with ease; and that he stood be-

neath a low roof quite as gracefully and like a supernatural creature as it was possible he could have done
in any lofty hall.

And perhaps it was the pleasure the good Spirit
had in showing off this power of his, or else it was his
own kind, generous, hearty nature, and his sympathy
with all poor men, that led him straight to Scrooge's
clerk's; for there he went, and took Scrooge with him,
holding to his robe; and on the threshold of the door
the Spirit smiled, and stopped to bless Bob Cratchit's
dwelling with the sprinklings of his torch. Think of
that! Bob had but fifteen 'Bob' a week himself; he
pocketed on Saturdays but fifteen copies of his Christian name; and yet the Ghost of Christmas Present
blessed his four-roomed house!

Then up rose Mrs. Cratchit, Cratchit's wife,
dressed out but poorly in a twice-turned gown, but
brave in ribbons, which are cheap, and make a goodly
show for sixpence; and she laid the cloth, assisted by
Belinda Cratchit, second of her daughters, also brave
in ribbons; while Master Peter Cratchit plunged a fork
into the saucepan of potatoes, and getting the corners
of his monstrous shirt-collar (Bob's private property,
conferred upon his son and heir in honour of the day,
into his mouth, rejoiced to find himself so gallantly
attired, and yearned to show his linen in the fashionable Parks. And now two smaller Cratchits, boy and
girl, came tearing in, screaming that outside the baker's

they had smelt the goose, and known it for their own; and basking in luxurious thoughts of sage and onion, these young Cratchits danced about the table, and exalted Master Peter Cratchit to the skies, while he (not proud, although his collars nearly choked him) blew the fire, until the slow potatoes, bubbling up, knocked loudly at the saucepan-lid to be let out and peeled.

'What has ever got your precious father, then?' said Mrs. Cratchit. 'And your brother, Tiny Tim? And Martha warn't as late last Christmas Day by half an hour!'

'Here's Martha, mother!' said a girl, appearing as she spoke.

'Here's Martha, mother!' cried the two young Cratchits. 'Hurrah! There's *such* a goose, Martha!'

'Why, bless your heart alive, my dear, how late you are!' said Mrs. Cratchit, kissing her a dozen times, and taking off her shawl and bonnet for her with officious zeal.

'We'd a deal of work to finish up last night,' replied the girl, 'and had to clear away this morning, mother!'

'Well! never mind so long as you are come,' said Mrs. Cratchit. 'Sit ye down before the fire, my dear, and have a warm, Lord bless ye!'

'No, no! There's father coming,' cried the two young Cratchits, who were everywhere at once. 'Hide, Martha, hide!'

So Martha hid herself, and in came little Bob, the father, with at least three feet of comforter, exclusive of the fringe, hanging down before him, and his thread-bare clothes darned up and brushed to look seasonable, and Tiny Tim upon his shoulder. Alas for Tiny Tim, he bore a little crutch, and had his limbs supported by an iron frame!

'Why, where's our Martha?' cried Bob Cratchit, looking around.

'Not coming,' said Mrs. Cratchit.

'Not coming!' said Bob, with a sudden declension in his high spirits; for he had been Tim's blood-horse all the way from church, and had come home rampant. 'Not coming upon Christmas Day!'

Martha didn't like to see him disappointed, if it were only in joke; so she came out prematurely from behind the closet door, and ran into his arms, while the two young Cratchits hustled Tiny Tim, and bore him off into the wash-house, that he might hear the pudding singing in the copper.

'And how did little Tim behave?' asked Mrs. Cratchit when she had rallied Bob on his credulity, and Bob had hugged his daughter to his heart's content.

'As good as gold,' said Bob, 'and better. Somehow, he gets thoughtful, sitting by himself so much, and thinks the strangest things you ever heard. He told me, coming home, that he hoped the people saw him in the church, because he was a cripple, and it might be pleasant to them to remember upon Christmas Day who made lame beggars walk and blind men see.'

Bob's voice was tremulous when he told them this, and trembled more when he said that Tiny Tim was growing strong and hearty.

His active little crutch was heard upon the floor, and back came Tiny Tim before another word was spoken, escorted by his brother and sister to his stool beside the fire; and while Bob, turning up his cuffs—as if, poor fellow, they were capable of being made more shabby—compounded some hot mixture in a jug with gin and lemons, and stirred it round and round, and put it on the hob to simmer, Master Peter and the two ubiquitous young Cratchits went to fetch the goose, with which they soon returned in high procession.

Such a bustle ensued that you might have thought a goose the rarest of all birds; a feathered phenomenon, to which a black swan was a matter of course—and, in truth, it was something very like it in that house. Mrs. Cratchit made the gravy (ready beforehand in a little saucepan) hissing hot; Master Pete mashed the potatoes with incredible vigour; Miss Belinda sweetened up the apple sauce; Martha dusted the hot plates; Bob took Tiny Tim beside him in a tiny corner at the table; the two young Cratchits set chairs for everybody, not forgetting themselves, and, mounting guard upon their posts, crammed spoons into their mouths, lest they should shriek for goose before their turn came to be helped. At last the dishes were set on, and grace was said. It was succeeded by a breathless pause, as Mrs. Cratchit, looking slowly all along the carving-knife, prepared to plunge it in the breast; but when she did, and when the long-expected gush of stuffing issued forth, one murmur of delight arose all round the board, and even Tiny Tim, excited by the two young Cratchits, beat on the table with the handle of his knife and feebly cried Hurrah!

There never was such a goose. Bob said he didn't believe there ever was such a goose cooked. Its tenderness and flavour, size and cheapness, were the themes of universal admiration. Eked out by apple sauce and mashed potatoes, it was a sufficient dinner for the whole family; indeed, as Mrs. Cratchit said with great delight (surveying one small atom of a bone upon the dish), they hadn't ate it all at last! Yet every one had had enough, and the youngest Cratchits, in particular, were steeped in sage and onion to the eyebrows! But now, the plates being changed by Miss Belinda, Mrs. Cratchit left the room alone—too nervous to bear witnesses—to take the pudding up, and bring it in.

Suppose it should not be done enough! Suppose it should break in turning out! Suppose somebody should have got over the wall of the back-yard and stolen it, while they were merry with the goose—a supposition at which the two young Cratchits became livid! All sorts of horrors were supposed.

Hallo! A great deal of steam! The pudding was out of the copper. A smell like a washing-day! That was the cloth. A smell like an eating-house and a pastry-cook's next door to each other, with a laundress's next door to that! That was the pudding! In half a minute Mrs. Cratchit entered—flushed, but smiling proudly—with the pudding, like a speckled cannon-ball, so hard and firm, blazing in half of half-a-quartern of ignited brandy, and bedight with Christmas holly stuck into the top.

Oh, a wonderful pudding! Bob Cratchit said, and calmly too, that he regarded it as the greatest success achieved by Mrs. Cratchit since their marriage. Mrs. Cratchit said that, now the weight was off her mind, she would confess she had her doubts about the quantity of flour. Everybody had something to say about it, but nobody said or thought it was at all a small pudding for a large family. It would have been flat heresy to do so. Any Cratchit would have blushed to hint at such a thing.

At last the dinner was all done, the cloth was cleared, the hearth swept, and the fire made up. The compound in the jug being tasted, and considered perfect, apples and oranges were put upon the table, and a shovel full of chestnuts on the fire. Then all the Cratchit family drew round the hearth in what Bob Cratchit called a circle, meaning half a one; and at Bob Cratchit's elbow stood the family display of glass. Two tumblers and a custard cup without a handle.

These held the hot stuff from the jug, however, as well as golden goblets would have done; and Bob served it out with beaming looks, while the chestnuts on the fire sputtered and cracked noisily. Then Bob proposed:

'A merry Christmas to us all, my dears. God bless us!'

Which all the family re-echoed.

'God bless us every one!' said Tiny Tim, the last of all.

He sat very close to his father's side, upon his little stool. Bob held his withered little hand to his, as if he loved the child, and wished to keep him by his side, and dreaded that he might be taken from him.

'Spirit,' said Scrooge, with an interest he had never felt before, 'tell me if Tiny Tim will live.'

'I see a vacant seat,' replied the Ghost, 'in the poor chimney corner, and a crutch without an owner, carefully preserved. If these shadows remain unaltered by the Future, the child will die.'

'No, no,' said Scrooge. 'Oh no, kind Spirit! say he will be spared.'

'If these shadows remain unaltered by the Future none other of my race,' returned the Ghost, 'will find him here. What then? If he be like to die, he had better do it, and decrease the surplus population.'

Scrooge hung his head to hear his own words quoted by the Spirit, and was overcome with penitence and grief.

'Man,' said the Ghost, 'if man you be in heart, not adamant, forbear that wicked cant until you have discovered what the surplus is, and where it is. Will you decide what men shall live, what men shall die? It may be that, in the sight of Heaven, you are more worthless and less fit to live than millions like this poor man's child. O God! to hear the insect on the leaf pronouncing on the too much life among his hungry brothers in the dust!'

Scrooge bent before the Ghost's rebuke, and, trembling, cast his eyes upon the ground. But he raised them speedily on hearing his own name.

'Mr. Scrooge!' said Bob. 'I'll give you Mr. Scrooge, the Founder of the Feast!'

'The Founder of the Feast, indeed!' cried Mrs. Cratchit, reddening. 'I wish I had him here. I'd give him a piece of my mind to feast upon, and I hope he'd have a good appetite for it.'

'My dear,' said Bob, 'the children! Christmas Day.'

'It should be Christmas Day, I am sure,' said she, 'on which one drinks the health of such an odious, stingy, hard, unfeeling man as Mr. Scrooge. You know he is, Robert! Nobody knows it better than you do, poor fellow!'

'My dear!' was Bob's mild answer. 'Christmas Day.'

'I'll drink his health for your sake and the Day's,' said Mrs. Cratchit, 'not for his. Long life to him! A merry Christmas and a happy New Year! He'll be very merry and very happy, I have no doubt!'

The children drank the toast after her. It was the first of their proceedings which had no heartiness in it. Tiny Tim drank it last of all, but he didn't care two-pence for it. Scrooge was the Ogre of the family. The mention of his name cast a dark shadow on the party, which was not dispelled for full five minutes.

After it had passed away they were ten times merrier than before, from the mere relief of Scrooge the Baleful being done with. Bob Cratchit told them how he had a situation in his eye for Master Peter, which would bring in, if obtained, full five-and-sixpence weekly. The two young Cratchits laughed tremendously at the idea of Peter's being a man of business; and Peter himself looked thoughtfully at the fire from between his collars, as if he were deliberating what particular investments he should favour when he came into the receipt of that bewildering income. Martha, who was a poor apprentice at a milliner's, then told them what kind of work she had to do, and how many hours she worked at a stretch, and how she meant to lie abed to-morrow morning for a good long rest; to-morrow being a holiday she passed at home. Also how she had seen a countess and a lord some days before, and how the lord 'was much about as tall as Peter'; at which Peter pulled up his collar so high that you couldn't have seen his head if you had been there. All this time the chestnuts and the jug went round and round; and by-and-by they had a song, about a lost child travelling in the snow, from Tiny Tim, who had a plaintive little voice, and sang it very well indeed.

There was nothing of high mark in this. They were not a handsome family; they were not well dressed; their shoes were far from being waterproof; their clothes were scanty; and Peter might have known, and very likely did, the inside of a pawnbroker's. But they were happy, grateful, pleased with one another, and contented with the time; and when they faded, and looked happier yet in the bright sprinklings of the Spirit's torch at parting, Scrooge had his eye upon them, and especially on Tiny Tim, until the last.

By this time it was getting dark, and snowing pretty heavily; and as Scrooge and the Spirit went along the streets, the brightness of the roaring fires in kitchens, parlours, and all sorts of rooms was wonderful. Here, the flickering of the blaze showed preparations for a cosy dinner, with hot plates baking through and through before the fire, and deep red curtains, ready to be drawn to shut out cold and darkness. There, all the children of the house were running out into the snow to meet their married sisters, brothers, cousins, uncles, aunts, and be the first to greet them. Here, again, were shadows on the window-blinds of guests assembling; and there a group of handsome girls, all hooded and fur-booted, and all chattering at once, tripped lightly off to some near neighbour's house; where, woe upon the single man who saw them enter—artful witches, well they knew it—in a glow!

But, if you had judged from the numbers of people on their way to friendly gatherings, you might have thought that no one was at home to give them welcome when they got there, instead of every house expecting company, and piling up its fires half-chimney high. Blessings on it, how the Ghost exulted! How it bared its breadth of breast, and opened its capacious palm, and floated on, outpouring with a generous hand its bright and harmless mirth on everything within its reach! The very lamplighter, who ran on before, dotting the dusky street with specks of light, and who was dressed to spend the evening somewhere, laughed out loudly as the Spirit passed, though little kenned the lamplighter that he had any company but Christmas.

And now, without a word of warning from the Ghost, they stood upon a bleak and desert moor, where monstrous masses of rude stone were cast about, as though it were the burial-place of giants; and water spread itself wheresoever it listed; or would have done so, but for the frost that held it prisoner; and nothing grew but moss and furze, and coarse, rank grass. Down in the west the setting sun had left a streak of fiery red, which glared upon the desolation for an instant, like a sullen eye, and frowning lower, lower, lower yet, was lost in the thick gloom of darkest night.

'What place is this?' asked Scrooge.

'A place where miners live, who labour in the bowels of the earth,' returned the Spirit. 'But they know me. See!'

A light shone from the window of a hut, and swiftly they advanced towards it. Passing through the wall of mud and stone, they found a cheerful company assembled around a glowing fire. An old, old man and woman, with their children and their children's children, and another generation beyond that, all decked out gaily in their holiday attire. The old man, in a voice that seldom rose above the howling of the wind upon the barren waste, was singing them a Christmas song; it had been a very old song when he was a boy; and from time to time they all joined in the chorus. So surely as they raised their voices, the old man got quite blithe and loud; and so surely as they stopped, his vigour sank again.

The Spirit did not tarry here, but bade Scrooge hold his robe, and, passing on above the moor, sped whither? Not to sea? To sea. To Scrooge's horror, looking back, he saw the last of the land, a frightful range of rocks, behind them; and his ears were deafened by the thundering of water, as it rolled and roared, and raged among the dreadful caverns it had worn, and fiercely tried to undermine the earth.

Built upon a dismal reef of sunken rocks, some league or so from shore, on which the waters chafed and dashed, the wild year through, there stood a solitary lighthouse. Great heaps of seaweed clung to its base, and storm-birds—born of the wind, one might suppose, as seaweed of the water—rose and fell about it, like the waves they skimmed.

But, even here, two men who watched the light had made a fire, that through the loophole in the thick stone wall shed out a ray of brightness on the awful sea. Joining their horny hands over the rough table at which they sat, they wished each other Merry Christmas in their can of grog; and one of them—the elder too, with his face all damaged and scarred with hard weather, as the figure-head of an old ship might be—struck up a sturdy song that was like a gale in itself.

Again the Ghost sped on, above the black and heaving sea—on, on—until being far away, as he told Scrooge, from any shore, they lighted on a ship. They stood beside the helmsman at the wheel, the look-out in the bow, the officers who had the watch; dark, ghostly figures in their several stations; but every man among them hummed a Christmas tune, or had a Christmas thought, or spoke below his breath to his companion of some bygone Christmas Day, with homeward hopes belonging to it. And every man on board, waking or sleeping, good or bad, had had a kinder word for one another on that day than on any day in the year; and had shared to some extent in its festivities; and had remembered those he cared for at a distance, and had known that they delighted to remember him.

It was a great surprise to Scrooge, while listening to the moaning of the wind, and thinking what a solemn thing it was to move on through the lonely darkness over an unknown abyss, whose depths were secrets as profound as death: it was a great surprise to Scrooge, while thus engaged, to hear a hearty laugh. It was a much greater surprise to Scrooge to recognise it as his own nephew's and to find himself in a bright, dry, gleaming room, with the Spirit standing smiling by his side, and looking at that same nephew with approving affability!

'Ha, ha!' laughed Scrooge's nephew. 'Ha, ha, ha!'

If you should happen, by any unlikely chance, to know a man more blessed in a laugh than Scrooge's nephew, all I can say is, I should like to know him too. Introduce him to me, and I'll cultivate his acquaintance.

It is a fair, even-handed, noble adjustment of things, that while there is infection in disease and sorrow, there is nothing in the world so irresistibly contagious as laughter and good-humour. When Scrooge's nephew laughed in this way—holding his sides, rolling his head, and twisting his face into the most extravagant contortions—Scrooge's niece, by marriage, laughed as heartily as he. And their assembled friends, being not a bit behindhand, roared out lustily.

'Ha, ha! Ha, ha, ha, ha!'

'He said that Christmas was a humbug, as I live!' cried Scrooge's nephew. 'He believed it, too!'

'More shame for him, Fred!' said Scrooge's niece indignantly. Bless those women! they never do anything by halves. They are always in earnest.

She was very pretty; exceedingly pretty. With a dimpled, surprised-looking, capital face; a ripe little mouth, that seemed made to be kissed—as no doubt it was; all kinds of good little dots about her chin, that melted into one another when she laughed; and the sunniest pair of eyes you ever saw in any little creature's head. Altogether she was what you would have called provoking, you know; but satisfactory, too. Oh, perfectly satisfactory!

'He's a comical old fellow,' said Scrooge's nephew, 'that's the truth; and not so pleasant as he might be. However, his offences carry their own punishment, and I have nothing to say against him.'

'I'm sure he is very rich, Fred,' hinted Scrooge's niece. 'At least, you always tell *me* so.'

'What of that, my dear?' said Scrooge's nephew. 'His wealth is of no use to him. He don't do any good with it. He don't make himself comfortable with it.

He hasn't the satisfaction of thinking—ha, ha, ha!—that he is ever going to benefit Us with it.'

'I have no patience with him,' observed Scrooge's niece. Scrooge's niece's sisters, and all the other ladies, expressed the same opinion.

'Oh, I have!' said Scrooge's nephew. 'I am sorry for him; I couldn't be angry with him if I tried. Who suffers by his ill whims? Himself always. Here he takes it into his head to dislike us, and he won't come and dine with us. What's the consequence? He don't lose much of a dinner.'

'Indeed, I think he loses a very good dinner,' interrupted Scrooge's niece. Everybody else said the same, and they must be allowed to have been competent judges, because they had just had dinner; and with the dessert upon the table, were clustered round the fire, by lamplight.

'Well! I am very glad to hear it,' said Scrooge's nephew, 'because I haven't any great faith in these young housekeepers. What do *you* say, Topper?'

Topper had clearly got his eye upon one of Scrooge's niece's sisters, for he answered that a bachelor was a wretched outcast, who had no right to express an opinion on the subject. Whereat Scrooge's niece's sister—the plump one with the lace tucker: not the one with the roses—blushed.

'Do go on, Fred,' said Scrooge's niece, clapping

her hands. 'He never finishes what he begins to say! He is such a ridiculous fellow!'

Scrooge's nephew revelled in another laugh, and as it was impossible to keep the infection off, though the plump sister tried hard to do it with aromatic vinegar, his example was unanimously followed.

'I was only going to say,' said Scrooge's nephew, 'that the consequence of his taking a dislike to us, and not making merry with us, is, as I think, that he loses some pleasant moments, which could do him no harm. I am sure he loses pleasanter companions than he can find in his own thoughts, either in his mouldy old office or his dusty chambers. I mean to give him the same chance every year, whether he likes it or not, for I pity him. He may rail at Christmas till he dies, but he can't help thinking better of it—I defy him—if he finds me going there, in good temper, year after year, and saying, "Uncle Scrooge, how are you?" If it only put him in the vein to leave his poor clerk fifty pounds, *that's* something; and I think I shook him yesterday.'

It was their turn to laugh now, at the notion of his shaking Scrooge. But being thoroughly good-natured, and not much caring what they laughed at, so that they laughed at any rate, he encouraged them in their merriment, and passed the bottle, joyously.

After tea they had some music. For they were a musical family, and knew what they were about when they sung a Glee or Catch, I can assure you: especially Topper, who could growl away in the bass like a good one, and never swell the large veins in his forehead, or get red in the face over it. Scrooge's niece played well upon the harp; and played, among other tunes, a simple little air (a mere nothing: you might learn to whistle it in two minutes) which had been familiar to the child who fetched Scrooge from the boarding-school, as he had been reminded by the Ghost of Christmas Past. When this strain of music sounded, all the things that Ghost had shown him came upon his mind; he softened more and more; and thought that if he could have listened to it often, years ago, he might have cultivated the kindnesses of life for his own happiness with his own hands, without resorting to the sexton's spade that buried Jacob Marley.

But they didn't devote the whole evening to music. After a while they played at forfeits; for it is good to be children sometimes, and never better than at Christmas, when its mighty Founder was a child himself. Stop! There was first a game at blindman's-bluff. Of course there was. And I no more believe Topper was really blind than I believe he had eyes in his boots. My opinion is, that it was a done thing between him and Scrooge's nephew; and that the Ghost of Christmas Present knew it. The way he went after that plump sister in the lace tucker was an outrage on the credulity of human nature. Knocking down the fire-irons, tumbling over the chairs, bumping up against the piano, smothering himself amongst the curtains, wherever she went, there went he! He always knew where the plump sister was. He wouldn't catch anybody else. If you had fallen up against him (as some of them did) on purpose, he would have made a feint of endeavouring to seize you, which would have been an affront to your understanding, and would instantly have sidled off in the direction of the plump sister. She often cried out that it wasn't fair; and it really was not. But when, at last, he caught her; when, in spite of all her silken rustlings, and her rapid flutterings past him, he got her into a corner whence there was no escape; then his conduct was the most execrable. For his pretending not to know her; his pretending that it was necessary to touch her headdress, and further to assure himself of her identity by pressing a certain ring upon her finger, and a certain chain about her neck; was vile, monstrous! No doubt she told him her opinion of it when, another blind man being in office, they were so very confidential together behind the curtains.

Scrooge's niece was not one of the blindman's-bluff party, but was made comfortable with a large chair and a footstool, in a snug corner where the Ghost and Scrooge were close behind her. But she joined in the forfeits, and loved her love to admiration with all the letters of the alphabet. Likewise at the game of How, When, and Where, she was very great, and, to the secret joy of Scrooge's nephew, beat her sisters hollow; though they were sharp girls too, as Topper could have told you. There might have been twenty people there, young and old, but they all played, and so did Scrooge; for wholly forgetting, in the interest he had in what was going on, that his voice made no sound in their ears, he sometimes came out with his guess quite loud, and very often guessed right, too; for the sharpest needle, best Whitechapel, warranted not to cut in the eye, was not sharper than Scrooge, blunt as he took it in his head to be.

The Ghost was greatly pleased to find him in this mood, and looked upon him with such favour that he begged like a boy to be allowed to stay until the guests departed. But this the Spirit said could not be done.

'Here is a new game,' said Scrooge. 'One half-hour, Spirit, only one!'

It was a game called Yes and No, where Scrooge's nephew had to think of something, and the rest must find out what, he only answering to their questions yes or no, as the case was. The brisk fire of questioning to which he was exposed elicited from him that he was thinking of an animal, a live animal, rather a disagreeable animal, a savage animal, an animal that growled and grunted sometimes, and talked sometimes and lived in London, and walked about the streets, and wasn't made a show of, and wasn't led by anybody, and didn't live in a menagerie, and was never killed in a market, and was not a horse, or an ass, or a cow, or a bull, or a tiger, or a dog, or a pig, or a cat, or a bear. At every fresh question that was put to him, this nephew burst into a fresh roar of laughter; and was so inexpressibly tickled, that he was obliged to get up off the sofa and stamp. At last the plump sister, falling into a similar state, cried out:

'I have found it out! I know what it is, Fred! I know what it is!'

'What is it?' cried Fred.

'It's your uncle Scro-o-o-o-oge.'

Which it certainly was. Admiration was the universal sentiment, though some objected that the reply to 'Is it a bear?' ought to have been 'Yes'; inasmuch as an answer in the negative was sufficient to have diverted their thoughts from Mr. Scrooge, supposing they had ever had any tendency that way.

'He has given us plenty of merriment, I am sure,' said Fred, 'and it would be ungrateful not to drink his health. Here is a glass of mulled wine ready to our hand at the moment; and I say, "Uncle Scrooge!" '

'Well! Uncle Scrooge!' they cried.

'A merry Christmas and a happy New Year to the old man, whatever he is!' said Scrooge's nephew. 'He wouldn't take it from me, but may he have it, nevertheless. Uncle Scrooge!'

Uncle Scrooge had imperceptibly become so gay and light of heart, that he would have pledged the unconscious company in return, and thanked them in an inaudible speech, if the Ghost had given him time. But the whole scene passed off in the breath of the last word spoken by his nephew; and he and the Spirit were again upon their travels.

Much they saw, and far they went, and many homes they visited, but always with a happy end. The Spirit stood beside sick-beds, and they were cheerful; on foreign lands, and they were close at home; by struggling men, and they were patient in their greater hope; by poverty, and it was rich. In almshouse, hospital, and gaol, in misery's every refuge, where vain man in his little brief authority had not made fast the door, and barred the Spirit out, he left his blessing and taught Scrooge his precepts.

It was a long night, if it were only a night; but Scrooge had his doubts of this, because the Christmas holidays appeared to be condensed into the space of time they passed together. It was strange, too, that, while Scrooge remained unaltered in his outward form, the Ghost grew older, clearly older. Scrooge had observed this change, but never spoke of it until they left a children's Twelfth-Night party, when, looking at the Spirit as they stood together in an open place, he noticed that its hair was grey.

'Are spirits' lives so short?' asked Scrooge.

'My life upon this globe is very brief,' replied the Ghost. 'It ends to-night.'

'To-night!' cried Scrooge.

'To-night at midnight. Hark! The time is drawing near.'

The chimes were ringing the three-quarters past eleven at that moment.

'Forgive me if I am not justified in what I ask,' said Scrooge, looking intently at the Spirit's robe, 'but I see something strange, and not belonging to yourself, protruding from your skirts. Is it a foot or a claw?'

'It might be a claw, for the flesh there is upon it,' was the Spirit's sorrowful reply. 'Look here!'

From the foldings of its robe it brought two children, wretched, abject, frightful, hideous, miserable. They knelt down at its feet, and clung upon the outside of its garment.

'Oh Man! look here! Look, look down here!' exclaimed the Ghost.

They were a boy and girl. Yellow, meagre, ragged, scowling, wolfish, but prostrate, too, in their humility. Where graceful youth should have filled their features out, and touched them with its freshest tints, a stale and shrivelled hand, like that of age, had pinched and twisted them, and pulled them into shreds. Where angels might have sat enthroned, devils lurked, and glared out menacing. No change, no degradation, no perversion of humanity in any grade, through all the mysteries of wonderful creation, has monsters half so horrible and dread.

Scrooge stared back, appalled. Having them shown to him in this way, he tried to say they were fine children, but the words choked themselves, rather than be parties to a lie of such enormous magnitude.

'Spirit! are they yours?' Scrooge could say no more.

'They are Man's,' said the Spirit, looking down upon them. 'And they cling to me, appealing from their fathers. This boy is Ignorance. The girl is Want. Beware of them both, and all of their degree, but most of all beware this boy, for on his brow I see that written which is Doom, unless the writing be erased. Deny it!' cried the Spirit, stretching out his hand towards the city. 'Slander those who tell it ye! Admit it for your factious purposes, and make it worse! And bide the end!'

'Have they no refuge or resource?' cried Scrooge.

'Are there no prisons?' said the Spirit, turning on him for the last time with his own words. 'Are there no workhouses?'

The bell struck Twelve.

Scrooge looked about him for the Ghost, and saw it not. As the last stroke ceased to vibrate, he remembered the prediction of old Jacob Marley, and, lifting up his eyes, beheld a solemn Phantom, draped and hooded, coming like a mist along the ground towards him.

# The Last of the Spirits

T he Phantom slowly, gravely, silently approached. When it came near him, Scrooge bent down upon his knee; for in the very air through which this Spirit moved it seemed to scatter gloom and mystery.

It was shrouded in a deep black garment, which concealed its head, its face, its form, and left nothing of it visible, save one outstretched hand. But for this, it would have been difficult to detach its figure from the night, and separate it from the darkness by which it was surrounded.

He felt that it was tall and stately when it came beside him, and that its mysterious presence filled him with a solemn dread. He knew no more, for the Spirit neither spoke nor moved.

'I am in the presence of the Ghost of Christmas Yet to Come?' said Scrooge.

The Spirit answered not, but pointed onward with its hand.

'You are about to show me shadows of the things that have not happened, but will happen in the time before us,' Scrooge pursued. 'Is that so, Spirit?'

The upper portion of the garment was contracted for an instant in its folds, as if the Spirit had inclined its head. That was the only answer he received.

Although well used to ghostly company by this time, Scrooge feared the silent shape so much that his legs trembled beneath him, and he found that he could hardly stand when he prepared to follow it. The Spirit paused a moment, as observing his condition, and giving him time to recover.

But Scrooge was all the worse for this. It thrilled him with a vague, uncertain horror to know that, behind the dusky shroud, there were ghostly eyes intently fixed upon him, while he, though he stretched his own to the utmost, could see nothing but a spectral hand and one great heap of black.

'Ghost of the Future!' he exclaimed, 'I fear you more than any spectre I have seen. But as I know your purpose is to do me good, and as I hope to live to be another man from what I was, I am prepared to bear your company, and do it with a thankful heart. Will you not speak to me?'

It gave him no reply. The hand was pointed straight before them.

'Lead on!' said Scrooge. 'Lead on! The night is waning fast, and it is precious time to me, I know. Lead on, Spirit!'

The Phantom moved away as it had come towards him. Scrooge followed in the shadow of its dress, which bore him up, he thought, and carried him along.

They scarcely seemed to enter the City; for the City rather seemed to spring up about them, and encompass them of its own act. But there they were in the heart of it; on 'Change, amongst the merchants, who hurried up and down, and chinked the money in their pockets, and conversed in groups, and looked at their watches, and trifled thoughtfully with their great gold seals, and so forth, as Scrooge had seen them often.

The Spirit stopped beside one little knot of business men. Observing that the hand was pointed to them, Scrooge advanced to listen to their talk.

'No,' said a great fat man with a monstrous chin, 'I don't know much about it either way. I only know he's dead.'

'When did he die?' inquired another.

'Last night, I believe.'

'Why, what was the matter with him?' asked a third, taking a vast quantity of snuff out of a very large snuff-box. 'I thought he'd never die.'

'God knows,' said the first, with a yawn.

'What has he done with his money?' asked a red-faced gentleman with a pendulous excrescence on the end of his nose, that shook like the gills of a turkey-cock.

'I haven't heard,' said the man with the large chin, yawning again. 'Left it to his company, perhaps. He hasn't left it to *me*. That's all I know.'

This pleasantry was received with a general laugh.

'It's likely to be a very cheap funeral,' said the same speaker; 'for, upon my life, I don't know of anybody to go to it. Suppose we make up a party, and volunteer?'

'I don't mind going if a lunch is provided,' observed the gentleman with the excrescence on his nose. 'But I must be fed if I make one.'

Another laugh.

'Well, I am the most disinterested among you, after all,' said the first speaker, 'for I never wear black gloves, and I never eat lunch. But I'll offer to go if anybody else will. When I come to think of it, I'm not at all sure that I wasn't his most particular friend; for we used to stop and speak whenever we met. Bye, bye!'

Speakers and listeners strolled away, and mixed with other groups. Scrooge knew the men, and looked towards the Spirit for an explanation.

The phantom glided on into a street. Its finger pointed to two persons meeting. Scrooge listened again, thinking that the explanation might lie here.

He knew these men, also, perfectly. They were men of business: very wealthy, and of great importance. He had made a point always of standing well in their esteem in a business point of view, that is; strictly in a business point of view.

'How are you?' said one.

'How are you?' returned the other.

'Well!' said the first, 'old Scratch has got his own at last, hey?'

'So I am told,' returned the second. 'Cold, isn't it?'

'Seasonable for Christmas-time. You are not a skater, I suppose?'

'No, no. Something else to think of. Good-morning!'

Not another word. That was their meeting, their conversation, and their parting.

Scrooge was at first inclined to be surprised that the Spirit should attach importance to conversations apparently so trivial; but feeling assured that they must have some hidden purpose, he set himself to consider what it was likely to be. They could scarcely be supposed to have any bearing on the death of Jacob, his old partner, for that was Past, and this Ghost's province was the Future. Nor could he think of any one immediately connected with himself to whom he could apply them. But nothing doubting that, to whomsoever they applied, they had some latent moral for his own improvement, he resolved to treasure up every word he heard, and everything he saw; and especially to observe the shadow of himself when it appeared. For he had an expectation that the conduct of his future self would give him the clue he missed, and would render the solution of these riddles easy.

He looked about in that very place for his own image, but another man stood in his accustomed corner; and though the clock pointed to his usual time of day for being there, he saw no likeness of himself among the multitudes that poured in through the Porch. It gave him little surprise, however; for he had been revolving in his mind a change of life, and thought and hoped he saw his new-born resolutions carried out in this.

Quiet and dark, beside him stood the Phantom, with its outstretched hand. When he roused himself from his thoughtful quest, he fancied, from the turn of the hand, and its situation in reference to himself, that the Unseen Eyes were looking at him keenly. It made him shudder, and feel very cold.

They left the busy scene, and went into an obscure part of the town, where Scrooge had never penetrated before, although he recognised its situation and its bad repute. The ways were foul and narrow; the shops and houses wretched; the people half naked, drunken, slipshod, ugly. Alleys and archways, like so many cesspools, disgorged their offences of smell and dirt, and life upon the straggling streets; and the whole quarter reeked with crime, with filth, and misery.

Far in this den of infamous resort, there was a low-browed, beetling shop, below a penthouse roof, where iron, old rags, bottles, bones, and greasy offal were bought. Upon the floor within were piled up heaps of rusty keys, nails, chains, hinges, files, scales, weights, and refuse iron of all kinds. Secrets that few would like to scrutinise were bred and hidden in mountains of unseemly rags, masses of corrupted fat, and sepulchres of bones. Sitting in among the wares he dealt in, by a charcoal stove made of old bricks, was a grey-haired rascal, nearly seventy years of age, who had screened himself from the cold air without by a frouzy curtaining of miscellaneous tatters hung upon a line, and smoked his pipe in all the luxury of calm retirement.

Scrooge and the Phantom came into the presence of this man, just as a woman with a heavy bundle slunk into the shop. But she had scarcely entered, when another woman, similarly laden, came in too; and she was closely followed by a man in faded black, who was no less startled by the sight of them than they had been upon the recognition of each other. After a short period of blank astonishment, in which the old man with the pipe had joined them, they all three burst into a laugh.

'Let the charwoman alone to be the first!' cried she who had entered first. 'Let the laundress alone to be the second; and let the undertaker's man alone to be the third. Look here, old Joe, here's a chance! If we haven't all three met here without meaning it!'

'You couldn't have met in a better place,' said old Joe, removing his pipe from his mouth. 'Come into the parlour. You were made free of it long ago, you know; and the other two an't strangers. Stop till I shut the door of the shop. Ah! how it skreeks! There an't such a rusty bit of metal in the place as its own hinges, I believe; and I'm sure there's no such old bones here as mine. Ha! ha! We're all suitable to our calling, we're well matched. Come into the parlour. Come into the parlour.'

The parlour was the space behind the screen of rags. The old man raked the fire together with an old stair-rod, and having trimmed his smoky lamp (for it was night) with the stem of his pipe, put it into his mouth again.

While he did this, the woman who had already spoken threw her bundle on the floor, and sat down in a flaunting manner on a stool, crossing her elbows on her knees, and looking with a bold defiance at the other two.

'What odds, then? What odds, Mrs. Dilber?' said the woman. 'Every person has a right to take care of themselves. *He* always did!'

'That's true, indeed!' said the laundress. 'No man more so.'

'Why, then, don't stand staring as if you was

afraid, woman! Who's the wiser? We're not going to pick holes in each other's coats, I suppose?'

'No, indeed!' said Mrs. Dilber and the man together. 'We should hope not.'

'Very well then!' cried the woman. 'That's enough. Who's the worse for the loss of a few things like these? Not a dead man, I suppose?'

'No, indeed,' said Mrs. Dilber, laughing.

'If he wanted to keep 'em after he was dead, a wicked old screw,' pursued the woman, 'why wasn't he natural in his lifetime? If he had been, he'd have had somebody to look after him when he was struck with Death, instead of lying gasping out his last there, alone by himself.'

'It's the truest word that ever was spoke,' said Mrs. Dilber. 'It's a judgment on him.'

'I wish it was a little heavier judgment,' replied the woman: 'and it should have been, you may depend upon it, if I could have laid my hands on anything else. Open that bundle, old Joe, and let me know the value of it. Speak out plain. I'm not afraid to be the first, nor afraid for them to see it. We knew pretty well that we were helping ourselves before we met here, I believe. It's no sin. Open the bundle, Joe.'

But the gallantry of her friends would not allow of this; and the man in faded black, mounting the breach first, produced *his* plunder. It was not extensive. A seal or two, a pencil-case, a pair of sleeve-buttons, and a brooch of no great value, were all. They were severally examined and appraised by old Joe, who chalked the sums he was disposed to give for each upon the wall, and added them up into a total when he found that there was nothing more to come.

'That's your account,' said Joe, 'and I wouldn't give another sixpence, if I was to be boiled for not doing it. Who's next?'

Mrs. Dilber was next. Sheets and towels, a little wearing apparel, two old fashioned silver teaspoons, a pair of sugar-tongs, and a few boots. Her account was stated on the wall in the same manner.

'I always give too much to ladies. It's a weakness of mine, and that's the way I ruin myself,' said old Joe. 'That's your account. If you asked me for another penny, and made it an open question, I'd repent of being so liberal, and knock off half-a-crown.'

'And now undo *my* bundle, Joe,' said the first woman.

Joe went down on his knees for the greater convenience of opening it, and, having unfastened a great many knots, dragged out a large heavy roll of some dark stuff.

'What do you call this?' said Joe. 'Bed-curtains?'

'Ah!' returned the woman, laughing and leaning forward on her crossed arms. 'Bed-curtains!'

'You don't mean to say you took 'em down, rings and all, with him lying there?' said Joe.

**330**

'Yes, I do,' replied the woman. 'Why not?'

'You were born to make your fortune,' said Joe, 'and you'll certainly do it.'

'I certainly shan't hold my hand, when I can get anything in it by reaching it out, for the sake of such a man as he was, I promise you, Joe,' returned the woman coolly. 'Don't drop that oil upon the blankets, now.'

'His blankets?' asked Joe.

'Whose else's do you think?' replied the woman. 'He isn't likely to take cold without 'em, I dare say.'

'I hope he didn't die of anything catching? Eh?' said old Joe, stopping in his work, and looking up.

'Don't you be afraid of that,' returned the woman. 'I an't so fond of his company that I'd loiter about him for such things, if he did. Ah! you may look through that shirt till your eyes ache, but you won't find a hole in it, nor a threadbare place. It's the best he had, and a fine one too. They'd have wasted it, if it hadn't been for me.'

'What do you call wasting of it?' asked old Joe.

'Putting it on him to be buried in, to be sure,' replied the woman, with a laugh. 'Somebody was fool enough to do it, but I took it off again. If calico an't good enough for such a purpose, it isn't good enough for anything. It's quite as becoming to the body. He can't look uglier than he did in that one.'

Scrooge listened to this dialogue in horror. As

they sat grouped about their spoil, in the scanty light afforded by the old man's lamp, he viewed them with a detestation and disgust which could hardly have been greater, though they had been obscene demons marketing the corpse itself.

'Ha, ha!' laughed the same woman when old Joe, producing a flannel bag with money in it, told out their several gains upon the ground. 'This is the end of it, you see! He frightened every one away from him when he was alive, to profit us when he was dead! Ha, ha, ha!'

'Spirit!' said Scrooge, shuddering from head to foot. 'I see, I see. The case of this unhappy man might be my own. My life tends that way now. Merciful heaven, what is this?'

He recoiled in terror, for the scene had changed, and now he almost touched a bed—a bare, uncurtained bed—on which, beneath a ragged sheet, there lay a something covered up, which, though it was dumb, announced itself in awful language.

The room was very dark, too dark to be observed with any accuracy, though Scrooge glanced round it in obedience to a secret impulse, anxious to know what kind of room it was. A pale light, rising in the outer air, fell straight upon the bed; and on it, plundered and bereft, unwatched, unwept, uncared for, was the body of this man.

Scrooge glanced towards the Phantom. Its steady

hand was pointed to the head. The cover was so carelessly adjusted that the slightest raising of it, the motion of a finger upon Scrooge's part, would have disclosed the face. He thought of it, felt how easy it would be to do, and longed to do it; but he had no more power to withdraw the veil than to dismiss the spectre at his side.

Oh, cold, cold, rigid, dreadful Death, set up thine altar here, and dress it with such terrors as thou hast at thy command; for this is thy dominion! But of the loved, revered, and honoured head thou canst not turn one hair to thy dread purposes, or make one feature odious. It is not that the hand is heavy, and will fall down when released; it is not that the heart and pulse are still; but that the hand was open, generous, and true; the heart brave, warm, and tender, and the pulse a man's. Strike, Shadow, strike! And see his good deeds springing from the wound, to sow the world with life immortal!

No voice pronounced these words in Scrooge's ears, and yet he heard them when he looked upon the bed. He thought, if this man could be raised up now, what would be his foremost thoughts? Avarice, hard dealing, griping cares? They have brought him to a rich end, truly!

He lay in the dark, empty house, with not a man, a woman, or a child to say he was kind to me in this or that, and for the memory of one kind word I will be kind to him. A cat was tearing at the door, and there was a sound of gnawing rats beneath the hearthstone. What *they* wanted in the room of death, and why they were so restless and disturbed, Scrooge did not dare to think.

'Spirit!' he said, 'this is a fearful place. In leaving it, I shall not leave its lesson, trust me. Let us go!'

Still the Ghost pointed with an unmoved finger to the head.

'I understand you,' Scrooge returned, 'and I would do it if I could. But I have not the power, Spirit. I have not the power.'

Again it seemed to look upon him.

'If there is any person in the town who feels emotion caused by this man's death,' said Scrooge, quite agonised, 'show that person to me, Spirit, I beseech you!'

The Phantom spread its dark robe before him for a moment, like a wing; and, withdrawing it, revealed a room by daylight, where a mother and her children were.

She was expecting some one, and with anxious eagerness; for she walked up and down the room, started at every sound, looked out from the window, glanced at the clock, tried, but in vain, to work with her needle, and could hardly bear the voices of her children in their play.

At length the long-expected knock was heard. She

hurried to the door, and met her husband; a man whose face was careworn and depressed, though he was young. There was a remarkable expression in it now; a kind of serious delight of which he felt ashamed, and which he struggled to repress.

He sat down to the dinner that had been hoarding for him by the fire, and when she asked him faintly what news (which was not until after a long silence), he appeared embarrassed how to answer.

'Is it good,' she said, 'or bad?' to help him.

'Bad,' he answered.

'We are quite ruined?'

'No. There is hope yet, Caroline.'

'If *he* relents,' she said, amazed, 'there is! Nothing is past hope, if such a miracle has happened.'

'He is past relenting,' said her husband. 'He is dead.'

She was a mild and patient creature, if her face spoke truth; but she was thankful in her soul to hear it, and she said so with clasped hands. She prayed forgiveness the next moment, and was sorry; but the first was the emotion of her heart.

'What the half-drunken woman, whom I told you of last night, said to me when I tried to see him and obtain a week's delay—and what I thought was a mere excuse to avoid me—turns out to have been quite true. He was not only very ill, but dying, then.'

'To whom will our debt be transferred?'

'I don't know. But, before that time, we shall be ready with the money; and even though we were not, it would be bad fortune indeed to find so merciless a creditor in his successor. We may sleep to-night with light hearts, Caroline!'

Yes. Soften it as they would, their hearts were lighter. The children's faces, hushed and clustered round to hear what they so little understood, were brighter; and it was a happier house for this man's death! The only emotion that the Ghost could show him, caused by the event, was one of pleasure.

'Let me see some tenderness connected with a death,' said Scrooge; 'or that dark chamber, Spirit, which we just left now, will be for ever present to me.'

The Ghost conducted him through several streets familiar to his feet; and as they went along, Scrooge looked here and there to find himself, but nowhere was he to be seen. They entered poor Bob Cratchit's house; the dwelling he had visited before; and found the mother and the children seated round the fire.

Quiet. Very quiet. The noisy little Cratchits were as still as statues in one corner, and sat looking up at Peter, who had a book before him. The mother and her daughters were engaged in sewing. But surely they were very quiet!

' "And he took a child, and set him in the midst of them." '

Where had Scrooge heard those words? He had

not dreamed them. The boy must have read them out as he and the Spirit crossed the threshold. Why did he not go on?

The mother laid her work upon the table, and put her hand up to her face.

'The colour hurts my eyes,' she said.

The colour? Ah, poor Tiny Tim!

'They're better now again,' said Cratchit's wife. 'It makes them weak by candle-light; and I wouldn't show weak eyes to your father when he comes home for the world. It must be near his time.'

'Past it rather,' Peter answered, shutting up his book. 'But I think he has walked a little slower than he used, these few last evenings, mother.'

They were very quiet again. At last she said, and in a steady, cheerful voice, that only faltered once:

'I have known him walk with—I have known him walk with Tiny Tim upon his shoulder very fast indeed.'

'And so have I,' cried Peter. 'Often.'

'And so have I,' exclaimed another. So had all.

'But he was very light to carry,' she resumed, intent upon her work, 'and his father loved him so, that it was no trouble, no trouble. And there is your father at the door!'

She hurried out to meet him; and little Bob in his comforter—he had need of it, poor fellow—came in. His tea was ready for him on the hob, and they all tried who should help him to it most. Then the two young Cratchits got upon his knees, and laid, each child, a little cheek against his face, as if they said, 'Don't mind it, father. Don't be grieved!'

Bob was very cheerful with them, and spoke pleasantly to all the family. He looked at the work upon the table, and praised the industry and speed of Mrs. Cratchit and the girls. They would be done long before Sunday, he said.

'Sunday! You went to-day, then, Robert?' said his wife.

'Yes, my dear,' returned Bob. 'I wish you could have gone. It would have done you good to see how green a place it is. But you'll see it often. I promised him that I would walk there on a Sunday. My little, little child!' cried Bob. 'My little child!'

He broke down all at once. He couldn't help it. If he could have helped it, he and his child would have been farther apart, perhaps, than they were.

He left the room, and went upstairs into the room above, which was lighted cheerfully, and hung with Christmas. There was a chair set close beside the child, and there were signs of some one having been there lately. Poor Bob sat down in it, and when he had thought a little and composed himself, he kissed the little face. He was reconciled to what had happened, and went down again quite happy.

They drew about the fire, and talked, the girls and

mother working still. Bob told them of the extraordinary kindness of Mr. Scrooge's nephew, whom he had scarcely seen but once, and who, meeting him in the street that day, and seeing that he looked a little—'just a little down, you know,' said Bob, inquired what had happened to distress him. 'On which,' said Bob, 'for he is the pleasantest-spoken gentleman you ever heard, I told him. "I am heartily sorry for it, Mr. Cratchit," he said, "and heartily sorry for your good wife." By-the-bye, how he ever knew *that* I don't know.'

'Knew what, my dear?'

'Why, that you were a good wife,' replied Bob.

'Everybody knows that,' said Peter.

'Very well observed, my boy!' cried Bob. 'I hope they do. "Heartily sorry," he said, "for your good wife. If I can be of service to you in any way," he said, giving me his card, "that's where I live. Pray come to me." Now, it wasn't,' cried Bob, 'for the sake of anything he might be able to do for us, so much as for his kind way, that this was quite delightful. It really seemed as if he had known our Tiny Tim, and felt with us.'

'I'm sure he's a good soul!' said Mrs. Cratchit.

'You would be sure of it, my dear,' returned Bob, 'if you saw and spoke to him. I shouldn't be at all surprised—mark what I say!—if he got Peter a better situation.'

'Only hear that, Peter,' said Mrs. Cratchit.

'And then,' cried one of the girls, 'Peter will be

keeping company with some one, and setting up for himself.'

'Get along with you!' retorted Peter, grinning.

'It's just as likely as not,' said Bob, 'one of these days; though there's plenty of time for that, my dear. But, however and whenever we part from one another, I am sure we shall none of us forget poor Tiny Tim—shall we—or this first parting that there was among us?'

'Never, father!' cried they all.

'And I know,' said Bob, 'I know, my dears, that when we recollect how patient and how mild he was; although he was a little, little child; we shall not quarrel easily among ourselves, and forget poor Tiny Tim in doing it.'

'No, never, father!' they all cried again.

'I am very happy,' said little Bob, 'I am very happy!'

Mrs. Cratchit kissed him, his daughters kissed him, the two young Cratchits kissed him, and Peter and himself shook hands. Spirit of Tiny Tim, thy childish essence was from God!

'Spectre,' said Scrooge, 'something informs me that our parting moment is at hand. I know it but I know not how. Tell me what man that was whom we saw lying dead?'

The Ghost of Christmas Yet to Come conveyed him, as before—though at a different time, he thought: indeed there seemed no order in these latter visions, save that they were in the Future—into the resorts of business men, but showed him not himself. Indeed, the Spirit did not stay for anything, but went straight on, as to the end just now desired, until besought by Scrooge to tarry for a moment.

'This court,' said Scrooge, 'through which we hurry now, is where my place of occupation is, and has been for a length of time. I see the house. Let me behold what I shall be in days to come.'

The Spirit stopped; the hand was pointed elsewhere.

'The house is yonder,' Scrooge exclaimed. 'Why do you point away?'

The inexorable finger underwent no change.

Scrooge hastened to the window of his office, and looked in. It was an office still, but not his. The furniture was not the same, and the figure in the chair was not himself. The Phantom pointed as before.

He joined it once again, and, wondering why and whither he had gone, accompanied it until they reached an iron gate. He paused to look round before entering.

A churchyard. Here, then, the wretched man, whose name he had now to learn, lay underneath the ground. It was a worthy place. Walled in by houses; overrun by grass and weeds, the growth of vegetation's death, not life; choked up with too much burying; fat with repleted appetite. A worthy place!

The Spirit stood among the graves, and pointed

down to One. He advanced towards it trembling. The Phantom was exactly as it had been, but he dreaded that he saw new meaning in its solemn shape.

'Before I draw nearer to that stone to which you point,' said Scrooge, 'answer me one question. Are these shadows of the things that Will be, or are they shadows of the things that May be only?'

Still the Ghost pointed downward to the grave by which it stood.

'Men's courses will foreshadow certain ends, to which, if persevered in, they must lead,' said Scrooge. 'But if the courses be departed from, the ends will change. Say it is thus with what you show me!'

The Spirit was immovable as ever.

Scrooge crept towards it, trembling as he went; and, following the finger, read upon the stone of the neglected grave his own name, EBENEZER SCROOGE.

'Am *I* that man who lay upon the bed?' he cried upon his knees.

The finger pointed from the grave to him, and back again.

'No, Spirit! Oh no, no!'

The finger still was there.

'Spirit!' he cried, tight clutching at its robe, 'hear me! I am not the man I was. I will not be the man I must have been but for this intercourse. Why show me this, if I am past all hope?'

For the first time the hand appeared to shake.

'Good Spirit,' he pursued, as down upon the ground he fell before it, 'your nature intercedes for me, and pities me. Assure me that I yet may change these shadows you have shown me by an altered life?'

The kind hand trembled.

'I will honour Christmas in my heart, and try to keep it all the year. I will live in the Past, the Present, and the Future. The Spirits of all Three shall strive within me. I will not shut out the lessons that they teach. Oh, tell me I may sponge away the writing on this stone!'

In his agony he caught the spectral hand. It sought to free itself, but he was strong in his entreaty, and detained it. The Spirit, stronger yet, repulsed him.

Holding up his hands in a last prayer to have his fate reversed, he saw an alteration in the Phantom's hood and dress. It shrunk, collapsed, and dwindled down into a bed-post.

## Stave Five:

## The End of It

 es! and the bed-post was his own. The bed was his own, the room was his own. Best and happiest of all, the Time before him was his own, to make amends in!

'I will live in the Past, the Present, and the Future!' Scrooge repeated as he scrambled out of bed. 'The Spirits of all Three shall strive within me. O Jacob Marley! Heaven and the Christmas Time be praised for this! I say it on my knees, old Jacob; on my knees!'

He was so fluttered and so glowing with his good intentions, that his broken voice would scarcely answer to his call. He had been sobbing violently in his conflict with the Spirit, and his face was wet with tears.

'They are not torn down,' cried Scrooge, folding one of his bed-curtains in his arms, 'They are not torn down, rings and all. They are here—I am here—the

344

shadows of the things that would have been may be dispelled. They will be. I know they will!'

His hands were busy with his garments all this time: turning them inside out, putting them on upside down, tearing them, mislaying them, making them parties to every kind of extravagance.

'I don't know what to do!' cried Scrooge, laughing and crying in the same breath, and making a perfect Laocoön of himself with his stockings. 'I am as light as a feather, I am as happy as an angel, I am as merry as a schoolboy, I am as giddy as a drunken man. A merry Christmas to everybody! A happy New Year to all the world! Hallo here! Whoop! Hallo!'

He had frisked into the sitting-room, and was now standing there, perfectly winded.

'There's the saucepan that the gruel was in!' cried Scrooge, starting off again, and going round the fireplace. 'There's the door by which the Ghost of Jacob Marley entered! There's the corner where the Ghost of Christmas Present sat! There's the window where I saw the wandering Spirits! It's all right, it's all true, it all happened. Ha, ha, ha!'

Really, for a man who had been out of practice for so many years, it was a splendid laugh, a most illustrious laugh. The father of a long, long line of brilliant laughs!

'I don't know what day of the month it is,' said Scrooge. 'I don't know how long I have been among the Spirits. I don't know anything. I'm quite a baby. Never mind. I don't care. I'd rather be a baby. Hallo! Whoop! Hallo here!'

He was checked in his transports by the churches ringing out the lustiest peals he had ever heard. Clash, clash, hammer; ding, dong, bell! Bell, dong, ding; hammer, clang, clash! Oh, glorious, glorious!

Running to the window, he opened it, and put out his head. No fog, no mist; clear, bright, jovial, stirring, cold; cold, piping for the blood to dance to; golden sunlight; heavenly sky; sweet fresh air; merry bells. Oh, glorious! Glorious!

'What's to-day?' cried Scrooge, calling downward to a boy in Sunday clothes, who perhaps had loitered in to look about him.

'EH?' returned the boy with all his might of wonder.

'What's to-day, my fine fellow?' said Scrooge.

'To-day!' replied the boy. 'Why, CHRISTMAS DAY.'

'It's Christmas Day!' said Scrooge to himself. 'I haven't missed it. The Spirits have done it all in one night. They can do anything they like. Of course they can. Of course they can. Hallo, my fine fellow!'

'Hallo!' returned the boy.

'Do you know the poulterer's in the next street but one, at the corner?' Scrooge inquired.

'I should hope I did,' replied the lad.

'An intelligent boy!' said Scrooge. 'A remarkable

346

boy! Do you know whether they've sold the prize tur-key that was hanging up there?—Not the little prize turkey: the big one?'

'What! the one as big as me?' returned the boy.

'What a delightful boy!' said Scrooge. 'It's a plea-sure to talk to him. Yes, my buck!'

'It's hanging there now,' replied the boy.

'Is it?' said Scrooge. 'Go and buy it.'

'Walk-ER!' exclaimed the boy.

'No, no,' said Scrooge. 'I am in earnest. Go and buy it, and tell 'em to bring it here, that I may give them the directions where to take it. Come back with the man, and I'll give you a shilling. Come back with him in less than five minutes, and I'll give you half-a-crown!'

The boy was off like a shot. He must have had a steady hand at a trigger who could have got a shot off half as fast.

'I'll send it to Bob Cratchit's,' whispered Scrooge, rubbing his hands, and splitting with a laugh. 'He shan't know who sends it. It's twice the size of Tiny Tim. Joe Miller never made such a joke as sending it to Bob's will be!'

The hand in which he wrote the address was not a steady one; but write it he did, somehow, and went downstairs to open the street-door, ready for the com-ing of the poulterer's man. As he stood there, waiting his arrival, the knocker caught his eye.

'I shall love it as long as I live!' cried Scrooge, patting it with his hand. 'I scarcely ever looked at it before. What an honest expression it has in its face! It's a wonderful knocker!—Here's the turkey. Hallo! Whoop! How are you! Merry Christmas!'

It *was* a turkey! He never could have stood upon his legs, that bird. He would have snapped 'em short off in a minute, like sticks of sealing-wax.

'Why, it's impossible to carry that to Camden Town,' said Scrooge. 'You must have a cab.'

The chuckle with which he said this, and the chuckle with which he paid for the turkey, and the chuckle with which he paid for the cab, and the chuckle with which he recompensed the boy, were only to be exceeded by the chuckle with which he sat down breathless in his chair again, and chuckled till he cried.

Shaving was not an easy task, for his hand continued to shake very much; and shaving requires attention, even when you don't dance while you are at it. But if he had cut the end of his nose off, he would have put a piece of sticking-plaster over it, and been quite satisfied.

He dressed himself 'all in his best,' and at last got out into the streets. The people were by this time pouring forth, as he had seen them with the Ghost of Christmas Present; and, walking with his hands behind him, Scrooge regarded every one with a delighted smile. He looked so irresistibly pleasant, in a word, that three or four good-humoured fellows said, 'Good-morning, sir! A merry Christmas to you!' And Scrooge said often afterwards that, of all the blithe sounds he had ever heard, those were the blithest in his ears.

He had not gone far when, coming on towards him, he beheld the portly gentleman who had walked into his counting-house the day before, and said, 'Scrooge and Marley's, I believe?' It sent a pang across his heart to think how this old gentleman would look upon him when they met; but he knew what path lay straight before him, and he took it.

'My dear sir,' said Scrooge, quickening his pace, and taking the old gentleman by both his hands, 'how do you do? I hope you succeeded yesterday. It was very kind of you. A merry Christmas to you, sir!'

'Mr. Scrooge?'

'Yes,' said Scrooge. 'That is my name, and I fear it may not be pleasant to you. Allow me to ask your pardon. And will you have the goodness—' Here Scrooge whispered in his ear.

'Lord bless me!' cried the gentleman, as if his breath were taken away. 'My dear Mr. Scrooge, are you serious?'

'If you please,' said Scrooge. 'Not a farthing less. A great many back-payments are included in it, I assure you. Will you do me that favour?'

'My dear sir,' said the other, shaking hands with him, 'I don't know what to say to such munifi—'

'Don't say anything, please,' retorted Scrooge. 'Come and see me. Will you come and see me?'

'I will!' cried the old gentleman. And it was clear he meant to do it.

'Thankee,'' said Scrooge. 'I am much obliged to you. I thank you fifty times. Bless you!'

He went to church, and walked about the streets, and watched the people hurrying to and fro, and patted the children on the head, and questioned beggars, and looked down into the kitchens of houses, and up to the windows; and found that everything could yield him pleasure. He had never dreamed that any walk—that anything—could give him so much happiness. In the afternoon he turned his steps towards his nephew's house.

He passed the door a dozen times before he had the courage to go up and knock. But he made a dash and did it.

'Is your master at home, my dear?' said Scrooge to the girl. 'Nice girl! Very.'

'Yes, sir.'

'Where is he, my love?' said Scrooge.

'He's in the dining-room, sir, along with mistress. I'll show you upstairs, if you please.'

'Thankee. He knows me,' said Scrooge, with his hand already on the dining-room lock. 'I'll go in here, my dear.'

He turned it gently, and sidled his face in round

the door. They were looking at the table (which was spread out in great array); for these young housekeepers are always nervous on such points, and like to see that everything is right.

'Fred!' said Scrooge.

Dear heart alive, how his niece by marriage started! Scrooge had forgotten, for the moment, about her sitting in the corner with the footstool, or he wouldn't have done it on any account.

'Why, bless my soul!' cried Fred, 'who's that?'

'It's I. Your uncle Scrooge. I have come to dinner. Will you let me in, Fred?'

Let him in! It is a mercy he didn't shake his arm off. He was at home in five minutes. Nothing could be heartier. His niece looked just the same. So did Topper when *he* came. So did the plump sister when *she* came. So did every one when *they* came. Wonderful party, wonderful games, wonderful unanimity, won-der-ful happiness!

But he was early at the office next morning. Oh, he was early there! If he could only be there first, and catch Bob Cratchit coming late! That was the thing he had set his heart upon.

And he did it; yes, he did! The clock struck nine. No Bob. A quarter past. No Bob. He was full eighteen minutes and a half behind his time. Scrooge sat with his door wide open, that he might see him come into the tank.

His hat was off before he opened the door; his comforter too. He was on his stool in a jiffy, driving away with his pen, as if he were trying to overtake nine o'clock.

'Hallo!' growled Scrooge in his accustomed voice as near as he could feign it. 'What do you mean by coming here at this time of day?'

'I am very sorry, sir,' said Bob. 'I *am* behind my time.'

'You are!' repeated Scrooge. 'Yes, I think you are. Step this way, sir, if you please.'

'It's only once a year, sir,' pleaded Bob, appearing from the tank. 'It shall not be repeated. I was making rather merry yesterday, sir.'

'Now, I'll tell you what, my friend,' said Scrooge. 'I am not going to stand this sort of thing any longer. And therefore,' he continued, leaping from his stool, and giving Bob such a dig in the waistcoat that he staggered back into the tank again—'and therefore I am about to raise your salary!'

Bob trembled, and got a little nearer to the ruler. He had a momentary idea of knocking Scrooge down with it, holding him, and calling to the people in the court for help and a strait-waistcoat.

'A merry Christmas, Bob!' said Scrooge, with an earnestness that could not be mistaken, as he clapped him on the back. 'A merrier Christmas, Bob, my good fellow, than I have given you for many a year! I'll raise your salary, and endeavour to assist your struggling family, and we will discuss your affairs this very afternoon, over a Christmas bowl of smoking bishop, Bob! Make up the fires and buy another coal-scuttle before you dot another i, Bob Cratchit!'

Scrooge was better than his word. He did it all, and infinitely more; and to Tiny Tim, who did NOT die, he was a second father. He became as good a friend, as good a master, and as good a man as the good old City knew, or any other good old city, town, or borough in the good old world. Some people laughed to see the alteration in him, but he let them laugh, and little heeded them; for he was wise enough to know that nothing ever happened on this globe, for good, at which some people did not have their fill of laughter in the outset; and knowing that such as these would be blind anyway, he thought it quite as well that they should wrinkle up their eyes in grins as have the malady in less attractive forms. His own heart laughed, and that was quite enough for him.

He had no further intercourse with Spirits, but lived upon the Total-Abstinence Principle ever afterwards; and it was always said of him that he knew how to keep Christmas well, if any man alive possessed the knowledge. May that be truly said of us, and all of us! And so, as Tiny Tim observed, God bless Us, Every One!

# About the Authors

HENRY VAN DYKE (1852–1933) wrote more than fifty books, many of which had implicit spiritual content, and the most popular being *The Story of the Other Wise Man*. An ordained Presbyterian minister, he pastored churches in Rhode Island and New York, then left the ministry to become Professor of English Literature at Princeton. There, he became a warm friend of Woodrow Wilson, a professorial colleague, who, upon being elected to the presidency, appointed van Dyke U.S. Minister to the Netherlands.

Probably best known for *Rebecca of Sunnybrook Farm*, KATE DOUGLAS SMITH WIGGIN (1856–1923) wrote thirty-nine books. Full of sweetness and flashes of homespun humor, they disclose a deep understanding of human nature. *The Birds' Christmas Carol* became a seasonal classic around the turn of the century and was published in multiple editions in various languages.

GRACE S. RICHMOND, an American novelist and short story writer, painted idyllic pictures of family life. Her stories usually were serialized in women's magazines. She wrote more than twenty-five books, which were equally popular in England.

CHARLES DICKENS (1812–1870), Victorian giant of letters, is almost synonymous with the celebration of Christmas. Although he earned popular success with *Pickwick Papers, Nicholas Nickleby, Oliver Twist, The Old Curiosity Shop,* and *Barnaby Rudge,* it was *A Christmas Carol,* written in only a few weeks, that catapulted Dickens to fame as England's greatest novelist. Scrooge's tale of reconciliation and forgiveness endures as the favorite Christmas novel of all time.